Black Inked Pearl
A Girl's Quest

A Magical Book of Lost Love …

An Epic Journey, An Ancient Mystery Reinterpreted
A Faerie Tale, a Parable, A Poem, A Nightmare, A Daydream
Can a Book be an Incantation or a Spell?
Espiritus, Veritas, and Dang'rous

A Work of Genius on Dream, Dementia and Truth

A Novel By
Ruth Finnegan

GARN PRESS
NEW YORK, NY

Published by Garn Press, LLC
New York, NY
www.garnpress.com

Garn Press and the Chapwoman logo are registered trademarks of Garn Press, LLC

Black Inked Pearl is a work of fiction. All situations, incidents, dialogues, and all characters, are products of the author's imagination and are not to be construed as real. Any references to historical events, real people, or real places are used fictitiously, and are not intended to depict actual events or to change the entirely fictional nature of the work. Other names, characters, places, and events are products of the author's imagination or are used fictitiously, and any resemblance to actual persons, living or dead, businesses, companies or events is entirely coincidental.

Book and cover design by Benjamin James Taylor
Cover image by Rubberball/Mike Kemp/Getty Images

Library of Congress Control Number: 2015941198

Publisher's Cataloging-in-Publication Data

Finnegan, Ruth.
    Black inked pearl : a girl's quest / Ruth
Finnegan.
        pages cm
    ISBN: 978-1-942146-17-9 (pbk.)
    ISBN: 978-1-942146-16-2 (hardcover)
    ISBN: 978-1-942146-18-6 (e-book)
    1. Fantasy literature, English—Fiction. 2.
Dreams—Fiction. 3. Love stories. 4. Spiritual life—
Fiction. 5. Epic literature—Fiction.   I. Title.
PS3606.I5594 B53 2015
813`.6—dc23
                                2015941198

in memoriam

John Ballard

of Nigeria, England, and Australia

Author's Note

I give thanks to my three wonderful daughters and their husbands, and to my five grandchildren who teach me what's what. One lives in the liminal space of New Zealand, a new world of technology and enterprise, yet an old land of ancient art and wisdom. It was the inspiration, along with African story-tellers and my native Ireland of saints and scholars, for so much of *Black-Inked Pearl*, which, Kublai Khan-like, arrived through my dreams.

Kate's epic journey through this story is interlaced with the eternity of love and the ambiguity between dream and reality, indicated by a style which grows more poetic, riddling and dreamlike as the story unfolds.

There are literary allusions throughout the book which are more fully explained in my book, *Why Do We Quote?* They are often references to texts learned by heart in my Quaker school where, unlike Kate's nuns, the teachers were all kind. Only some of the many allusions in the novel are annotated, left to my readers, if they so choose, to winkle them out.

New words and spellings are deliberate, a play with language, allowed (*it seems*) to poets and verbal artists, as in, for example, Gerald Manley Hopkins' poetry or James Joyce's prose. Many of these words are also allusive in sense, especially sound.

Kate, together with her earthly author, sometimes likes to use Anglo-Saxon/Teutonic plural endings, also at times old spellings, when she feels they sound better – the same with the extensions, separations and abbreviations of words. These sonic and poeticke dimensions are integral to the writing.

Often, especially in the later portions of the novel, Kate's experiences are conveyed in a series of Homeric-like similes, sometimes in direct translation from the *Odyssey* or *Iliad*, sometimes modeled anew on this rightly famous literary form. Both repetition and the recurrent epithets characterizing Homer's heroes are features of his epic style, imitated, as is the biblical tone of the nineteenth-century translations in which I first read Homer, in parts of the novel.

Finally my heartfelt thanks to Denny Taylor, and to wonderful Garn Press and all who sail in her. I hope my readers enjoy the magical story of Kate's quest for her lost love as much as I enjoyed writing it.

Ruth Finnegan
June, 2015

Contents

"Since brass, nor stone, nor earth, nor boundless sea,
But sad mortality o'ersways their power,
How with this rage shall beauty hold a plea,
Whose action is no stronger than a flower?...
Oh none, unless this miracle have might,
That in black ink my love may still shine bright."

Shakespeare: from *Sonnet 65*

"Whatever pearl you seek
look for the pearl within the pearl"

Rumi: from *The Dome of the Inner Sky*
(from the Persian)

PART I

THE START

1

... *she couldn't* ...

Donegal shore by wild Atlantic sea. Today. Or long ago. Engrained in her heart. Beautiful. Storm, waves, seagulls crying, long black hair he loved tossed and tangled in the wind, maybe that had confused her? Could she blame that? (*Oh her hair, her hair, was not that part of her story? ... it seemed ... somehow ... and her nails ... digging into her hand ...*).

His arms. In the mist. His head bending to her, his mouth ready to ...

'NO!!'

She was too young she was not ready she was afraid she was terrified only fifteen not ready yet she must go now immediate like a brother nice-impossible too young sea too loud storm tangle-hair she was too young now run run run ...

Panic, running, panic, running, running. Footmarks. Footprints in sand, vanishing filling, seeping salt water, tears (*hers his, who knows?*) vanished gone-now path no-prints no back no way.

One glimpse back, oh careful Kate, his shape lust-lost in the sea's mist (*surely somewhere beyond would be sun, salvation, no-cold?*).

Would he follow? No!!

She turned to go back. Perhaps it wouldn't be so bad …

But he was lost (*lost …*) in the mist. Her footmarks, the way, lost in the water …

PART II

BEGINNING

2

An ordinary girl and a magic world

That was not how it was meant to be. Well of course. Kate knew she wasn't some famous heroine on an epic search through sea and land to find a great lover. Or journeying in Homeric lands for a treasure like as a seabird. Or turning into a Business Woman *par excellence*, feted by peers, in demand, best fee earner ever.

Or even a pearl in heaven …

No! She knew her fate was a quiet, gentle one. Among the paths of faerie, Tír na nÓg, enchanted dreams and histories, with steeds galloping noiseless away into the far distant mists (*oh, mists … how could they stir her?*), boats slipping silently over dim horizons, the sea (*oh the sea …*).

Just an ordinary girl. In a magical world.

It was just to sit silent on the shore, scooping coarse sand grains in her hands, falling them through her fingers, grain by grain, counted, countless. Or feeling the clouds and the moon, numbering the stars ...

Numbering? No!! She had never been able to cope with numbers.

Yes you got it right. She'd never been *any* use with figures. Not!! That was just her, Kate, take it or leave it! Oh that she could have left it and learnt her sums then when she was seven!

Well did she remember too, no, not the numbers, no no, nor the miles (*no metrics then-a-days*), but sitting on that tight bench with the five others, names cut in the ink stained wood (*ink-stained when the wells were always dry and they traced their letters in pencil?*), four Juniors on the bench in front, three Big Girls so clever behind and Infants with their teacher to one side, stove with its no-heat to th' other.

There the seven-year Kate was set to learning 'parsing' and grammar 'analysis' and the counties of Ireland and mental arithmetic and calculating the pounds shillings and pence of compound interest (*what good was that?*). And miracle, she was good at it *all*, even 13-times tables. But once onto *useful* arithmeticking – hopeless.

For then, one day ...

'Now class, multiply 3679 by 107, add 13, divide by 575, find the lowest common denominator, then highest common factor, take away 13 and – *well done* Hilary, you're the first, who's next? Kate? You're usually close on ...'

But Kate wept. She was there all right – but of all that bench of bright-dull girls she'd forgotten to subtract the 13, fateful, unfortunate, number. Humiliation! She was only seven. And wasn't there something magical, symbolic about the sum, something deep in her life she could not see? Some tragedy, some forgotten thing. Like parallel lines, token of her life. She wept again.

And since that day – no good at all with numbers, used or useless (*such is education you know*).

But walking to school was a marvel, going home too. The bogs and man-insect-catching (*would she ever?*) butterwort, marsh grass, heart's ease, hawkweed, myrtle, asphodel. And the wondrous thistles and the gorse, the ever-flowering hill gorse. And everywhere, everywhere the heather, God's heaven-gift.

Then leaps down the hills and over the turf cuttings and the bogs, more bogs, shoe stuck in mud, carried home, kind 'uncle' arms, son from the carpenter's workshop three fields away – 'uncle', no her first adult Admirer, little did she know – but her childhood friend of her heart, brother-seeming, ever there – we will hear more of *him*. Barefoot was better like her companions, no stuck-in-mud stumble over ruts sandals pierced through by the bumpy-path-thorns. 'Ragged urchins' her mother called them – huh? Better dressed than her with tweeds, generation-handed, 'gainst winter hail, quick-dry hair on heads.

Past the bull, fierce, fearsome, bolt in his rickety shed, no not bolted, don't you see him staring at the splintered door, locks just just just about to burst. How they laughed and shouted and rapped to stir the beast, and told her of the bull that had gored the man beyond the headland to death, ''cos he'd been teasing it,' said her ma, 'never you fear,' but she did.

And even if she passed the geese (*golden? No!! Not for her, she knew already that mythic end wasn't her life*), geese, most aggressive of beasts, rushing her with wings, great wings, spread wide, pecking at legs under her knee-high skirt, threatening higher (*that was why she always … thoughts flickered away …*). So all her life she was afraid of that, of geese, an' all that.

The schoolroom. And the COLD. But she'd remembered that already.

Oh she'd forgotten Big Jim, tallest strongest deepest voiced of all, son of the little hunchback carpenter along the way, sitting down with the infants. Treated gently by all. Only laughed at occasionally. Fine youth he's been an' all till his friends tied him to a calf's back to watch them career down the hill and fall. Since then he had been, well ... Even attacked his father once, what horror, but mostly quiet except his stammer-stutter, couldn't voice the words crowding his brain. Alas – but p'raps he had been retard already to be thus afflicted by his fellows? And do we not know that Ireland is the Land not just of Scholars but also of the stupid-blessed, the Saints?

The way back was delight. The geese slept. So perhaps did the bull, quiet in his shed, even the boys didn't try to rouse him. And the damson-purple sloes on the high blackthorn, freeze-delighting her mouth. And leaping through the bogs with his hand come to meet her from his separate school (*religion!*) then – *his* home – listening to magic slow crochets of piano on the wind up gramophone (*'His Master's Voice' – oh, and hers*) his father had thrown out as useless – heaven's gift: together, not-cold. Paradise.

Then bogs and more bogs, home of the turf fires they could sometimes afford. Red pimpernels by the bog-side, mountain goats silhouetted on the top crags, early moon just showing, impossibly slim, symbol of something. She'd started to read now – properly, not those daytime school primers but myths of great heroes, the Odyssey of the age of gold (*her childhood indeed*), and most tragic of all tragicks the Iliad (*no need for numbers, she wept for Priam*), wept then laughed for Alcestis, lived and died with Cúchulainn, hero of Ireland. So she knew something of sacred symbols – for others, not for her.

And then, alone now, for that childhood's friend lived the other headland-side, but his songs cajoled her tread, and her heart, treading across the final, named, most fertile field where mythic Diarmaid slept with his love Grainne (*oh memories ...*), home of the sea-gulled plough, the waving oats, sky-root flax most azure of flowers, and seeing the wisping corkscrew smoke of blazing fire. Miracle orchids, hazels, birch and old old oaks, centuries, unimaginable time to a seven-year-old and tracing the secret fairies' path under the spring's thickets to find the violets and soft primrose and sweet sweet sorrel flowers in the ivoried glade, image of heaven.

The gentle place, the wood of fairie, Tír na nÓg, the ever-youth.

And, oh, it was little tender Holly, the silver bitch named after the magic tree by the door, with its bitter witches' fruit but silvered bark. Holly the sweet, the faithful, never leaping or excited, who lay by her mother's feet content, talked to her with her lovely eyes – one blue, one brown – and minded the childers in that Irish land when her mother must search out the cow (*oh, searching ... could she match her ma? Not for a milk-cow but ... impossible quest was it not?*) or the wanderer donkey through the bog at night, Holly who loved them till her cruel death, who would ever be by them and welcome them home. Like Kate was welcomed today.

And by her mother's ever-smile.

3

The great art

Next, convent school, away from home, away from him. First step from the fairyland of home. Cycling to reach it with quiet father through Donegal lanes in rain, snow, ice. Gales, mist, showers. Thorn-burst tyres. The gaiters her mother knitted against the cold (*cold – 'the enemy' her mother called it, she was right*). But sun, sun that was what she always recalled. And rain.

But the convent. There she learned – not to count (*never!*) but the resonances of words. How lovely. How had she, the reader, not felt it before? Quoting, imitation, tradition, allusion, reminiscence (*ah …*), echoes through all literature, ritual, culture. Others' words in speeches, religious things, high art (*low art too you unpopular snob! She'd learnt her convent lesson well. No, not 'popular' – humble, poor, Christ's sheep that even priests forgot*).

And were not Milton and Wordsworth crammed with allusions and parallels. Or who could new-compose Pope's poems or Coleridge or Milton either, and not draw on others' words? And countless others too, Words they learned in parrot minds 'fore e'er they broke their morning's fast. Did not Renaissance arts or Greek or African recycle others' texts? Shakespeare too and Bible, yes – of that the nuns spoke not.

Allusion, they taught – and they were right – is ubiquitous: sermons brimmed with biblical bits, writings that are naught but quotation. 'In what sense or senses might that be said to be wrong? Discuss in the light of your own reading and reflection' they said, 'and don't forget to include quotations now!'

Fantasy is quote you know and image – a lesson played out with her life.

'Puns?' spoke up Kate, bravely.

'No' they said fiercely, 'puns is different, puns is for punishment and punitive-ness and puncheingness.'

'Punch and Judy?' asked Kate all innocence. (*That'd be a good pun wouldn't it?*)

'Behave yourself miss, or you'll not miss (*miss?*) your pune- ish-ment, you dead won't an' all.' And punctuation, 'Essential, girls, for proper finished ladies.' And punting with phallic, er, punic poles in the 'Ford er, Cam.' Ha ha, but they didn't see the joke – well Sister Clare (*their 'Sissy'*) stifled a little giggle, but she was only a new girl. And Punic warriors and (*shudder*) punks, and, and – oh all those-punnyfunnyfings. 'Just you watch it young miss no thinking here ...'

And those recycling myths of loss and quests and sainthood an' heaven lost and re-found again. 'However you define it,' they continued solemnly looking quite uplifted but blushing slightly, 'quotation and transformations interpenetrate (*hmm ...*) the arts and rites of humankind, creators and hearers evoke, play on, the words and voices of the others.' As she did.

Kate agreed, a new insight into the novels and poems that she adored. But it was, actually, all rather grand for a young writer-reader like her. It wasn't as if these mythic tales of love or quests or loss could ever have meaning for *her* life. Why did that memory (*memory?*) make her shudder? What nonsense! Bury it!

Like all else in life, quoting was there to be controlled (*that was better*), trammeled by human reason. So often applauded but it was dang'rous too. By the wrong person (*lower orders!*), out of place, or number (*ha!*), or time. Saying wrong thing to wrong person. 'Freedom' said the motto over the school side gate, 'is the right to say what the hearer does not want to hear,' or something like that. Guided her for life. Not that she would ever dare – even if she *did* know what she thought. Much much better, far better, give in to others' views, give them their space, that was her nature wasn't it? Why else be Kate?

Suited her OK that they went on an' on about sacrifice. And giving giving giving. That was *her* all right, her, Kate.

Or showing off. *Not* her! She would never make pretentious-ness of her learning even if she could quote scripture and Greek and Latin plays in the original. Even love poetry (*oh-oh*). Catul-lus under the desk – no not *Lesbia*, but with him, him, with him, not there, f'rever entangled heart … 'neath the oak's great arching branches ('*arch*'! – *for her-him only ever*), Catullus' love, a friend, a brother, a – no!. And as for 'plagiarism', well, that's what they call it now – used to be 'inspiration' like Handel's Messiah or Milton's 'hand of God'.

And platypus too, no sorry 'parody', mock quotes. How we rolled in the aisles then as they showed us – relief to our solemned nun-ned dumbned lessons there – James Stephens' 'Wordsworth', and told us (*serious now*) to track its 'original' for the two (*two?*) voices, that of the deep, and that of (*oh great!*) an old half-witted sheep, and then, quite right:

> "*good Lord! I'd rather be*
> *quite unacquainted with the A.B.C.*
> *than write such hopeless rubbish as thy worst.*"

But she was actually on Mr W's side, so was her verse …

Quotation is always with us, they went on and on – regurgitation, copying, theft, appropriation (*that's kinder?*), imitation, inspirati-on. 'Collage' they said, and 'sampling' too, the po mo lingo now. Did not writers for centuries burnish the dark as well as the bright polish of repeating others' words?

'A fine quotation is a diamond on the finger of a man of wit, a pebble in the hand of a fool,' we parroted after.

Kate agreed really but quoting wasn't her thing! And she would not, she decidedly would *not* give in to that malarkey, would not allow her well-ordered career to mimic one of those shady recycled tales. NEVER!

They learned much of the glories of God's creation. Of the vertebrates and invertebrates, the birds and beasts of the earth, shells and creatures of the sea, the worms that slide beneath the ground and the snakes over it, the insects of the sky. And they spoke with hushed breath of angels and archangels, of heaven – and of God himself. Kate and the others listened but weren't much impressed – or anyway seemed not to be, it wasn't the done thing.

And then the nuns told them to treat even the rough and hairy and beetle-like (*uuuugh!*) as if they were – angels! Fat chance!

And the nuns prophesied to them of the *Fall of Pride* – not vanity, not self-worth, not boastful-of-God or Pilgrim with Mr Vainglorious-For-Truth, but *Pride*. Male pride that riseth erect in the passion of night, falls to nothing under the star, the lull, the fall of morn. Why were they hiding their faces? Blushes. What did the nuns know that they didn't? (*Hiding?*).

The students (*yes, they were called that now, wonder of wonders!*) couldn't tell the reason. But it certainly felt right for a giggle behind the boat shed. Yes Ireland, so of course a lake, or was it the sea estuary with tides up and down and mountains around? Nothing so lovely, in Kate's eyes at least. (*Oh – attend there!*). So they did. Giggle that is. By the sheds, the shores, the palace gardens. They knew their duty as pious learners. And never forgot the lesson, though now, perhaps ... did it *maybe* have a deeper meaning?

Theological, anyway not erot-, whatever that was ...

They made her cut her long hair – 'pride' they said and made her shiver – the only thing of herself she loved. 'Mortification of the Flesh' they said – brings you nearer God.' Fat chance again. What *was* 'flesh' anyhow? Must she be vegetarian and not mortify the meat on Fridays, lent, five-thousand-feeding? Now *that* was mordentification if anything was!

But mostly she loved her schooldays. Even the boat-shed ditties they knew were wrong were right. Like:

> Wen u is i, nd I is u, how gr8 th luv, btxt uz 2

And better because somehow naughtier (*don't tell the worst. Later. Maybe*):

> u r so swete like mrshmllows 2 eat, 2 scoff
> s a treet 2 eat so farwll u sweet am off

Sad really. Not Catullus of course.

The nuns didn't understand texts, or so they said, good thing (*just u wait!*), but confistikated phones anyway (*and that's why, dear children, mobiles weren't there till 39 years after. So now you know. Education isn't for nothing you know ...*)

They were growing up and developing, er, er, 'figures'. Not 'cleavages', that isn't the right attitude at all at all now girls. So when they heard us rhyming on they didn't pay us no attention they didna, 'just a skipping game, mens sana and all that', it was their duty to see to our physical – well, not *too* physical – needs, converted into teachers by God himself with heaven round the corner for the non-sinner-runners, the non-physical. No marathon runs for them. Or us.

We loved the rhythm and certainly knew what it meant for those in the know, for I knew that you knew that I saw that you saw my, er, cleavage. And the shocked but wondrfly descriptive (*was it?*) exclamation at the end, and the kiss or was it prohibiti-on? We knew it was naughty but we *loved* it – what anyone saw we never knew. But anyway, away we skipped nipped sipped ripped quipped all the more:

I nu u nu I saw u saw, ma clevj, X, OooooO

Easier, even for the nuns, was:

hi is it u, if so hi I luv ya tru

A little suspicious but not too bad, 'specially if, sensible us, we didn't seem to be making too much of it. That was before they took away the phones of course, but the beat never left us.

And on the loo wall (*giggle wriggle piddle*):

If you sprinkle
As you tinkle
Be a sweetie
Wipe the seatie

Quite so. What better use of that high nunless funless genre?

Those wonderful poems, even if they *were* from the Bible (*not from mobiles, don't get me wrong*). Psalms. The love of mountains, oh the dreaming hills of the North West. The Song of Solomon. And those other songs, even if they did call them hymns. And that amazing one she'd found all on her own and hid in her heart:

"Amazing Grace, how sweet the sound,
That saved a wretch like me,
I once was lost, but now am found,
Was blind, but now, I see....
The earth shall soon dissolve like snow,
The sun forbear to shine,
But God, who call'd me here below,
Will be for ever mine."

She loved the bit about the sun forgetting to shine (*well he did, didn't he, for days on end in Donegal?*), made just for her.

Or the song the sea sang when she walked on the shore, promising great things for her life, for her, only if she'd just look up when …

And that – a classic model they called it, Elizabethan genre, special subject 'the Sonnet'. She knew Shakespeare was thinking just of her and and – was it of someone else too, or just the Irish summers?

> *"Shall I compare thee to a summer's day?*
> *Thou art more lovely and more temperate: …*
> *But thy eternal summer shall not fade,*
> *Nor lose possession of that fair thou ow'st, …*
> *So long as men can breathe, or eyes can see,*
> *So long lives this, and this gives life to thee."*

She couldn't follow it all but knew the printers had got the last line wrong – trust them to obsess about ink-writ this or that rather than lifelong love. She knew better and amended it in her heart. But of course she didn't tell the nuns. Or even him when she saw him next (*not often now*). Or her friends behind the boat shed.

Well anyway, she survived, her heart full of many things.

And then the slogan over the door at the rear. 'It's *rear*, do not say backside, even backside, girls. Even if pray God you don't know what it means. Vulgar.'

> *"That whereof one cannot speak,*
> *thereof one must be silent."*

Or something like that.

What a bleak saying, worse even than 'all hope abandon …' which Kate positively liked. Think of all the wonderful words and places that followed. She'd love to visit hell one day, and it'd be warm there wouldn't it? Anyway it was TRIPE. As if there could ever ever be a time when words, speaking, couldn't help. You can talk about *anything*, well she could anyway, and well did her teachers know it! Suited the nuns though. Well maybe not Sis Clairey, still new. Ish. Though with her it'd be a giggle more like. She was human – so far.

Well anyway Kate pushed it from her mind. Firmly. Not for her.

'Lean and mean,' they said next, 'lean and mean's the motto for your figures and your prose. Only then will girls achieve finishment. Mind ye it well!'

So they, they crossed out all Kate's lovely indulgences, sent her to the bottom of the class, lucky no longer the corner or the hat.

'No more treats for you miss till at least three-quarters cut. Down. Cut down. And detention till you write us out 200 times, your best be-Irished uncial calligraphy.' Well it *is* beautiful but not after hundreds of times …

And this shall be your text – 'Hail Mary' – oh yes, 50 of those too, they're short at least.

'I must not, must not never use three words, or four, when one, one will do. I must shun from all long sentences until I am a nun. I must be lean and meaner like a nun. I MUST NOT!'

She tried, she really did, and missed her supper – 'lean' indeed! And all her sleep. And breakfast too. For the first try didn't pass, she'd missed a 'not' in the second line:

'Too clever by half miss, cut y'rsel' didn' y' now, that kind o' slyness'll end you in the ditch, the dirt-filled shough (*they went all Irish when they were special-uplifted*) so it will now, up to yir knees now and serve y' right now.'

The second didn't either, she'd counted wrong hadn't she now (*oh Kate Kate*), and written it once too often (*oh Kate, numbers!*).

And Kate wept. Well no she didn't, she wasn't seven now. Big Girl, back row. But nearly. Well, just think – language not like numbers, language th' nearest thing to God bar music, language greatest gift to man, language too deep 'n dear for tears. Well perhaps she did weep, just a little in the dark o' the night for her dear blind mentors and what they missed.

Then the nuns told them again – their 'leit motif' (*big word!*) it was – hushed as if it was secret, mythic, of the Fall of Pride, not vanity again (*didah didah didah didah …*). Well alright, she did never forget the less'n, un-understood, if now …

Oh! her name on the redboard – sinboard! 'Miss Cath-erine to see HeadNun. H.E.N.'

Her own full name. It was serious then. Called to Her-Eminence-Now, or was it High Excellent Nun, even Mother Hen – how *dare* she take that scared-sacred mother-name?

'And what my dear (*'my dear' – it was really serious*) would you say was your besetting sin? My dear?' she asked. (*Gently perhaps, well nuns aren't gentle but you know what I mean – trying*).

'Er. Er. Er. Too much reading, or er, er (*what would sound good?*), er, love?' (*Well that was sort-of true – she thought of him*).

'No, my dearest lamb (*worse still*), it is impatience. Im-pat-i-ence. And OverTheTopness.'

Kate had never heard of that, not one of the Deadly sins, perhaps she only qualified for second-class ones, or was it the same as pride perhaps? Pride, perhaps pride pride perhaps prancing riding priding p'rading raiding down the precious years and … a lovely ring …

'*Attend!*. IM-PAT-I-ENCE. Do you not skip to the end to see the finish and not stay for the middle, the meat?'

'Er, er, but not in lent. And I always read the beginning.'

'Dear. And what of those lines, your overweeningness and thinking to improve Our Grammar, given by God Himsel?' Irishness overcame her when she was moved. Avertin' sin. Her Vocation, Her (*she meant 'her' of course*) 'Callin'.

Kate hung her head. HeadWitch, er, HeadNun *right*. Her sins were indeed as scarlet, scarlet woman, scarlet, scartle, scampering scarletting scartling scarletting down the ages, rages, sages, mages, wisemen, stars … oh yes and Catherine's gridir'ning, wheeling, feeling, lightning, stabs, and fireworks, er, and …

'Yes sister, no sister, I confess it, *mea culpa culpissima* sister.'
And ran for it (*oh Kate Kate, impatience again, overweening, too
fast by half down corridor and centuries and, er, hallowed halls*).
Not waiting for the more kindly tone, 'I *will* say for ye, that y'are
"organized" there. Aye y'are.'

H.E.N. hadn't mentioned her darning – good at that she
was, but not worth noticing. How wrong she was we shall see. In
heaven. No darners there. All'd gone down to the darn-, the damned darning-ned dungeons below, where there was wailing and
gnashing of teeth and much darning and dashing and socking
of men's heads and heels. Well heels would always need darners,
even down there, wouldn't they? Poor Kate, good at it but not her
thing. Anyway too much praise would turn young damsels' heads,
even make them think they weren't the destined darners. Elect for
instance or summin' like that.

That blue-black motto – 'Courage, Gaiety, and a Quiet Mind'
– by the convent door, the one they never used, just for visitors,
who all had little text prints given to them before they left. It was
actually quite good in spite being up there.

Quite what convents had to do with gaiety or 'gaydom' Kate
couldn't think, though she liked that word (*had she just made it
up?*). Quiet minds all right, empty … full of information of course,
cleverness, 'wise words' and texts and hail-to-Mary's. But no music
there, not really. (*Yes, that's what I mean – empty*).

Strange – with all that there she couldn't quite help but love the
nuns. Teachers. Misguided – but isn't that the best of educati-on?

They thought that text would be the handhold for their girls
for life. With a *deo gratias* at the end, and a pious clasping of hands.

Not for her. Rituals had more meaning than she liked to admit.
It was true. But she didn't know where she was going or who was
going with her or who she would love or who she would marry –
there was a song or was it a snog? Her spelling wasn't too wonderful

either and as for touch typing, forget it! That kind of singing was not allowed so naturally she loved it but couldn't quite remember, was it down by some Salley-Alley-Palley Gardens or something, near the boat shed, by the river?

Anyway, what she held for life or what life (*life?*) held for her she'd no idea, but she longed to know … She knew nothing, bless'd ign'rance, the rest so full of knowledge.

Ev'n so, the vision she learned there was to love, ever seeking ever-giving. Others first, for them, of never giving up even a thousand lines. Like the horns on the hilltops, the goats leaping, hers was to endure. To the end. She knew all ends were bitter, but OK, she would learn to like bitterness. Perhaps it wouldn't be so bad.

Then the nuns explained that all the proper poetry was for *men* – about them. So thus it was and she observed the rule. But secretly she thought the poem that she'd made up by herself (*and she a girl, fifteen she was*), made for herself, was really truly fully – for her (*she put a man in lest the nuns found it*):

> *I am on a path*
> *lovely with basil and nettle*
> *I cannot tell where it may go*
> *perhaps to a swamp*
> *or an impassable river*
> *a high hill*
> *with sight of the sea*
> *I only know*
> *it will not go back*
> *and I must tread on.*
>
> *So was it 'fore my life began*
> *so is it now I am a man*
> *so will it go when I am gone*
> *'pon this world's track*
> *no longer on.*

Remember me.

'Remember me.' A saying for her life.

4

Africa, a story and a tsunami

So Kate grew in wisdom and beauty and forgot the strand and her dear loved friend. But though *she* forgot, we will learn more of *him*, and had he not his own success?

And, beautiful, she soon had many loves. Not close. But sort-of love. And kept them at a distance. Light were they all, to her. But they did well enough. For now. 'For now?' 'Enough?' She would not think of that …

She flourished in her profession and her business prospered – she was 'organized,' just like they said. And she interacted daily, as required, with the social media. And she had money to travel to 'make more contacts' – she wouldn't admit it was just a holiday.

Africa. The Congo! She knew that 'age old lost world tribal-time-immemorial back-to-our-roots' image was all wrong. Victorian patronizing – were the Victorians always wrong? But still. Still there was a tug to her heart that she hardly knew. Or would not know.

So she journeyed. And *did* Africa. And might the age-old

(*watch-it*), er, great Congo river hold something of that, ah, time-less truth in its ever ever-flow? She'd known only the little canal ones, 'leats' they were called, rhymed with her golden Keats, those wonder Drake-made water-carriers of the Dartmoor hills. She'd seen them once, her mother took them, a far cry from Donegal, and yet another place of fairies.

They flowed in her mind now, unresisted, as she sat by that mighty dustless flowing river of Africa. No dust here (*oh that relief at least*), bringing the water from that black ink darkest land to the light of the sea's salving flow, loos'ning hearts for what was to come. So little did she know, that innocent convent girl, that not-Congo Irish girl!

She stood by its waters, never the same flow twice (*not for nothing had she learned her classics – that was before*), exile from her own leat-bound chain-ed heart. She wept. Why? How could she tell?

'Contacts,' that was the thing, concentrate now high power-girl, fee-earning income generator. Listen to that rag-piggery water-carrier, what mumbling there? Karang, was that his black'moor name? Something 'bout Adami and Yifa (*coincidence, funny fings in Africa you know … well, listen you!*).

'Tell you a story, Kati?'

How did he know that name, that fate-destined, awful name, persona, hers – oh no, remember she was Kath-ar-ine, Kathryn (*for mates*), high earner, top MBA, twice over top-pest student, part-time of course, top earner that year too, twice would you believe! Never sell yourself short she knew …

'A story for you. About when the earth came out, how after long we were brought out, we mortals, how after long we came to do work, how we lived. I am going to tell it this evening.

You see – God was once up above up there – look. In the whole world then there were no people. So God said, "I will take people to there."

What he brought out were two human beings – one man, one

woman. What were their names? The man – he was Adami. The woman, the sweet one (*Kate struggled*) – she was Yifa.

Well, he set them down in a most beautiful sweet place, trees crowded into the shade by the stream. For her, for our sweet lady the queen of heaven, he had brought them out, they came and lived there, in the beautiful glade. But they found nothing to eat. So they went to God and made him formal obeisance as for a request, a heartiest prayer.

"We have come here to you."

"Any trouble?"

"No. no, *no* trouble. No, the reason we have come is this: you brought us out, you went and put us on the earth here, but – hunger! Nothing to eat. Will we not die tomorrow?"

So God said, "I will give you food."

He came and showed them the trees in fruit, the whole fruiting autumn glade. He showed them the fruit of every tree. For them to eat.

"This is your food."

Then he pointed to one tree. He showed them and said, "Don't eat this one!" It was like an orange, when it was in fruit it was red. "Don't eat this one! This is prohibited. You are not to eat it."

Adami said, "All right." Yifa said the same, but you know women, "Just looking …"

They lived there for long – they ate the fruits of the trees. They did no work. They did nothing except just live there, except that when they were hungry they went and ate.

Then a snake got up there. He came and made love with the woman, with Yifa. They travelled far in that love.

Then the snake came near, the speckled spattered sneaky snake. He came and said to Yifa, winning – whenever did you see him lose?

"Do you never eat from this tree?"

Yifa said, "No. We do not eat it. We were told that we should not eat it. It is taboo'd."

Then the snake said, "Oh you! That tree – eat from it!"

Yifa said, "We do not eat it."

"Eat it! Would I lie to you? We share in love you and I. Just eat it. There's nothing wrong about it."

Yifa said, imploring – it's hard to go against your love – "We do not eat it. If we eat it we are doing something wrong."

The snake said, "Not at all. Just eat."

So she agreed.

Then the snake picked it, carefully, sweetly, lovingly. He looked at it with his glittering coils below, bright head poised, tongue flickering – you know snakes (*she didn't*), devilish but oh so winning.

So the snake gave it to her (*so, so, no, oh no, thought Kate, she had not turned her back after all, why dreams uncontrolled, he could master – but no, no thought of … of … of … that, mastering, she was all right so long as she didn't know the name. Or the number, there anyway she was safe*).

The snake gave it to Yifa.

She said, "You eat first."

That would make it all right wouldn't it? It didn't.

So – he bit. Into it.

Yifa took it. She held it in her hand (*oh the sound of the waves, the blown spume, the cold rain – in Africa?*).

She ate.

Adami came back. "What are doing Woman, Woman-of-Mine. WIFE!!! We mustn't ever eat that one!"

"Not at all," said Yifa. Lightly. "Just eat, there y'are. There's nothing wrong about it."

He refused but – you know women – she let down her hair (*like mine once, for him, like for him*) and wheedled him.

So – you know men. He ate.

Now God was sitting up above, a snooze after nut an' apple lunch, not payin' heed.

He looked over his parapet. A thoughtful angel had put it

there to catch him when he fell off his rocking chair and the cats weren't around to rescue him from mid-air, you know what cats are like, they'd all sneaked off duty to play with the knitting wool, little monkeys, time they had a dog to keep them up to er, scratch, but cats always win, it's the eyes you know.

Well anyway Ms Kate, he woke with a jump and saw O-O-Oh!!

He saw *exactly* what had happened. His people, so lovingly set in the beautiful garden, hoed and planted by his hundred, er, wives. And they'd transgressed his prohibition! Impedimented the light for every wandering bark. False! Flouted him …

Down below Adami's heart was shaking. His knees were limping too.

Yifa was looking the other way, Kate probably too, she preferred to avoid emotions, especially strong ones. And especially if they might be hers.

Adami whispered, "When G-God comes here tomorrow, he'll know we've done something horridly wrong."

So when he saw God coming Adami hid himself. He crouched down in the bushes, straggly, good for hide-and-seek. Hadn't the snake and Yifa …? 'nuff said.

Actually they both hid. Yifa too. She knew she had done nothing wrong, but well …

God arrived and called, calling the man, "Adami! Adami!"

Adami was afraid to reply – for he had eaten from the tree.

God called again.

"Adami! Adami!"

He was afraid to reply.

God called again: "Yifa! Yifa!"

They were both too afraid to reply.

Then at last Adami replied – terrified. He came out.

"Adami!"

"Yes?"

"What made you eat from that tree? I told you you were not

to eat it. You ate it all the same. What made you do it?"

"Ah, my father. It was not *me*. It was the woman who gave it to me." (*Just like a man thought Kate*). "Of course I refused, I said, 'I do not eat this.' (*How self-righteous he was*). She told me, 'Just eat it.' *She's* the one to punish, not me."

God called Yifa: "Come here!"

She came, she trembled, she tried to throw herself at his feet like women do, but he was up to those feminine wiles, had had enough of them in heaven I'd say.

"What made you give him from that tree for him to eat?"

"It wasn't *me*, my father (*just like a woman*), it was the snake. Oh and I kept refusing, so I did and did and did, for *hours*. But he kept on and on and on at me (*you know, lovers …*) and I … I …"

So then God called the snake – a real court of law it was – and asked him about what had occurred. God listened, his head to one side, his red hat over his brows.

The evidence had been heard. Heard. The case was finished. Finished in those old days of the beginning of the world. And all the heavenly host agreed on the verdict "GUILTY. Guilty as Sin. As human original sin. As apple stolen. As love accomplished, er, denied."

So they left the garden, that sweet glade. Adami and Yifa.

So that is why God's people suffer. We have to work. The sun burns us, the rain soaks us, we struggle through the rivers, and a sore devil with no face, 'Emoti-on' is his name, he haunts us each day. And if we try to run we must face him and be stretched on the rack and burned with passion and brands before we can eat. Ha!

We endure that suffering – if we want to eat we have to struggle for long long long, seven years, centuries. It started with the snake. That first woe, first original sin, it started there (*it was really the snake, you know not us, how unfair was God*).

So you see how we live, we people, working – that was how it began.

So that is it, amen.'

He said his people had learnt that story many many genera-
tions before from a priest who had come from the place where the
sky meets the earth, and where sailing ships slip over the edge into
the Black Hole and the Kraken's ravening maw. Or perhaps it was
his grandfather who told the priest and he took it away with him.
Who knows?

Kate was entranced. By the place, by the sweet tones, by the
mystery of it all. Why did the tale perturb her so.? Of what possible
significance could it be for *her*?

There were some words at the end that for sure *were* for her. Or
her own. Fleeting shreds of a dream remembered not remembered,
spray of the sea, Milky Way melting to the dawn, a man's arms.
(*No!*). The words fled away from her. Could she find meaning in
a crude African tale? Never while her mind was unshuttered and
her calm control, her own busy life, her aims her (*no no, not her
dreams*), her 'mission' held unfettered sway.

She reflected. Calmly. Of course. 'Age old myth of tribal Africa.
Primitive. Childish.' Why should it stir her? Adam, Eve, apple?
Snake? But it was 'Adami' that pierced her, how could that name
feel so close? So far ?

She must rid her mind of the troubling dreams that came again
and again to torment-inspire her (*hopes …? No not that*).

She looked again. That young girl slim, immature, narrow
beads low on loins, necklace over small jutting breasts, near-ripe
for marriage. Balancing water from the great river for her brothers,
such ease such grace.

What beauty, what innocence of this world's passions, the
crude emotions seat of misleadingness. Little would she know of
sacred myths of earth.

The girl was singing now? Some song, young and suited to
her innocence, a song of maidens' play with childlike friends, of
Nausicaa's ball and shore. Kate crept closer to listen to such sweet

singing, dreamlike, entrancing as she had never before known. It was about the origin of death – and, alas, she thought of love. And of the death of love's passion. She sang:

> *Once in the old old days*
> *or ere the world'd begun*
> *lived people free of death and sin*
> *and free of love and passi-on.*
> *For so God willed.*
>
> *He willed no death in th' earth, no sin*
> *his will to win*
> *he mixed a charm of magicked leaves*
> *so there should be no sin or death*
> *in world begin.*
> *For so God willed.*
>
> *An innocent sweet maid to carry it*
> *Kateki she*
> *without e'er sin of passi-on*
> *on earth to be.*
> *For so God willed.*
>
> *So on she went, bowl on her head*
> *to bring to us our freedom here*
> *see innocence and grace now come*
> *and passi-on e'er banned to be.*
> *For so God willed.*
>
> *But snake, see, willed it otherwise*
> *he tripped the maid, seduced her there*
> *laid in the bushes' tangled sin*
> *without a thought, a dread, a care.*
> *And thus was herb in those days shed*
> *spilled in the wilderness of love*

so ne'er could men released from dread
or sin or passi-on ever be.
For so God ...

Her voice faltered and died, but Kate completed it:

'*... so God willed.*'

Oh, but did he, could he, wish death, sin, p-passion on the world? (*On her – that thought wasn't there* ...).

Emoti-on – it fitted the rhythm. And the rhyme, did they have rhyme in African verse? She'd heard they didn't but was it somehow there? And had that young uneducated girl – African, she must be uneducated – not yet been instructed in the elders' ways, in the dread initiation bush?

And passion, oh passi-on, oh passing-by (*him passing by? Oh but he would not ... never*), impasse-ion – what artifice, what play on words – no not for her. That would be against the inmost dwellings of her soul, her *mind*, the aptness in which she had her life and being.

The old man cross-legged 'neath the twisty thorn tree raised up his quavering tones above the river's tumble.

'Once upon a time there were ...'

Kate was barely listening now, she had too much (*what?*) to trouble her ...

'And in their travel they ventured deep in the bush. They crossed one river. They crossed another. They came to a third. And the young girl threw her child so the crocodiles would not devour them there. They came out. They went again into the bush, *de-e-eep* under the arch of the green-growing arching trees and then ...'

'*N-o-ooh!*'

Kate heard the scream bounce along the edges of the universe. Penetrate the earth with her agony.

An arch!

It was *her dream*, hidden, oft surfaced oft submerged, concealed resisted forgotten come-yet-again dream – and again, again again again to torture her.

Could *he* not leave her in peace?

As she was. In her life, controlled, ordered managed her own. Helping others. Care. Friendship. Keeping separate, sep-ar-ate.

Leave her as she was!! In control of her life. Even the scientists agreed. Had she not read that learned article last week, corroborating her convictions? Is not science always so? Except – oh except *eppur si muove* ... But to the point, she read it back to herself:

> "Happiness – you know it when you see it, but it's hard to define. You might call it a sense of well-being, of optimism or of meaningfulness in life, although those could also be treated as separate entities. But whatever happiness is, we know that we want it, and that is just somehow good.
>
> We know that we do not always have control over our happiness."

There was more but she couldn't quite recall. Technical stuff, numbers, double blindnesses (*not for her*). Happiness was 'under her control', that's what they were saying, wasn't it? Well, as far as she was concerned it *was*!

Scream again, unearthly, yes unearthly. Destroying the universe. Unheard but all the worse for that. How can you control what you cannot hear? Again. And again. From hell. Not upper earth.

'I no longer exist. I exist – in hell.'

Aaaah ah! Ah! Ah! Ah! ...

She remembered her dream, that dream (*from where? Don't imagine, don't think ...*) she had forced herself so many many many times to resist forget bury.

Then yet again she entered under some great curved St Pancras arch-ed roof, dreamed then in her dream long e'er that roof was first ev'n thought. Or great museum dome. Her hand, see there, was gentle on his arm, unfelt and calmed, on dear friend's arm, supporting her, befriending all her separated life. Accustomed. Gentle. Undemanding there. Was not friendship God's great gift to us, to all mankind?

But then, *explosi-on* in paean, curse, destruction, demolition of her life, her harnessed harvest garnered happiness.

For next she dream-ed that they walked as one beneath that high and arching roof for station built, together here and hand on hand, the gentle hand of friend, and then I felt (*oh she was I, and I was she, for such is Dream*), I touched, I turned, no friend but lover, lover passionate and burned, with fire to love …

So she awoke (*I did?*). But *she* was the one who dreamed again.

> *We walked as one*
> *beneath the high and archen tilt*
> *of stars and milken way*
> *from heaven built, for our delight*
> *and long I felt his hand on mine*
> *the gentling hand of friend*
> *through many years.*
>
> *But then I turned*
> *no friend, nor foe, but lover*
> *passionate and burned*
> *with love for … me.*

So I awoke.

> *I dreamed of walking once again*
> *with gentling friendship's hand in mine, as one*
> *within the oak tree's mighty roots*
> *its branches, arches, leaves*

once born of acorn ready set
with its roots and branches
waiting there, for us.

So then I turned
and met the pain the joy!
For 'twas not friend
but lover walking there.

Then I awoke.

Then dreamed again, the last
of walking quiet in friendship
all desire now past and gone
for evermore.

But look!
We were within the great and orb-ed veins
of hearte's blood and tears and beats
aorta sending labyrinthine breath to lungs, to heart
his gentling hand on mine so still so tranquil near
and oh but look, we walk within my heart.

But this time, this time, oh this time, she did not want to wake.

And then, then by that great river of old Africa, then a great change came over Kate.

Hurricane. Earthquake. Maelstrom. Volcano, a millionfold erupting with moltenest burningest lava. Tsunami sweeping all before.

Words cannot tell it, but for the first time Kate saw her life. Her loves, her hates, her trials and successes, there, by the river they passed one by one before her eyes. And her feelings erupted in phoenixsome firesome fearsomen words, molten lava like she had never known:

I long for you

(oh and she did and she did and she did)
I long for you as one
by hurricane oppressed
lost in the storm-crossed ocean
by storm and wind distress'd
goes without rudder sail-less
no friend no love in sight.

She was lost. Not now the cool dispassionate one wherein her self-pride lay. She was different, changed, migrated. Utterly. She was no longer herself, no self, no-nothing. No nowhere. (*Even numbers didn't matter to her no more, how strange*).

She no longer existed. Where had she gone?

Oh grief on the sea
where waves heave and roll.
How come I to shore?
How can I land whole?
Not broken and torment
not hurted and torn
and swim to be safe
midst clashes and noise
'f storm and o' typhoon
and taste of the joys
of life not of death
of love not of drown.

Where was the final line, the resolution? Could she continue? Could she run? But his shadow followed close after hound of hell, of heaven, she knew not what on her heels, no place to hide.

Words struggled, tsunami words she could not utter but knew knew knew, in what could such fires erupt but in poetry, words not of muses but the furies, Erinyes, forced look in the very mirror of her heart:

I needed not say I loved him
those years ago
I need not remind you now
– for you know.

I need not tell you of joys and tears
of loves and longing those centuri'd years
I did not tell you in calm or in blow
I was too young
those years ago.

I did not speak of love and longing
ah – you know.

How could she be so blind deaf so unfeeling? No, not unfeeling, feeling over-mastered, not like him the controlling of the chariot pair, but the more she closed her eyes, her grey eyes – had he not once called them beautiful?

Now was too late for she saw what destiny held for her, had held all along. She recalled his words, bitter words she saw now, she had thought it only a ditty, person-switched in irony, lightly cobbled to stop the boredom of a summer evening amid the nightingales of the meadowsweet. How she had been wrong!

I said it was friendship
but you wanted love
I said that I'd thought of you
when you wanted – above
above kingdoms and treasures
and heavens and earths
and care b'yond all measures
and throne-place and shrine
b'yond sorrows and mirths
that heart my beloved
that cannot be mine.

For then at last the tsunami revealed to her those passions she had denied. The verse was the wrong way, was written upside in the water, floating away ... For the heart that was wanted was *his*, the one that – oh how well how heart-piercedly expressed – could no longer be hers.

Submerged for seven years, seven by that fateful storm-torn day. Was she not born to love him?

He was hidden. Ever. In the mist. His face in shadow. Always. Even when he had let her see him. In the sea-mist. Seven years gone. Invisible. Invisible to *her*. For her only. For always always there. Dream, sea song, *l* ... *love*. There. She had said it.

So indeed she must search, seek. How else to know him, see the fragrance, hear the warmth of him through the cold gloom of a schoolroom or the table of a humble meal, his head's dawn-glow in the meeting hall or the great museum's dome?

And again words tormented her, why why why must the poets sing such pain? And again ...

Caught in love's chains that fearsome ring

But she scarcely knew him! Not in this life. Not-speaking when she was a girl and he a boy, so beautiful, a youth, separated by the emptiness of a classroom, a hiatus of life's years, a seven-year-eternity, the stuff of fairy – but this was real! Just those sparse hours when they met again, table-divided meal. How little it was!

And yet she had known him in the womb, since the sun and planets began or the Milky Way shone in the sky, from before death or sin had come to the world or the universe was made. Before God existed she was his.

She knew his inner being, all. Better than herself (*'as easy might I from myself depart ...',* oh quotation quotation, *why had not the nuns taught her how to avoid – for all their 'mortification of the flesh' they knew not it seemed*). His likes, his hates. His Mozart piano love they'd heard as one, and the hills and the stars and the sea.

I close my eyelids
free of day's care
So tranquille smooth
and soon to sleep and dream.

Oh but the night, the dreams
the terrors there
pulled down in damp
of clutching sea grass
down to drown and swamp
amidst the wreck and wrack
the storms the hurricanes of life
the lot and strife of being
the quagmire mires and
damping sucking swamps again,
where I must sink forgotten
ever more forgot
and gone, no surface left.

Ah me, what woe
to undergo in sleep and dream
ah will he never turn, look back
to care for me?

And God spoke again, she caught the echo through the ink-tangle-murmur of the sea.

'Severance, yes sever-ance, severe-ance, severest wound of all. The first lesson dear child: it is through your wounds that the light enters, hast thou not learned of the great Persian sage of old?' (*She hadn't, he hadn't either, else he would of ...*).

'Rumi,' he added kindly.

'Rumi? Wha-a t?' But he was pronouncing (*'pronouncing'? Oh, words again*).

'And second: is not language beautiful? Bethink thee once

more, again, of sever-ance, it is thy fate my child. Without thy sev-erance how can *per*-severance be? Perseverance. That too will be your fate …' (*Your? A prophecy?*).

God's words echoed in the fade of the waves, the water over her steps, the unrelenting relenting sky …

Now it was for *her* to seek, to find. She set her lips hard. She called on all her capricorned horned obstinancy of per-sever-ance (*God was right …*), not for naught were the leaping goats on the hill, avoided the passive-herd sheep. And the standing one, so still so quiet so contained. So knowing of sin. *They* knew what they had done, and what was still to do. Well, *she* would leap too, leap to the skies, the heavens till the lightning ceased and stars fell from the sky.

She would find *him*.

And then? She could not think, that was for the gods.

She prayed, how she prayed. Never before. Never before talked with God. Never before in her sweet entwinement had need.

And God harkened and answered, she had no words but he knew her need.

'To find him dear child? The road will be long, oh long, many years, centuries, eras of what they number (*oh, number!*) of human living. But if you will agree to meet these two conditions …' (*Two, two only? Not the three of fairyland, not seven, eight, two oh how easy. How undeserved*).

'First, you will not know yourself till all these things be accom-plished. In God's time.' ('*Das beste zeit*' – *so Kate thought it, the nuns hadn't known about German capitals had they? Or genders*).

'Do you accept?'

She accepted indeed. Eager. Not know herself! What more blessed fate? And 'all things accomplished', so far away, that would never come (*she was still quite young wasn't she! Her mother would've known better*).

'And second, dearest child – how hard this will be – you will not see his face until … until the ending, the black-inked ending that I in my great mercy have willed for you.'

She didn't like to ask if 'you' was singular or plural (*oh Kate Kate, numbers!*). Was it just for her, or ... or ... for both?

'Do you agree?'

She hesitated. That dear face? More known to her than her own. But she knew she would never forget. If only his face had not been in the cloud's shadow that day, cloud over the sea, mist rising, not her fault at all? (*Oh oh foretaste of her mist-full mist-tranced agony*).

But what could she do?

'Must it be?'

Oh anything rather than that. Not not see his strong left hand, his hair, his ... (*double negative indeed*).

'It *must*,' said God, quite sternly now.

'Or never see him in the flesh again – in heaven, that is another matter, not even I can prevent it – but never on earth, not arm, not face, not hair, not ...' (*Oh oh she knew it well from those nuns' tales, and not hide, hiding, hide-ance either, oh oh, never again*).

She drew a ... a bravened breath. She thought of those goats on hills, her mother's smile.

'I *will*,' she said.

And her voice echoed down the centuries, ready for another's 'I will, I do.' His voice.

Well at least ... but she could no longer recall that sweet face of love, those darken eyes, that soft hair tousled in the wind.

Kate looked around. She was alone with her grief. But a seed and small small seedling, a kernel was growing in the garden of her grief. She would not could not rest. But ever onwards, upwards, downwards, roundwards she must go – to find him.

No rest for her. What rest could *she* have, the guilty, the benighted, the accursed? All life she must pursue him, the phantom, the unloving, the no-longer-loving.

The no-longer-loving. That was the hell-est thing. Hurricane.

Her own accursed cursed curse.

And she *would* seek him. Through hazards of this earth's strife, through war and famine and pestilence, sin and innocence, and… and passion too, and the innermost secret thoughts of her mind. For was she not a creature of the mind? Of calm. Of quiet pursuits (*pursuits …*). All passion spent.

'Your heart my beloved that cannot be mine.'

Oh oh oh. So she had thought. She had been wrong. She had been too young.

> *Sap of my sap*
> *of my soul*
> *silk strands on maypole wrapt*
> *on tree of life*
> *my soul.*

> *How hard and hard again*
> *that long night's pain*
> *to climb perforce t' the very brink*
> *of th' passion'te hurricane*
> *t' stumble again and sink*
> *all knowing, all consenting*
> *in that tormented sea*
> *to fall again, to drown*
> *to lose again her very self.*

And now that she had seen her heart's desire, what now? What now? She had walked away. Run. But her life's quest was to follow, to find him, to kneel for forgiveness. Let her count him her ways, her travails through the earth, and tell the ways she loved him.

How strange that she had not known that sacred *him*. Not to be touched. *Noli me tangere.*

Proud. 'Pride comes before the Fall,' the nuns said. (*Giggle … all we knew!*).

It's harder by far for the proud. (*And he was proud was he not? Just look! That uplifted head, that scorning look*).

And do not volcanoes ever spew forth molten verse?

Blessèd the humble in heart
for it's theirs to inherit the earth
bless'd my submission to you
to your love, to your care, to your art
of loving and grieving
and joying and leaving
to pass-by at last for my heart
who must stoop to the love that is theirs?

For the rightful the stone-cover'd road
for the virtuous the cross-threating crowd
for them not the giv'd but receiving
for them the hard stoop to the meek.
O how can he bear to bend down t'me?
But come now from calvary's tree
for your sorr'ful your penitent love.

Oh why and why again the unending grinding round, sails of the windmill, tides flow and ebb, season after uncaring season, moon around the Earth?

Why why why and *how* had she grown a deny-er, a-crippled of the passion man lives by, the feel-emotions even God and shepherds love? Maybe not sheep? Lambs? Oh that time when together, as one, they saw a lamb born. First, the horror then the miracle, hard wool and stagger first, then little feet and mother's milk. And then then they rode together – tried, on the fierce ram's back – and were swept off, one then one more, by low branches over the sack-clothed back. (*No saddles or bridles then or hardhats-on, while the other laughed and ran to help – who knows?*).

But no, her mind had been on 'higher things'.

Her mother had seen it had she not? Forbidding Kate to read too young, to seek instead the fragrance of the skies, the fields, the bluest, flax, its color captured from the sky – only the fiercest twists could unroot *that* – the unrolled and rolling magics of the northerned lights, gorse-covered hills, soft primrose, birches, larch emotion-drenched and hazel hazel sprouting everywhere.

And that soft lullaby from Garten Vale, sung to her dream:

> *"Sleep my babe as the red bee hums*
> *The silent twilight's fall*
> *And Aiyvell from the wild hills comes*
> *To hold the world in thrall*
> *Oh sleep my child, my own, my dear*
> *My love my heart's desire*
> *As crickets sing you lullaby*
> *Beside the dying fire"*

Would she ever have that peace again?

She didn't remember the words right but the melody was in her heart, a tune of liberation and freedom. And wouldn't it have been Columba then that she sang to, founder of the Derry oak grove, Kate's maiden city.

How her heart was wrung, how could she have been so wrong to walkwalkwalkwalk … away? To turn the light out, ever out.

And now she knew it – she loved him.

She loved him she loved him she loved him, till she died.

Again and again and again must she return in dream, in flesh, to that pained strand. Her agony her penance. Her God's grace-given dream-nightmare. Could she never find the peace of a quiet heart, that ever fruitless prayer of lost souls all the ages?

> *I am torn by love and torment raged in a torrent sea*
> *Oh Lord, for a quiet mind and your serenitie.*

PART III

JOURNEY FOR THE HIDDEN

5

Hidden – at St Pancras International

And so her quest began. To see his face. Be near at last.

So now she waited waited waiting there for him. By archen roof once more. Centuries, eons, the beginning of the world. Seven years, it was a period indeed. But it was the appointed day, he would come.

Would he know her? Would he reveal himself to her at last? And oh – would he forgive her?

This was a good table, she would see as soon as he … And yes he would come, he would know her.

Or was it the right table? … 117 or 118? (*Kate had never been any good at figures – well did she recall those mental 'rithmetic tests in her little Donegal school – or names either*).

But no matter. Feast on that lovely scent through the open window, and the Italian food waiting for her. And here came the waiter with the menu.

Oh oh, now her love was coming, coming after seven years,

up from the rose garden Eurostar platform through the meeters-and-greeters.

Would he know she was there? Was he expecting her? Would he, oh would he know her? Was he still angry?

She had been too young. No no, untrue. No excuse to offer. She had walked away. Not even with another. Just walked away across the storm-filled shore. Seven years.

Would she have changed? Would he?

He had not.

Upright. Slim. Sedate ever. Pacing fleet-foot, lofty, lord, through the crowds, stooping stopping for a rosebud from the ragged girl accosting only him, looking in her eyes (*oh!*) as she fastened it to his coat, kissing her cheek (*oh oh!*), exclaiming at the thorn (*a thorn? – but then – do not thorn and rose ever lie together?*).

And just look! Hadn't he picked the only one with a thorn? How like him!

He had seen her! Seven years … Not recognition. Merely a need for lunch. The waiter spied him, brought him near.

'May I? May I join you? Hmm, excuse me, is this seat free, do you mind if I sit here?'

She stood, leapt, oh LEAPT from the table, to his arms, to his kiss, to his embrace.

'Huh?'

'Oh oh. I'm sorry, sorry, I didn't mean, I didn't … I couldn't … I'm so sorry … help it. Please, please my apologies.'

What embarrassment, what blushful, red-faced shame, and she beyond the years of *un*-wisdom. What would her mother have said? Worse, her brother? The waiter – even the young Italian waiter – would have seen this customer's behavior, six paces away. Even among St Pancras International's greeters and farewellers and fairwalkers, this was not seemly conduct.

Oh, had he remembered after all? (*Seven years …?*).

'Kate,' he said (*did he not, should he not, had he not? Her dream*), 'more fragrant than even I imagined, the thyme, that long journey from Paris, Europe. The forever days in Africa and the dry Sahara I remembered you, far away, gone far into that silent land away, counting my ways to love you.'

'Let us sit then. The waiter brings our menu, four paces away.'

'Been here long? Waiting for what? I missed my train. (*His figures were always right, the hand of God*). I caught the next train. Would I have missed you?'

'No, no, yes, no, yes, maybe. It is the appointed day.'

'This is fun then! Let us pretend to be a long-married couple. We might be meeting for our diamond anniversary, a secret assignment before home. Or maybe going to that hotel I spied not far away, you saw it? If ...'

'I did,' she said. (*Or didn't she?*).

'What to choose? Are you hungry? Soup – red pepper and goat cheese, yes please. Fish cakes for starter?'

'Yes, for me, and yes – wine. Sparkling, celebrating.'

The waiter arrived. Opportunity? She was quite attractive, seemed receptive, even too much so, good clothes, figure. Hmm ... maybe ...

'A celebration waiter! Sparkling rosé, a bottle. Large glasses please.' (*Seven years, can you believe?*). 'Do you recommend the special today?'

Perhaps he did, perhaps he didn't. He knew it was a rhetorical question – people don't ask waiters questions, and they've made up their minds anyway. Always. This couple looked smart enough, she with her youthful figure and he with his handsome face. They looked happy – though surely not up for much at their age. Forties, but well-preserved. Good for a decent tip?

'Your rose. It's lovely!' said Kate. 'Where does it come from? Surely St Pancras PLC doesn't allow barefoot girls on the platform?' (*Girls! Seven years waiting, and now he ...*).

'Yes, beautiful. Smell! Oh I've pricked your hand, I'm so sorry.

No all right, I see it's nothing.' (*A little love prick, think of it like that*).

'Yes,' she said.

'It wasn't meant to be,' he said. (*Didn't he?*).

'Let me fasten it to your larch-green coat, goes beautifully. Such a sweet rose. Flown in this morning from Kenya, picked in the freshest of the valley's dew, look, sweet golden petals with apricot rims, maygold she said they were called.'

'Perhaps in some other age and time,' she said. (*She did? She would have said, wouldn't she ...?*).

'To you Kate. Nice wine even if it is Italian. And what next?'

'But well ... I'm not really ... really. But do please do yourself, you've travelled so much further.'

He hadn't – had she not come the watery way across the Irish sea from storm-ridden Donegal where they'd climbed the peaks together? Muckish the pig's back. Errigal the Ancient.

And oh, how could he forget, or she, that sight down swooning from fear and delight, the sea kelp waving in the ocean's swell, fish darting among it, no closer than their darting thoughts, and seen the sea and he'd caught her fall in his arms and not hesitated or drawn his knife (*oh ... his knife ...*).

And yes she admitted it, she *was* tired ... the nearby hotel ... (*and so it would indeed after seven years*). Yes yes, and lying aside the cliff's edge on a floor of fragrant thyme, feeling all its soft harsh roots below, reaching perhaps down to eternity in the sweet scent-sent of thyme of ever-time. He would not have forgotten, even if she nearly had. That thyme fragrance, the substance of the air upholding them, their twining thoughts, their one-some ever one-iness.

'Waiter, just coffee please, cappuccino for you Kate? For me black with Strega and cream please – oh, for you too, needed I guess.' (*He was kind ...*).

The waiter hasted off, no hurry now for tips, they didn't look good for anything much he decided. Just move 'em on, lucrative ones waiting. Good thing they were finished, bring bill quick? He hovered. For once.

'Aren't stations wonderful?' said she. 'All those reunions! After … after sevensome years.'

'Farewells too.' (*That Donegal strand, that Oxford garden by the lake? Alas!*)

'Thank you waiter, that was quick. Thank you. Can we have the bill? My card. No I'll sign (*never remember number, no good with figures*), can't expect you to have anything but euros after your long journey. Next time perhaps?' (*Could there be? She could wait for him to the end of the world – but would he? Flower-girls. Witches. Princesses*).

She signed. Full name (*today, so far, she had remembered it when needed, those were the days you could sign for it all, avoid numbers, good thing. And his was … was …?*), address, telephone (*why that?*), bank numbers all recorded. They wouldn't lose track of them, ever, would they (*why would they want to?*). A discount next time there?

'Goodbye sir and madam, *thank you* now.' One euro! What did they think a man was?

'Careful – remember your card, you nearly forgot didn't you?' (*Same as ever Kate, demented! Love it!*)

She took the card, might need it.

Trod side by side. (*once more, so natural*), high heels along hard surface-noise (*heels at your age Kate?*). But their gait, oh it was Kate running, twenty-year speed, flying over the pavement, he fast after. (*Seven years ago on that sea-lapped sea-wracked heart-wracked shore, she'd run*).

To the hotel's steps, stiff major domo, soft yellow scarf, spotted gold tie, hat.

'Please to enter honored Sir and Madame, let me help you up the steps, not designed for high heels, ha ha.' (*Awkward – 'honored'? he was paid to fawn*). Fast to reception, card. Quick.

Did they have reservations?

Yes yes, all arranged, meeting here, staying (*surely we would come together today this very hour, this very instant. Booked seven years ago, surely they remembered? And surely we would meet here in this age and time? Destiny*).

Where was he? Oh the Gents. Of course. His case still there, no need to panic. Or help. After seven years she could surely manage even an English hotel.

'Mine,' she said. 'It's here, you reminded me! As always!' (*No cards in old days of course, just pennies in those days it was, it was*).

'Yes madam? I do apologize, the software is not working, out of our control. But yes of course I can take a mechanical print instead, hotel not full you see. Thank you. Which would you prefer, 118? 117? Both *beautiful* double rooms, windows, lovely view, thyme-fragrance from rose bed, fine ... Oh you don't mind?' (*Strange but never can account for foreigners – if indeed they were, something funny about them certainly*).

'Whichever ...'

Would she never get on?

Up in lift. Together. Not daring to look, hotel staff member escorting them. Suspicious? Monitoring? Daytime? But OK, going for his lunch, taking it early, wouldn't recall. Pointer to direction, she no good with figures, directions all those years (*wasn't it seven?*), might not have managed otherwise ...

... 117, 118?

Inside door. How she remembered melting to him ... seven years ... she had been too young. Heaven, sun above dew frosted meadows, rivers sparkling light. Face, oh face still shadow, but firm soft arms, seven seven years, eternities ...

'Yes,' she said.

Waking in heart's happiness, rose-lit dawn, rose-thyme fragrance, light. Footsteps by the sea. *Light?* Words piercing her brain from hospital-radio, piercey voice, ugh ... she thought she could make out the words now, just:

"An unknown gentleman was found in St Pancras Hotel this morning. The Police do not suspect foul play but urgently want to trace him. Anyone with information is requested to contact the nearest police station giving reference number (*she was no good with figures even if she did know anything – and did she?*), or if they wish to remain anonymous to telephone the free number. Crimestoppers UK, number ... (*not again – didn't they know she was no good with figures?*).

The hotel has been unable to trace him due to a computer failure, beyond their control of course, the human-operated printer was defective for a few seconds this morning and the name remains unreadable despite our best efforts (*always best*). The only clue is a yellow rose in his jacket, maygold, but it has now disappeared, its provenance remains a mystery. These roses hail only from Kenya in December and the flight by the World's Favorite Airline was cancelled for an unexplained mechanical fault. This puzzling case is likely to remain on the police books for some months ...

A statement issued by the St Pancras World Hotel explained that Lessons would be Learned. The operative concerned has been sent north of Watford for re-training. The hotel is fully open for business, all guests welcome, with a special discount on the raised prices for the summer season. By then the rose beds will be flowered, fully unique, first in St Pancras."

The fragrance through the open window, the rose garden, even hospitals open windows in December. She knew the maygold rose had been picked from among the little crawling beetles in Kenya just that morning for a pittance to support an extended family and troop of schoolchildren, carried on heads to market.

But she was too tired to tell them. Pleasanter to go to sleep and dream.

Bed 117 or 118? They were right she *was* confused.

6

The cliff

She remembered now.

Today, or was it yesterday? Or a hundred years thence? Or hence? She had clambered the sandy slope in terror (*she was only 15, too young, too young*), scrabbling scrambling, falling, climbing, wild rose fragrance, leaves, thorns. No one to comfort, to soothe, to balm her rose pierced hand.

She had abandoned him. Or was it herself? Good not-good? She no longer knew.

Gulls calling their young, the fluffing ones, teaching them fly, feather flying in the wing.

As if, as if that meant to mean something. She looked into her mind, her knowing of herself …

So tender so caring and loving
but – frighted so sore in the night
to take on another's loving.
so frightened by the light

of other's love so freely
so freely given thee.
'Oh get behind me Satan'
that cannot be for me.

For me clear freedom's wand'rings
for me the skies' expanse
I will not take your loving
I will not join the dance
a dance of two mingl'ng freely
to joy the night away
in love and passion blending
and whisper soft to say
'I love you so my darling ...'

And oh, to see the feather
its softest tend'rest curl
in womb entwined, oh tranquil,
and then, at last – unfurl.

But she would not think about that.

Could she know him more and deeper now than when they met as one? As childhood friend and playmate on the cliffs, the great chasms worn by Atlantic storm, or as ... as lovers? Just by searching, questing him? Might the calling of his name be still its answer there? No magic, only ... *she must not think.*

If he had followed. If she had seen him in the mist, not hiding in the mist, the spray, the rain. If she had not run ... (*she was too young*). If she had turned when he looked at her, with his sea-dark longing eyes ...

Was she dreaming? Was the search, the invisible vision so strong, was at last his love revealing, disclosing his hidden-ness? No, impossible

7

In the sea's hide-ance

So she stood again upon the cliff's front and gazed back at herself. Herself standing. Unmoving. Terrified. Of him of herself of him of her fifteen years of her seven years of what she had done.

Glance back to that wakeful Kate-ful fateful day? Was he standing there? Still, stillness, hidden stillness still. Surely he would follow her.

Yes, yes? The tiny figure swaying, moving … Fig-ure, fig yes fig, ever from Garden of Eden, the very image of love.

A pair …Pear, yes, oh that punning peering pear of ancient rhyme in convent college gardens. Pear of temptation. Pair-pear of love, of Garden of Eden, age-old tree, what was it but the fruit of that old appled pear for the middle middling muddl'ng wigg'ling mankind-ages. Pear of love, of longingnessing.

What was it the nuns had taught them, she who loved music, loved the image?

"Tasting a pear is an adventure fraught with anxiety.

As the opera lover yearns to witness, but seldom,
if ever, experiences the ultimate synthesis of music
and drama, so the pear connoisseur strives to obtain,
but seldom gets to consume, the perfect fruit at its
optimum state of maturity and stage of ripeness, to
produce the perfect proportion of texture, acidity,
and sweetness."

And did it not come in antiquity too and function with the fig
and the apple as the symbolic sacred of fruits?

For thus spake Homer, king of poets, lord of the image-simile:

"Without the courtyard by the door is a great garden,
of four plough-gates, and a hedge runs round on
either side. And there grow tall trees blossoming,
pear-trees and pomegranates, and apple-trees with
bright fruits, and sweet figs, and olives in their
bloom …

Pear upon pear waxes old, and apple on apple, yea,
and cluster ripens upon cluster of the grape, and
fig upon fig.… These were the splendid gifts of the
gods in the palace of the king."

No pair-ed-pear for her. Only the wind and the shimmering
dream-making entrancifying light falsifying her eyes, swirling
mists.

She … She would go back. She knew it.

But not yet. *He* must. Must feel her so tangible present-absence,
hear her silence, see her unmoved mover to remove, see it from
her stand, grasp at last why she turned from him. Why had she?

Why was it? She just needed to remind herself as she stood
there.

Just so she would understand.

But she *didn't* understand.

She was afraid.

But she did at least see – *he* would not be coming after her.

Not for her a shared arrival at the gates of gold with the man she loved. As she had always dreamed (*ah dreams, Kate, dreams so potent, so overcoming reality, could she call them up once more, her at the gate, he walking towards her with shining face and sandal torn … past, present, passing, passed …*).

She called again, again those potent words. Repetition, she had read, makes ritual …

Dearest of all thou art
amore delectissime
look down, still kind, on me
ev'n me, the one
who set thee on the tree
yet still from womb I see thee come
in oak-tree's bend
in woodway's wend
to clone my loving heart.

Dear twin oh come you back
if thou art kindly still
come now on music's way
in notes as sweet as you
only in heaven found
divinest sound
to me to you
of keyboard fugue.

Oh as I fall
come now in Yacob's stair
and dream
to hold me safe
my struggling soul, I sue

to thee above,
to wrestle back
to you.

To save from fall to catch me true
to wrest me back again to you
and back to God, to heaven again
the last and best of all …

He did not turn.

He did not come.

Oh, she knew so well that proud unyielding mien, that nose-lift high, the hidden scorp-concealing fast-beat heart-beat blood-beat flaming there. Still hiding. No morning star for rising shining meet … but LUCIFER himself (*no ghost, how else could skeleton live and move?*).

She had lost him. Lost in God's earth.

Had not her passionful passi-on-tsunami freed, resolved …?

Resolved yes resolution, now she'd *run* to him, easy down slope, straight to his arms dear eyes unhiding, tell how she loved him lovedhimlovedlovedhimalwayshad it was just her emotions hidden restrained now leaping *leaping* …

Running. Joyous. *Leap* to his arms.

But, a halt a shiver …

What was that?

Voices. Floating to her above. That delay from sight, that dreaming tracing echo.

'Ahoy there. Any room for a passenger? I'll pay my way no fear. Or work if you'd like it! Ahooooy!'

No answer. Did she still have time? That fateful sound-lapse.

'Ahoy, no worries I know your pirate trade, bootlegging drugging. Entrance-e-ment your ware. I could do with it tonight good friend, take me with you.'

The moon shone on his head, his grandeur-uprighteousnesses,

unyieldance, was there a dew-glint on his cheek, half-seen so starlit?

He was so beautiful so beautiful, dark eyes of sea his panther tread his mouth that understood all but never opened in a laugh (*her grievous fault*), his darkened face half-seen, oh oh …

'Sell me of those wares good peddler, I need your phantasmagoria this night, turn nightmare to enchanted-ment so I forget her for one night's span.'

'… forget her!' He remembered! After seven years, no one hundred and eighteen, no one more (*less?*), no it was now it was all happening, only minutes since she walked ran staggered relented unran and … (*Oh that lag of time*).

She stopped her running to remember. *Why* had she run? She must remember. *Why* was it?

They were right. She'd never been any good with numbers.

Or time.

Or emotion.

But his were checked, rider-controlled. Emotions his. Would he teach her? But could she learn? And what use was that-a-way if he'd said, 'Kate! Catherine! Attend!'

Run. Stumble. Kneel. Reach out. No not, boat slipped away. Going, going. Ju… just snatch rope-end. Unraveling oh oh o-oh, her life too … Voice faint across water.

'I have forgotten her. Already.'

She struggled, oh she struggled, strained reined sprained her heart her hand, her limbs, held on, cut her right hand she would she would she would. But the rope of his boat, his dear boat, his dear body slipping swimming slimmening shimmering spinning – oh winning, grinning away from her fingers … that verse from …

And the magic turn of tide, neap and flood together, no closer than they two, they one. Oh and those days, those how-do-I love-thee days?

Yes they spoke of 'liking' and 'friendship', sibling-like. But love oh love and love and love and love was what they meant, she knew it now. Oh, oh for all those ways to hold not-hold. See the too-sweetn'ing words from sentimental spinster-spinning teachers, *they'd* ne'er encountered 'affairs of the heart' (*so light, just novels' happenings*), the breaking broken shatterance.

That day when they'd stood entwined no closeness greater, head on his shoulder his face agleam for her, in sun, in lightening, in just-for-her, and when she shuddered at the edge of that high cliff, too far for her unbridgened chasm, oh then he'd held her fast. Oh her, oh only her. And she was safe, too close for touch, his arm around her shoulder, his whole arm, so safe-secure, above the whirl spurl whirl whorl spoiling knit of ocean's waving. And the weed and wrack and wreck, the pearls below the sea's so ever-given wealth.

So could she keep him still? The known unknown. Go back?

Almost could see his sweet and secret face, in his abandon he had forgot his hiding of it.

Joy …

But the moon went behind a cloud (*oh, tale of her life*) and hid his face too. She could not see him now. Shadowed, forever-always. Oh she could only see him … going. Vanishing.

> *Between the wid'ning gap*
> *the waters swilling the side*
> *the ships as they fell apart*
> *and chasms growing a-wide*
> *then wider benexte us.*
>
> *Between us.*
>
> *Oh sparkling sea*
> *Oh empty bed*
> *sunrise of beauty*
> *and lone sunset red*
> *ships aparting to far-off sands*
> *no heed to voices or stretchinghands.*

Rope slipping from fingers, rough fibre on hands, that are pulling and gripping, fumbling and rasping, struggling and nipping, twisting and slipping, fading and grasping, going and holding, and going and going, and holding and …

Holding? That was the illusion. Holding indeed – she would never hold him.

Her 'holding' was an empty hand.. Clutching gripping as if vain fool she could hold him back, keep him to her.

She saw the moon rise, sweet crescent, *dulce inexpertis*, sweet and delicate to those who see her not, not feel her cruel watching crescent. How could *she*, the cool, collected, feel thus so? *She* was not one to be Emotions-ruled, no they were steeds to be controlled, wild horses for a charioteer's cool rein-reign.

Poor fool she'd woven a sweet dream, a fantasy. This very shore. No storm now, just hurr'c-ane volcano, molten lava, flood tide flooding. She saw herself, again the wordstormenting one. By the side of the sea. Was it her? Another dreamer-singer? For as she stood there, on that same shore …

I dreamed of a babe, small child
sobbing and crying abandoned
lost alone by the sea I put hand to his breast and
soothed him
but it needed still more and still more
as we stood by the side of the sea.

I searched, searched
combing the high tide
to find by the side of the sea
a wondrous shell of ocean
God's creature for you and for me.

Pearl ring'd in our tears
so lovely, so fragile so strong

so washed in the sea's wild waves
braving the tide and the sand.

So we knelt by the sea by that shell
so delicate, fragile, so strong
the home of a God-loved creature
in the slime, the bottom-most sea
　living his long life in worship and longing
Oh, some thing to see.

For 'twas God created the shell
with pink opening wings and the sound of the sea
for heaven, for earth, for our selves
created for love to dwell in.

I gave to my love and asked him …
he would not yet bend to kiss
but looked with his sea-dark eyes
at me and our shell
with its love-ly wings and the sound of the waves
as we knelt by the side of the sea.

She could hear it, that heavenly shell, the sea's echoing, floating, to haunt her, coming quiet from deep-sea fastnesses, the clutching hand of ocean, oh, clutching … in his black cat black sea pearl ship, in the closing fastening shell lips, heart shut to her …

She could not bear it. Oh, words words, easy to say, words, for those bearing unbearable, and still bearing, still … What else to do?

Smaller, going, smallest, slipping stealing stillening away.

Unbearable.

She could not clearly see the ship-name, was it 'Pearl'? 'B … Pearl'? Yes, 'Black' it must be 'Black', black were the sails, black the mast, black the sky, black the sea, black the rocks. Black her heart.

'Black Pearl.'

Why had she not looked at the number on the stern she could, oh she could, what, call the life guards, the ship-at-sea team, the SOS, sailors duty bound to rescue were they not. Oh no, Morse code no more, what was it now? A number? (*But she ... well, you know by now ...*).

Mayday?

Oh, but nevermore would she see another May, those sweet May queens in innocent garlands, no love to chain *their* hearts or hide or daunt or haunt their stepping dance as they paired (*oh, paired peered peared*) under the arches, larches, she recalled it well. Oh but – how many ...?

Yes, she would note down the number on the stern, but – oh why had she not done it when she could see, it was ju-u-ust slipping out of sight now, jujitsu-ing away as the ship bowed to the breeze, wondrous sails, and that little fig figure on the mast. Why had she stood woolgathering about figs and pears and nuns and images (*oh that theoretical stuff, she'd never managed it, not from those school bench days so cold and now too late, too ...*).

But the flag?

Too late. Story of her life.

Sea on the shore. Just sea. Just breaking waves (*breaking – something breaking, broke ...*). Breaking, again again again. On the shore. Unheeding in the coign of the cliff. What cared the unending waves, breaking for eternity?

Dolphins and whales leaping and winging round the ship, in the sky.

Her not-her watching, turned away, unbearing.

The sail. The mast. The mast tip going ...

Then – only dolphins and whales leaping, only empty sky the only-sky, grey for the joy that had gone, the emptiness of sea.

Alone with the sky.

The ever-seeing sky, blue with his eyes.

Seagulls in clouds. Aerated airy airen winds. And beat'n beaten wings. What did they care?

Sweet pinks, thrift-flowers of cliff and cloud. Harebells – how they had rung for them in that old faerie time. Why should they care?

Empty sea. Just – sky.

Where have you gone love white blossom sweet as slumber I cannot see you?

He was gone.

She lay in the sharp bent-grass above the tide's march, razor leaves cut-ting her hands. And oh it was so cold, so cold, would she ever be warmed again? And they once so close so warm, so one, separated by no sea, no chasm. No ice-hand then on her heart. Never the end of that coldiness again.

Would new mothers ever sleep again? But that alas was never hers, was she now too old? But oh for her womb to hold the fruit of his loins … but it would never never never happen now.

And why why *why* had he not followed her then in that fraught time of old? She'd looked back had she not? To see if he would come? (*Oh she was so cold*). Pride. Obstinance. Headlongstance. Lucifer, well he deserved that fall (*the snake, that beautiful beautiful snake, Lucifer with the apple – she would not think …*). But that was him, never revealing. Like him.

Oh how she remembered – that firstest memory of their sand-castling on the shore, stamping the sea edge, then deeper, deeper, rolling strolling wholing souling together their own not-own bodies in the waves. The laughter spray.

The two little-uns on the sea's edge, splashing her, delight, she crying to her mum. But he ran on his toddler feet and gived her a little wet kiss. And she was comforted.

Oh, memories …

'I'm going to marry you,' he'd said, 'when I am old,' and she'd agreed. The mothers shook their heads and knew their sects would never mix, and laughed indulgently at their sweet babes.

Sore parting then – religion sore! – he went to another school.

But they shared their learning, and learned the more. How could they not in their united minds?

And she'd come leaping to him through the bogs, he first across that chasmed cut, the impossible space, then she to follow. Impossible, impassible for her, too wide. But he, oh he! Look there, oh there his arms awaited her, his whole strong arms, and so she leapt. And he enfoldend her as she fell short, caressed and praised her, stroked her hair.

For as convolvulus roots dig deep in the Earth's heart, ne'er torn uproot, and in the world grow spiraling untwistable in th' ether till burst out in morning's glore.

So were they twined.

As the starlight of the milken way that runs forever through the sky falls as one to the Earth, as the spray of the wave mingles in undivided mist, as the tree's sap feeds as one its branchen leaves and the birds of the sky.

So were they not divided.

And as dear twins sleep, in their womb content, ever together and closest of all creatures of the world till torn apart by that harsh cut of birth.

No no, she couldn't bear it.

Or, as a woman weaves sweet threads in intricate patterning not to be unpicked, as the Earth turns in eternal motion to the sun (*that was her, that was her, her, Kate*), as ebb tide and flood follow ever together with the sky's moon.

So were they eternally bound and grown as one, not to be parted, not by God himself.

Oh oh, but they *were*. Parted. Her doing. Why, why was she so young, so untrusting, so separated now from him, from her twin, her dear, eternally beloved. *Her* doing, she must try to understand.

For the day had come when his gaze altered and became keen and ardent, a man proud in his youth and love (*and she only a – a little girl? a child?*). So they played the more and walked by the sea in the sun and the storm, and he pulled down her hair and tangled it in the sound of the sea, and loved it. And waited. But she looked only to the sea's lovelinesses, its wrack, its whorls, its spurls, and did not see his look.

Until … until he turned to look and bended his head and … NO!

She did not understand.

She tried to send a blessing after him beautiful star of the sea. 'Don't go, don't go, don't leave me.'

'*Stella maris* star of the ocean my life, my sea as sunlight sets as moon turns round, Oh keep him safe. Oh guard thou me.'

But her words caught in a jagged jag of the rock, a snarl on the snarling road, late prick of winter thorn.

Oh and herself, she could not speak for sobs, try again.

'Oh moon or shine, Oh sink or swim, Oh through the brine lord, keep thou him.'

A last blessing, the Irish one her mother had sung to cradle her:

> *My love my dear*
> *now shed no tear*
> *for I am with you*
> *you need not fear.*

Oh, but she was cold. Chilled to the bone as her mother would have said ('*cold is the enemy*') setting her before the fire. And the ship – oh the ship, not even its masthead, its pennant. Vanished, vanished. Gone.

Put out the light.

And then, put out the light.

People die of being frozen do they not? Of grief more like.

8

Hidden - in Ye Olde Gentlemen's Residences

Aahh, to have furs warming her. She didn't want to leave her warm chauffeur driven-car – how strange it was to have got so rich, she, Kate, Irish country girl. But at least she could be warm. And her dear chauffeur so patient and so kind, treating her always as a respected employer, never as a woman … unlike … the thought flickered away into the sea, a sail. She heard the gulls crying on a lost beach.

Might this be the very day her quest was to end? Seven years. She felt it in her heart, perhaps at last, at last … but what would he say? Would he forgive her? Reveal himself, his name, his face, his number? That secret number, clue to his heart, the one she could never master?

She leaned forward.

'This looks like it Russell. Can you see the name through the smog? Yes, that looks like it, impressive frontage, Olde Gentlemen's

Residences. Oh yes, "Limited" of course, or is it PLC? It don't, doesn't, look very restful to me, but well …'

'Are you sure you're up to it Madam? You look so tired this afternoon. Missing just one wouldn't make any difference. After all it *is* the end of the week, they'll be closing down.' He knew he wouldn't win, but he had to try she looked so forlorn, and hadn't she cut her hand too? Something long and sharp, but he'd best pretend not to see.

'I don't think so. But you're right, that would be wonderful. I would so love a warm hot bath and early night. Maybe …'

Quick, reverse down street, turn at the end.

'Can you manage? Oh oh, careful! We only just missed that car coming out of the back entrance there.'

'Of course Madam.' (*What did she take him for, a cab-driver?*)

'A hot bath … but no, have to be a shower. If I missed one, he might be …'

Russell knew he wouldn't be, so did she he supposed, but she was so stubborn. It wouldn't be an up-market looking place like this in this superior end of London now, would it, that was for sure, and probably too correct and old fashioned to have anything as sensible as a lift. At least there should be a young attractive-look receptionist anyway.

'… just to say I've ticked it off, only take a moment, look at records, not worth turning I'll walk.'

'In those heels Madam? Of course I'll turn her, I'll keep 'er warm for you.'

'Won't be long, Russell, promise, just look in the door so I can say I've been, then my bath, oh … Oh I'm so fatigued …'

He watched her go, picked up the credit card she'd dropped (*as per usual!*) as she tangled up her furs getting out – the poor dear, typical. Gave it back, stuffed it in her pocket she did, ready to fall out again any minute. Oh well, women! Hopeless with anything with numbers on. How she was still rolling-n-riches he couldn't make out. Oh well, not his business.

Be ages if he knew anything of women. Titivating in the Ladies not that that was really her nowadays. But she did look tired poor thing. His training didn't permit him to think of her that way, but he was a man after all. And she so well turned out to visit all those dreary dusty homes, day after day after day, and that long hair of hers, with a hat on today to cover her exhaustion he guessed, and the rouge on her too. He'd love to just, er, to just talk kindly to her to wipe that strain from her. Must be awful to be a health visitor (*if that's what she was*), he knew she'd keep at it till she dropped. Oh well, at least it was a job to keep his young family warm.

In the Residence-Apartments (*the Olde Residences mind you*) all was busy. Talk shows how *very* busy they were, is it not always so? God knew better of course, what with all the things he had to do up there, all those doings misdoings of the world to watch out for only he knew what true busy-ness was.

Voices. From 'The Residence'?

'... Number 18 – you know his city-wealth and skill-ness at the Animal-Trust-Accounts – not well today. Too numbering. Accountancy (*lucrative of course*). Called in to take day off, they couldn't say no to such a high achiever. Sally says he's on an' on about some Kath or was it Kate? Anyway, someone years and years ago by the sea with hair flying in the storm and missing him apparently, if you can believe Sal. I think he must of bin in love with her though she didn't return it, obviously. What did he expect? She hasn't been near him for years as far as I can make out, but he's convinced she'll be coming to see him one of these days poor old thing.'

'Oh well, these clever counting folks will have their fancies, do no harm I suppose though course there's nothing in it. I'll admit he's quite pleasant with it, only wish his relations took some notice might help sort out the good memories from the bad. He wears a ring but I s'pose his wife's gone off with summon else.'

'Well that's the lot then Mr Waldrop, all quiet on the western front, ha ha. Let Sally go home to her family now?'

'Yes yes.' He needed to be busy too – 'fussiness' (*sshh, 'self-importance' was what she called it*). 'Yes, quite so Miss Smith, if you've checked she's got through everything. How about the mess in the top corridor? And that query over the flowers for number 18?'

'Oh just a little mix-up, went to 12 (*slide over the corridor question*), we'll fix it, he won't notice.'

'No no Miss Smith that would be *quite* against the quality care we guarantee our residents. And governmental guidelines of course (*never ignore government guidelines Miss Smith. HLTHCARE/ GOV/30097/4/UK latest issue*). Please see to it yourself …'

'Sa-a-alleee! One thing before you go …' Shout loud, not shrill of course, that would never do.

'Oh! Oh well. Anything for a quiet life. Well as quiet as a Gentlemen's Residence would ever permit. Worth it for the money I suppose! Even if I do wonder sometimes …'

'I think our residents are so fortunate, don't you agree?'

'Certainly Mr Waldrop. Yes *indeed* Mr Waldrop.' (*And a lift in salary might make us all more comfortable, and a drop in yours I tell you Mr Waldrop …*).

At the door. Tall figure. Kate. Enquiring …

'Sorry, ooh, didn't see you. May I help you Madame?'

'… your records? Please?'

'Er – well, we don't …' (*Good clothes. Fur. Lucrative*). 'Certainly, Mrs? Er? Mrs Faulkner?' (*Inspector? Oh and Mr Waldrop at home by now*). Apar-t-e-ments, yes, yes, that's it …'

'Oh oh. Yes. Yes I see … No, I'm quite all right. Ju-ust a moment … Is this …?'

'118-7, yes I know what you mean, strange numbering ha ha, a *lot* of our residents, ha ha … May I take your coat, what *lovely* fur, and the rosebud so delectable pinned with the *beautiful* brooch, clasp a bit loose perhaps, can I …?' (*What a find that would be*). 'No? that's fine, I'd better warn you, Mrs Faulkner, I heard he was a bit extra wandery this morning. But pleasant, pleasant, Mrs Faulkner, you've nothing to be afraid of.'

'I don't think I'll be afraid. No thank you so much Miss Miss er, I'll cope, I'd rather be on my own anyway. No, not a number, just the direction if you please. Yes I understand. 3rd floor, sorry-lift-under-maintenance, corridor, on right at end, thank you, on the right, yes. Yes, thank you. No no don't come …'

Swift up stairs, lock of hair escaped, furs in breeze behind.

And oh … (*seven years*). To look in his dear eyes (*would he let her at last?*). Feel his firm arms (*two arms, shred of memory …*), two whole arms. Would he let her see him? Oh oh would he …?

Could it be at last at last her heart's desire – that precious mortal heavenly rite of love? Of revealingment. To kiss those loving eyes, touch cheek with gentle hands? Dry tears with long hair, so long, lovely, remembered? Or rejection again again, that armor plate too strong, unyielding pride?

> *Does first sweet love ev'r perish?*
> *Or drown deep down in the sea?*

What happened behind that half-closed door no man knows. What was it? Who knows but themselves? All that was heard was a door snap-shut and Kate downing the stairs, hair storm-flown, smooth dress, one silver glint, uncluttered brooch (*it was loose thought Miss Smith, what a waste …*).

'Thank you Miss Smith, all is well.' (*She'd been a minute, a century, a life*).

'Would you like to put your hat straight Mrs er, Mrs Faulkner? Oh and … er, some of our visitors like er …' (*Saucer closer – careful now, not too surreptitious*).

'Yes, a cheque or cash. A card if that's the only way …' She knew the residents were *much* too opulent to need anything – but well, always worth a try, 'If at first …' She was full of homely wisdom was Smithie, well known for it.

'Oh, oh sorry, must have lost my card. Cheque book in car, I think. Russell will know.'

'I wouldn't want to press you of course Mrs er Faulkner. I can assure you that *everything* goes direct towards our gentlemen's "little comforts" they do so appreciate them – and their kind patrons too of course.' (*That usually works ...*).

'Oh? Good here's my purse, Le-e-t's see, I'd like to do something worthwhile. Is this a valid coin? Not a farthing anyway, so hard to keep up with inflation and things. Here and please buy some er, some bottles of whiskey or something to treat your good gentlemen.'

Mr Waldrop would have a fit! Even *she* was a trifle cross. One euro!! That wouldn't even do to touch up the un-greyed curl only her stylist knew about so she might as well pass it on. For once.

But graciousness above all – that's what they'd said at Finishing School. 'Courtesy is everything Miss S especially when you're in the wrong.'

'Thank you *so* much Mrs Faulkner, that will do *so* nicely Mrs Faulkner. We can buy *lovely* treats for our dear folks and say they came from you Mrs Faulkner.' (*Scrooge!*). 'Mr Waldrop – our C.E.O. you know – will be overcome, and I just *know* our most distinguished Chairman, er Chair, will be writing to thank you personally.' She was drafting the standard thing in her head as she spoke, tomorrow would put in post, couldn't go till Monday, why would people come on a Friday just when all sensible people were winding down ...?

'A pleasure Miss er, Miss Smith, so glad to be of help.'

'And if you would just be so very kind Mrs Faulkner as to sign our Guest Book Mrs Faulkner. Thank you Mrs Faulkner, oh and can I get a plaster for that little cut you have there, if you just pop off your pretty ring (*yes I can hold it*), just little but we can't be *too* careful now can we? Ooh *Catherine*, my favorite name Mrs Faulkner (*it wasn't*), would that be a C or a K now Mrs Faulkner? Ooh, *Kate* when you were young? How touching. I'm sure it brought back memories for our old gentleman up there Mrs er, Faulkend. And what a *lovely* brooch, can I –?'

But Mrs F was already at the door, try fast get away! Away from heart's delight-despair, sleep-guardian-watch.

'Goodbye then Miss er, er, Smith. Thank you very … is that your phone? Must run.'

She'd made it! Away. Away from the …

White trunk on Donegal road
black ashen buds
Oh that my heart would burst
with your green leaf cloud,
not with my grief.

Miss Smith's voice intruding yet again, wak'ning her:

Yes you saw me afar
coming through milky way
through station rainbow dome,
through the trammeling trees
coming from distance at last to your love
and then – you put out the Light
and then again put out the Light.

Quick down steps. Russell dear man holding door, sink into cushions. So tired. Warm. Miss er, Smith's voice on the phone fading …

'*Y-e-es* OGRE here, er, Ye Old*e* Gentlemen's Rest Home, yes with an 'e', yes, yes. *Miss Smith speaking, can-I-help-you?*' She had to get that phrase in, got paid by phrase-clicks, how about getting them to press numbers, that'd be more lucrative wouldn't it?

'No! Old-e Gentilhommes Resi-*dance.*' She preferred it that way, sounded so sweet and French. 'Yes *olde*, no no, not our *gentlemen*, the building, the family establishment, we like to think we are …'

'Yes quite right, it's Miss-Smith, yes Miss.' (*No bed-hopping for her, oh how dare he?*). 'Oh yes ...'

'Yes, common, ha ha.' (*Had she heard that one before? They were so original. Ha!*).

'How original, we'll have to get you on the staff here we will ...' (*And she'd change her name to Saucepan Man. Except that she liked 'Miss Smith' it had an upright straight feel to it. You could be sure no mercenary goings on there. Yes her name had always been Smith-like, er handy. Names matter you know – more homely wisdom. Ha, 'home-ly'*).

Back to the matter in hand (*her hand of course, don't be so slow*).

'*What* a cheat!' Smithie was actually quite cross! And she's picked up the ring from where I'd so neatly got it laid, you'd think it had some special meaning for her, silly old codgerfogie. And what on earth will Mr W$ say?'

Mr W$ was her pet name for him, Mr DoubleU-DollarEyes, but only Miss Smith knew *that*. Not that he'd know of course, didn't have a clue did he about expenses, hers of course that is, present-day cost of living and all. It wasn't all oldie meals or blood pressuring she'd have him know.

She added the measly bit to her purse after all. Not a bad haul this week. She was good with numbers, just as well, highly valued that in this responsible position of hers. She needed a bit of a top-up by now, a girl had to live these days. What a good thing Mrs F'd dropped her credit card.

'I suppose it *would* be quite nice if his Kate *did* come to see him sometime.' (*She had flashes of humanity sometimes*). 'He's always saying he'll not meet death's door (*quite flowery he gets at times, wild flowery*), that he'd not die till he'd seen her again, looked in her eyes once more.' (*Oh dear, humanity again, she'd have to watch it, couldn't afford that kind of malarkey in her position*). 'Not that he'd be up to anything improper at his age old dear, oh dear me no! And they could do with the extra room ...'

Bother that phone, trust it's something worth the fuss. 'Yes? What? Oh? No ... suchlike goings on *not* permitted at weekends ...'

Just shut the door, Sally'll deal with it Monday morning.'

End of story.

'Poor rich folks, they have their fancies, don't they. Not that I think there's anything in it. Medically speaking.'

9

Sleep the revealer

He hadn't recognized her when she came, hadn't seen her even. Standing a wraith at the door. Holding the flowers. Delivery girl? You don't *see* delivery girls. Even in Gentlemen's Residences.

And him so up-market now. Look at his tiptop apartment – Wow! She hadn't thought it of him (*lying on soft-hard heather, poor, asleep in sun. And rain*). But why not then? After all she too …

He had slept. The miracle. Slept as she watched, peaceful, quiet like an angel (*as once …?*). So *he* was tired too? Growing old? Grown old waiting for her? And his hair, so thick … where was it now? Yet only thirties surely oh? And still so beautiful, so beautiful, so beautiful …

Seven years. Seven long short years. How could he be looking old? So old from waiting for her? His lovely hair, tufts only. But God's mercy, blessing, greatest grace of all, he *slept*. Here before her very eyes, eyes that had longed and longed to see, fingers to touch, ears to … oh, how were hearing, and poetry, and music so bound in with him ...? And the sea?

Awake he would not be seen. By her. Pride. Lucifer the Beautiful, the Scorpion. Always soft heart beneath his armored arms. Only his mother saw his gentle-ness, the sweetness at his core, his care for his lambs, his gentle stillness. His mother knew, she the make-less maiden, Queen of Heaven. She, she was the one (*oh miracle oh miracle*), who saw him true.

> "*He came all so still*
> *where his mother was,*
> *as dew in April*
> *that falleth on the grass.*
>
> *He came all so still*
> *where his mother lay,*
> *as dew in April*
> *that falleth on the spray.*
>
> *He came all so still*
> *to his mother borne,*
> *as dew in April*
> *that falleth on the thorne.*"

Enough of that. She had to puzzle out – worse than numbers even ... Was it Lucifer then? Adam? Christ? (*She muddled up, what would her teachers say? Adam. She struggled to retrieve that filleting dream-straw ...*).

She knew there was truth somewhere in all that. *Veritas domini* but not for her. Would he ever ever show himself? The scorpion heart? The hidden-shining-star over a stable (*somehow*)?

And she was only Kate, too weak, too distant, too pure too sullied to see that fragrant timeless thymingstillness, to set her eyes on that holy gentleness.

But – now she *could* look on him. For while he slept sometimes his mother, burdened with her heavenly duties, would entrust the

care to her. Even here, here where she stood in the Old Gentlemen's gentle magical place. And when he slept – ah then then, then
she could gaze unhindered at his beauty. Then his loveliness was
revealed, all armor gone. Sweet night. His lovely form, loveliest eyes:
even in sleep she could not mistake their sea dark fragrance, quiet,
stilled, like the sea troubled, stormy raging, gentled.

And now I watch alone
for God and she
are gone to other guards
or perhaps to rest.

They need it
those cares and weals of earthly kind
to guard and cure
and mitigate.

I watch alone
tasked with my holy guard
watcher entrust' by God Himself
o'er beauty.
He is so beautiful so beautiful so beautiful
that fingernail but now was torn
bit, sinned against
Oh who could sin 'gainst that, so perfected
so beautiful?

But there by his bed?
Lying so low, so tossed, so neg-lected
what can it be
so beautiful, so beautiful
so beautiful-not-beautiful?

Sacred-divine
dare I whisper it?

It is his soul.

Whisper it softly, wake him not
it is his soul
his soul his very soul
laid there to rest him while he sleeps.

For could he sleep so heavy laden down
with sin in's wounded wounding self
by me by him by sin alone
his soul-full sins his heavy guilt?

Oh beauty, beauty lying there
may I not take your stains, and fast'n
your sins upon myself to bear
to free your load and share your weight?
So might you rest, asleep, at last.

She remembered the text her mother had made her learn:

"He shall feed his flock ..."

And then the explanation – it meant *something* for sure not
sure, though not for *her* by now.

Even the prospect of facing Miss, er, Smith at the stairfoot
could not despoil the moment or the joy of the prayer from her
grief-full heart:

All those burdens on you
heavy-laden tortured rack
caring all for others
taking them on your back.

Will you not lay down now
give them over free
lay on another's back now

lay them onto me?

10

College gardens and the sound not-sound of the sea

Why could others sleep but not her? Her mind went back. To when she first entered trembling the hallowed paths of Oxford.

'Go find your tutor,' they told her, 'the test is to locate her room, double suite 117, be sure to go to the sitting room.' (*Sitting? Sleeping…? 118 for sure, for sure?*).

Oh it was *so* confusing, quad flowers (*in December? Magic Oxford*), frost, snow-fog, slips, door-wouldn't-open, where-stairs? Up panting. Just-in-time, last one coming out, so clevercleversure, conf'dence, London-culture gang, no chance for *her*, knew it was no good, why had she …? And her with her just three years of Greek, others their lives …

'Well and Miss Katharine, had you seen this unseen translation before?'

T- truth, lie, obfuscation (*you need big words for Oxford-Entrance whether you know them or not*), smokescreen.

'We-ell, er, y-e-es …' (*Shame faced. As if she'd somehow been caught out, er, cheating*).

'How did …?'

'There was just a something about the turn of phrase …'

'YES' – hadn't her mother always said, 'When in doubt tell the truth'? Not otherwise of course – her mother was the one who had the telling of the polite, well, notlies, whitenesses, her father too upright. It was her mother who had the imagination (*alas, what dreams, nightmares, imaginations that brought to her mind*).

But attend! What was she saying?

'… must improve your grasp of Greek grammar, no swimming off on pretext of diving into German Miss Katharine. And I hope you *always* spell your name the *Greek* way.'

Kate hesitated. Not sure what that meant.

'Yes of course Miss Senior Tutor.'

She did know her birth certificate had 'Catherine'? Wild thought, would they want to check that ? Thank goodness, in the end they didn't. Just had to make sure she always signed 'Katharaine', er, 'Katharine' (*spelling almost as bad as numbers*).

'When you come,' ('*when*'?!) 'we will start you all with spelling and accents.' (*Ouch, then she'd be hopeless, how could she change her Irish – oh, Greek accents, oh relief!*).

Not an auspicious start.

But she did improve her grammar and her accents, even her accent (*traitor!*). And she outstripped those clever clever schoolboys who'd privileged Greek verse in their cradles. And sucks to London-Culture too (*sorry … but for her a convent taught little Irish girl!*). And popular too – honest! And men running after her, yes truly, true! And wondrous life and spires of learning op'ning up before her eyes, all amidst those dreaming libraries and rooves.

Enchantment!

So all those years it was in her mind that she an Irish-really girl could match them (*it was not numbers now, she was free of that*). Even recall the sound of … the thought perished, moved on to that massive inspiration from that German-bred tome the Great Greek Dictionary. English from the beautiful Greek. And it *was* beautiful was it not? Even if its sound and beauty had leached out in English-ed translating.

'No no, not Helen Waddell from mediaeval lyrics, lovely,' she'd cried.

'NO!' (*Shocked*). 'That's *late*, that's *vulgar*, doesn't count, not *Latin*.'

But wonders! Late or early, what's that matter? Homer – oh his similes, his epithets, his repetitions, that's how you love the heroes, love their places, their souls, their persons. Then wonder of wonders, Aeschylus – was any man more danced, that miracle human-divine glory bringing words, music, meter and movement to one? Theocritus' loves, and Virgil's and Sappho's and Catullus Catullus Catullus (*no not Lesbia but – the thought, fractioning away to the sea …*).

From this she learned to love. Not love as the body or the soul can learn, the bond one human with another that she'd known, a girl, but love of the word, the mind. And she experienced it too. How could men not flock to her, bees willing if she would but let them taste her honey?

One came closer. Soon his ring upon her finger. Forgetting. Left hand. For that is the hand of the heart, is it not? The emotion she had not yet learned – that was before she knew, before great Africk's mighty river.

And she was happy too. And watched with friends the enactments of true loves, and false, and humorous too in the beautiful gardens of the town. Are not all Shakespeare plays about love?

'The Tempest' and the 'Midsummer Night's Dream' (*oh, dream*) with magic on the cut-kept lawns, the heart-rend of Coriolanus caught anew beneath the moonlight's rise above grey walls, 'As You Like It,' entrancing transformations and the sound of lovers' oars across the lake, the searing of Othello only too real because (*don't think …*)

For there came the day when she sat high on scaffolt-seat to see again the agony of jealousy, Othello there (*ah, scaffold indeed, but she had not seen it then*), with her one true love, that strand at last forgiven – but she did not know it, did not recall. Her ever-love from schooled days. From 17. Or less. Come late, for her to Oxenford. Far from the sounding of the sea.

He had not forgot.

When the play ended, he knew it, he would walk with her among the deer in the garden under the moon, and he would turn her to him with gentle touch, and he would kiss her. And she would respond. He knew it, it was God's destiny for them. For ever. And then on that day, or it might be another, he would ask her to marry him. And he knew she would say, 'Yes.' He could forget that other strand, the sound of the sea, that other moon and mist and rain.

He knew it would be so. It was the plan God had laid for him. Had his father not told him so?

'When the time is ripe.'

He looked at her as she sat by him watching the players, by his right side. Soon she would take her rightful place, the beloved's. Had not his mother instructed him in the answer to that fraught question?

> *Why is it, Jehovah my lord*
> *that a man must stand*
> *fast on the right*
> *and she on his leftes hand?*
>
> *So is't in the syn'gogue's wedding's day*
> *he right, she left*
> (man always right, you know!)
> *and so they play*
> *they would have it so*

through life's all-way
as man and wife.

I've asked the rabbis
but they don't know
I've looked at my life
from fin'sh to start
and now I can tell you
now that I know!

It's so it's so that a man
can hold his wife
can hold his wife
his dearest of life
his own hande's wife
right next to his heart.

And she had told him too that when he saw his desire in the
place where he heard the sound of the sea, that sound of miracle,
then she, that very she, would be his love. Would love him for ever.
And would never fail him.

And so indeed. There she sat. And in his mind he saw her
fully for the first time, at the side she would ever be in God's kingdom and the world's. And she, his mother, would welcome her to
her home in heaven (*and teach her to spin he thought, just a little
sourly – but his heart was so filled with joy he cast that aside*). And
he bethought him not that the words of all women, even a mother,
can mislead. For he did not hear sound of the sea, nor the waves.
Not in Oxenford.

And are not the horn dream-gates too ever-close, opening wide
for dreamers, beguiling them with lies? And we know not, we know
not, even now – ask the birds of the air – which was the gate for
the dreams of Kate, or if the long wait by the gates of heaven had
purified what of dross remained in that sore sweet soul.

So he looked in the beauteous garden in the home of the spires of dreams, he looked to the lovely girl at his side, by his right. He looked in the pride and glory of his love. At her beautiful left hand lying there so still, the hand he would hold next his heart for her life and his and all of heaven's, the hand with the vein linked to her heart in God's unending, unbending, plan.

And as he looked again with all his heart's love and joy he saw – he saw another man's ring on her finger.

PART IV

ABOVE

11

Kingdom of beasts

That was before she knew. Before the gust that blew her mind and tied her soul, revealed to her God's plan, there, all the time, her destiny.

'When the time is right.' (*'God's time is the best time.' She had never believed it, she knew those old saws were just there to control the young*).

But for now she must seek him. Implore forgiveness. How could she have been so blind, so waywarding? Her life, her death, repentance, sorrow, mourning, penitence, distress, were all his not hers. But his the hurt. For no undoing, no way back.

Whence comes it lord
this loading guilt?
Weighting my shoulders
and hands and feet
my e-ver-y move whereby I live?
How comes I'm fill't

nor food nor eat
but faint from lack,
and chains iron-built
each day with guilt?

I've done my part
sure-ly oh lord?
Giv'n to the poor
and rich ones too
shown mercy so
held back my sword
from weak and strong
and all along
still heavied by thee?

Spread love around
to all who sought
or wrought
your works
and who did not?

Spilt on the ground
my heart-es' love
and lifes' blood
for him who would
and who would not?

Suff-er the gift
below, above
of peac-es' might,
to flight, to free
fly 'mongst the stars
of heaven above
for sight, oh lord, at last for love
of thee?

No sins luxuriant
I, as others do of pride or lie
t' ndulge, repenten, or descry
'n atonement dear
to nearen thee.

What must I do
dear lord to see
thee close at hand
to stand more near
and come
to thee?

Must I still stay
till sinning done,
away, alone
th' unpardon'd one?
Why must I still
tread weighted down?

Oh God, my God
with this drear guilt?
Oh God, my God
how can I come
atoned to thee?
your mercy fast
bring here to me
as so I ask.
Or could it be
it be at last,
cut free?

She had caused him hurt. He whom it was her task, from God himself, to cherish, keep from harm. So had she wounded him, to death.

So why repentance now? Sorrow for sin? Too late. Nothing, no thing in heaven or earth or hell, in sea or sky, in past, in here hereafter could remove that wound.

Her love that she had pierced, be-thorned, dragged nigh to death.

How might she seek him now? Oh where in hell – for there it must be – should she now creep?

'You are right,' said God, 'seek him there. In hell, your hell. Set yourself now amongst the lowest of the beasts, perchance you will find him there. Or yourself at least. And amidst the gusts of poetic words too – that were more difficult my child. Perchance you may prevail.'

'???', looked Kate.

'Seven tasks I set you if you're to find him. And one, the most difficult of them all. Accomplish them, *all* of them, and you may find him. Answer the exactest tasks I ask, nor deviate, not once. To find the love in each, its words, and show them me, is that not right? Fail one – there's no coming back, that is the end. Not one! Exact. Do you agree?'

So she agreed there (*no choice whatever told her God …*). Surely she could manage seven, was seven not that of myth, of fairy tale? Just seven. How light a task from all her travailing. To win her love nothing was too much. And now with ease? How light indeed.

So she began.

God said 'A worm. A worm first.'

Worms? Those herm'phrodites? What love is there?

So – a worm? Two-sexy there, unite in love, what greater fate could befall than that? God's grace indeed. (*Too sexy?*).

So days there, or 'twas centuries perhaps, she labored the earth, tilling the soil for human plough, for garden green, for delectation – and contempt (*a worm!!!*). For her – to be at one, no need for two, with him for whom existence lay. To be at one again, as once in youth, her maiden bliss.

'You have done well my child' said God. He'd thought it hard, not joy (*she knew herself, no need for words …*). 'Now move on up, towards the light a bit.' For still she was below the ground, no sky in sight.

'No no,' said God. 'Five senses, now bethink them now, consider now, consider how our days are spent and how the spring … Now move to words, you're bless-ed now, towards the light of men.'

She strove again and listened to the moles' sweet song, that ne'er before was heard by mortal ear, and drew her words from their singing's sweet:

> *I sing of a mole's dear sight*
> *what, no sight lord?*
> *Then how moles live their lives*
> *under the sward?*
>
> *Are not those eyes there*
> *how can that be?*
> *So large, but – sightless?*
> *Oh! Lord, I see …*
>
> *Of hearing then?*
> *Oh ears so fine*
> *they catch the sounds*
> *of prey to dine*
> *on fare so fine*
> *for sense of taste*
> *t'eclipse it all.*
>
> *Not sight then,*
> *hearing only?*
> *And taste as well?*
> *So then – of touch?*
> *Can e'er we tell*
> *of mol-ens' touch?*

Oh beauteous touch
that velvet love
Oh sweetest heart
Oh love above
all senses five.

'You have done well my daughter.' So God spoke.

'Now the third test. So to the fishes of the sea, the sea not earth, great school for men and beasts and waves and trawls and ships. This one will be hard for you. Harden your heart think of the prize – perchance you will prevail.' (*For so he hoped*).

So she hardened her heart indeed and God put the next in her mind, for she thought of destiny, of fish glinting at her from deep ocean bed – her fateful fatal fate more like. And this time she sang for him, for herself, for her misfortunate:

He has gone my lovely shark
my so beautiful beautiful catch
with his shining scales and grey-silvered loins
away from me.

Oh come Oh come my love to me
did I not catch you?
But you just swim away
with silver loins.

Her catch, her not-catch, oh alas alas. But 'No,' she said, 'not shark, too – sharkey.' A beautiful whale, replace with *that*?

My beautiful leaping whale
I'll follow wherever you go
leap to the ends of the world
t'where the waters no longer flow
O my sweetest my dearest heart
so curving so tender so true

that heaven-ward sea-ward leap!
Can any man sing like you?

I may not swim like you do
but e'en for your dear love's sake
so longing so faithful, so true
I'll follow along in your wake
go to wherever you go
follow your sorrowing joy
your dreaming, your trancing sleep
strive still to match your leap
your flight o'er the blue-dark sea
follow where ever you go
leap past the ends of the world
where the waters no longer flow
to you.

It was a bit of an, er, leap in the dark, but God was pleased and counted on his fingers (*counted – oh …*). '*Three!* And now – the vertebrates, the landed ones.'

She knew what *they* were (*not for nothing that Donegal school*), and she was glad she'd escaped the insects, since there was *something* there … the great and greatest insect. Anyway it was good. For her.

'What would you like, a bird or mammal?' (*Divert the childers – give them choices for those decisions they had to make anyway*).

'A … a bird?' For was he not eagle, soaring, roaming flighting eagle, phoenix fire-ing?

'Attend Kate!' (*Just like schooldays, why could she not get them from her head? – Well God was rather school-masterish wasn't he?*).

'They are important. Think of doves. So *I* will sing this time.'

So he struck up with his beautiful bass voice (*well it had been beautiful, a bit cracked now but Kate didn't like to say*). And – somehow – he sang of something eagle-like after all, such was … (*best no comment*):

Great albatross with double wing
hold me secure and safe
soft to your feathered breast
not fallen but lov-ed close.

Fly to the high cliffs hidings
see sharks in the deepest sea
whales gamb'lling in deep mid ocean
eagl's in that secr't eyr-ie.

'Now a deer,' he said, 'symbol of all that is good and innocent. Humble. Loving. Sing me of a deer, the fourth.' (*Good thing he was doing the numbers bit*).

She did her best and her voice was improving with practice ('*use it or lose it' the nuns had told her – they were thinking of prayer of course*) – but why was it always fleeing fleeting away, Like dreams?

For the fifth she'd *really* wanted something fiercer, harder, tenderer, like her dear gentle love. (*Listening to bird song in the oak grove, looking at sweet blue eggs in hidden nest. Together. Miracle*). God favored tigers burning bright, but he gave way and with the next, oh the next (*she gasped in delight, dismay, despair – when would she see him more?*), came *her* song:

O beautiful loan-some wolf
carry me safe to your nest
holding me soft in your jaws
as babe looking up from your breast.
bring me soon to your western lair
holden secure in your arms
flighting me swift through the air,
safe to your home in the west.

There was love there wasn't there? She turned to God.

'I'd never seen it before. Ravening wolves. Man eating. Ravening each other too? But no now I see it, teamwork, fidelity, a pair

rearing their young, love, my love carrying me in tender jaws …
Oh …'

But again he had not revealed his face, only the hold of great
jaws. The wolf was her love was he not, not? But again – refusing.
She could not, never, see his sweeten face, his sullied soul, head
bending … NO, she would not think … But still it came, unquiet
heart … *Inquietum cor meum est*:

He had it right
Augustine then
how can hearts rest
of money, market
lucre based
of fight, of haste
of profit profitless
and waste?

For can souls rest
when man to man
must eye tear out
and limb en-flame
must hate and harm
must kill and bomb
exploit and maim
heród the child
debauch the girls
unknot the man
cruce'fix the tree
and so it was
since world began.

how can hearts sleep
how can they rest
until they lie

at rest in thee?

Unquiet her heart. He would not reveal himself. Not his name. Not his number. Not his face.

She saw last a gibbon at sunrise, set there by God at the first dawn, or perhaps it was the second, of his world's new day. Nearing the end of her quest, she saw in her mind the stately pyramid of her existence, soon to reach Man in her sevenfold task (*oh, her love … he would surely be there, number in vain the beast, he would be there*).

So she sang – with longing with despair with hope, in the very dawn of the world:

> *Love-ely gibbon's height*
> *'bove on your bough midst th' winter stars*
> *with your beautiful sea blue eyes*
> *your long soft hair*
> *to clutch me silk'n to your breast*
> *t' carry me sweet to your love*
> *in this world's first-ever morn.*

She might not see his face, but this was indeed true love. Love as she knew it, wanted it. Her destiny. But she mistook. For had not God pronounced one more task for her (*oh – numbers*). Seven seven, surely she had accomplished the all seven, surely the nuns had said that was forgiveness? Seven.

One more to be sure, like her lines? But was not eight, the eightsome bob, the infinity, too wearisome, no longer beautiful?

'Not so,' said God, 'for consider this, most beautiful lines by my arch-poet of heavens singing the world's infinity, of mathematics, love, the figured reel, know you not the eightsome symbol of infinity?'

> *Is not mathematics beautiful*
> (she trembled and hid her eyes)
> *did God not give it t'us*

for figures of eight
for his hating
mating
lusting
loving
creatures
math'ticians
of his create.

So do you think
I'll find
stant at the gate
God 's halo
now with mine
in fig of eight?

That fig so beautiful
two separ-ate
two matching matchless
join-ed
loin-ed
twisting wisting
rings.

Entwined across a Meeting House
where first we saw
each other's mutu'l worshipping
where God 's true brings
once single be'ngs toge'er
to one enwoven
in fig of eight.

to hear Bach joined
in countless counting massing G
sep'rate and beautiful

to glory God
with contrapuntal harmony
eight voices, separ-ate
and joined.

That many years
of rings again
to ringings separate circles joined
might once as one
enfolt in two
one lonely nought
too separ-ate
too dearsome bought
o'er countless noughtful soughtful years
be now one mind
int'linked, in-twined.

That reel of eight
two circles join'd
in equal first,
identick magickal of reels
in endless matchless mateless
dateless
inter-signed
with noughts' eternity
geo'metric
in
IN-FIN-I-TY.

'Enough,' said God, kindly. 'You have done well. But now for the last, one last one only now. You have done well, you have reached, near-reached, the goal that was set before you.'

For (*oh Kate Kate*) she had miscounted. Not eightsome were needed but SEVEN. And no, not *seven* she'd accomplish-ed but six, six only. *Six.*

'Yes, you have done well,' said God, 'one only remains, the easiest. My dear breed of insect, cleverest, swarmingest, wiliest of my creatures, you will find them soon. Choose!'

But she wasn't good at insects. Could he not let her off, give her a different number, capita wasn't it called, she *never* could make them out, oh NUMBERS!! Was an ant an insect? Spiders? Oh and scorpions, surely they were the kings, she could love a scorpi-on. She began her song ...

> *Others may stop*
> *at his hard hard shell*
> *impenetrable, but she*
> *she, the beloved*
> *she knew his hidden entrances*
> *and exits too*
> *to watch him sleep*
> *his hidden secret*
> *hurted soul*
> *his softnesses ...*

How she knew it she could not tell. But she did. She stopped. It wasn't very good. God looked – uncertain. Perhaps it was not right. Not her destined song. She could not dare or risk. She must not mistake. Mistake.

'Choose for me Lord, I wish to do thy will in my singing'

Fatal mistake. All else she could have managed but – A BEETLE?!!!

So she was set to seek him (*ugh*) among the beetles (*oh but she didn't like beetles ...*).

'Not so,' said God. 'Do you not know of my insect band? The cleverest, bravest most ingenious of all my creatures.'

'Yes Lord,' she said and humbly too (*but did not believe*).

So God made the song to persuade her, mocking her ignorance, challenging her (*how could she not know, or the nuns either?*).

'A beetle lord? A beetle POEM? You must be joking. For – I don't LIKE beetles. Not hate, but worse dislike. Slimy, slithery, roach-ey,' she said to him.

'Ignorant girl! Not slimey and slithery,' he said to her slo-o-owly, VERY slowly, so she'd understand (*'Oh get on,' thought Kate – tenterhooks weren't in it …*). 'InSECT'ivore, not saur – (*look wikiped*).'

'Well an'way – hard, lots legs, all right, not hooks or tenters-tentacles, but tickly, sixly, thin an' horrid,' said Kate.

'Get real you mortal you! They're thousands an' hundreds an' milli-ons, more beetl's than all oth'r cr'aturs – d'you live here on this earth at all? More beetles than …'

'Oh all right all right then, then, you sky-lord (*not liv'ng on earth, that's for sure*), I'll try…'

But even for God, even for herself, even for her search her fatal fateful fatesomest search – she could not.

She wept tears of bitterest anguish, moisture after dewdrop after torrent from her eyes, she cried to the heavens, she called even to the insect clouds to the bees. Why why why had she not remembered *them*, were easy for song, millions on millions of honey-nectar-befed, and sipping the flowers. The makers of all anthologies and *florilegia* sweet.

Too late. Oh Kate, always too late.

'You have failed your task,' said the Lord, 'at the last hurdle. No longer may you go forward. It is finished. Your love has reached its end.'

12

The larches of God

But she wept all the more and cried and fell at his knees and begged him, implored.

As the tide sweeps over the flat sand, as the wind blows gently through the trees yet makes them bend, as the light creeps up from darkness to flood the world.

So is the mercy of God.

And so cried she before him.

As the pearl rises from the grit of the ocean, from the dust, the dirt, as the shell nurtures it like the seed of a lovely tree, as for every thing in Earth and in Heaven and in the great garden of the Lord (*that touched him a little, for God is a great gardener*) there is a season, night as to morning, moon as to milky way, dawn as to the limpid dusk.

So is the Ruth of God.

Then she said, 'May I not sing, Lord, from my own heart, my imagination given as a gift by you to the sons of man? For you have forgot the most beautiful of all, the trees of the forest, the springtime of the year, the autumn, gold needles on the ground, then hid in snow for frost to come that they may grow green again, the most beauteous thing in God 's, er, in Your, creation?'

And so she sang:

> *Spring of the year*
> *of youthful'st love*
> *of springs abounding*
> *here above*
> *the earth, the heavens,*
> *Oh worldly sweet*
> *Oh dear'st delight*
> *the soften sward of loving firsts*
> *of larch and birch*
> *and greenest leaf.*

God listened, and his heart melted, just a little.

> *Oh then the summer*
> *season sure of love and marr'ge*
> *for children meet, for family*
> *grandchildr'n then, and then the prize*
> *of pen and sword. And then the fall*
> *of life, of season*
> *callen back by ageing bone*
> *to walk alone*
> *once more.*

A tear touched God's eye. She might be a bit bemused-like, and innumerate, but she had it right.

> *But f' now we walk again*
> *your touch, your arms enfold*
> *not springtime's loving now*
> *but autumn's sweeten'd gold.*

God listened, leaning his cheek on his hand, remembering his love of young days.

She ceased. And he relented.

'Pass my child, and God go with you in your quest. For did you not sing twice of my great fishes and now move my heart, even the great heart of the Mighty of Mightiness, King of the Universe, Creator of Heaven and Earth. Eminence of the Jewelled Throne.' (*That was enough – for now – to show he didn't give in easily, that His Merciful Ruth was quite something*).

'You have many trials yet to pass, up and ever up towards the light as you see more, of Him, of Me, heat of the sun through the nine circles of hell that you well know my child, the Gorgons' fearsome gaze turning all to stone.' (*I am safe from them at least, thought Kate, my heart is already stone*).

'The sirens' sweet voices beguiling the stoutest mariners – perhaps you will find him there, combing their long tresses for them, for still he loves long hair.'

'You have much to learn my child and may not progress till you have tasted sweet of it. Of my great mercy must you come to that great site of knowledge e'er yet complete your quest. For the learning of those black-robed ones ...'

(*He meant the nuns – God isn't always up with the latest lingo you know, far less the fashion trade*).

'... try as they might, was not yet enough for journeying to heaven.'

'So go ye now on your quest and perchance you may prevail, for love may yet conquer all. Love not of worms or of beasts or of birds – but of man, of that one, that only man. But not of my will, child,' he added hastily, in case she thought he was all-forgiving or merciful or something.

'But of the one that is greater than me, almighty. Men call it – destiny. And beyond that, for this is what I call it – love.'

13

The Great Book

So he instructed his dear Saint Columb the psalter scribe, who
loved oak groves, winged by his sweet dove. He led her from the
kingdom of beasts – she looked back longing at the wolf, to see his
face, but was hurried along on wing-ed feet. He was leading her to
the great hall to see the heavenly archive.

Vaulted it was, soaring beyond the skies below, reaching above
to the great oceans that encircle the world, arching to the borders
of the stellar way. Gently Columb guided her, too humble to say his
full name and title, and opened the great doors. Never locked they
were for who could carry out that might of memory?

'God wills that you should know all beasts upon the earth, all
trees (*yes, you were right, it touched us all*), all creatures of his make
before you may pass on. So you may understand what you see. It
will be many years dear mortal one.'

Then he showed her the record chamber. Row upon row lay
there, scroll after scroll, parchment, papyrus, skin, paper, and by
the side drawings in sand and bead count, lacerie, writings upon

stone, miracle-glow pictographs, there was no end. Heaped they were, piled, to the very peak of knowledge.

See here Great Book of Plants and next it Rocks. Books of the Sea Salts and the sweet Sand Grains. Of Cats, and Siamese and Snakes and Centipedes. A side room for the Insect Archive, wondrous fruits of God's great wisenesses. The Termite Book on intricate-wrought stand, cunning-framed by insect art. Of Ants and Beetles (*oh … so God was right*) and the slim Book of Scorpions – the one God comes to read in sleep-lacked nights. For he loves the scorpions, outside proud shell, impenetrable by craft or wit, within soft humble heart.

Kate looked for The Book of Mankind. Surely it would take center place?

'Yes indeed, dear child,' he said, 'not all will look, they have not courage or the curiosity. But God commanded that you see and mark it well. But first,' he lowered his voice, 'he has ordered that you see the mystery of mystery, the chiefest heart of this great cathedral of wisdom.'

And with careful reverence, the greatest even in this holy of holies, he carefully lifted down the cunningly wrought chest. Carved it was with friezes not of animals but of singers. Of Neanderthal women pipers, children a-song, cave men with – somehow like lyres? – fishermen with nets and conch shells, savage drums, and flutes, cymbals, tambourines, lutes and all. And at its heart a curious sign, most secret of them all – even here may not reveal it – of the human voice.

'But but,' said Kate, bewildered now, 'how is this? Surely the great Book is the record of *living* creatures, the great creations of God. This is – oh well beautiful, 'tis true, but but – not breath, alive, the *espiritus*, the soul, the air of the worship of God which is the task of all living beings of the world … the great world.'

For everything within that great cathedral hall was, to her, great.

'Listen my innocent,' he said 'was ever greater life or greater worship, greater breath-ed life than music's breath? Listen and carry in your heart. For do you not know the power of song, that most enchant enchanted magical of gifts God granted us? And you, select among the few, given back in your own guerdon now of praise.'

And it was true, she had – tried. The larch tree nodded its stately head too, but she did not see. So she harkened and the air around her seemed to ring with living – yes living – sound, too great for ears to hear, mind to recall, even her body to dance, for was not dance the music twin, child of all muses? But not too great for her heart to resound.

> *Chords are so love-ly*
> *God – gift to humankind*
> *sep'rate so perfect and together*
> *when join to one*
> *'n Handelli-an pavane*
> *in wondrous unison*
> *greater than separ-ate*
> *chord of the heart*
> *love-one.*

> *But ah! – but counterpoint*
> *miraculous multitude*
> *fount'n sparks in th' air*
> *or ocean spray and sands*
> *and bubbling reversals back*
> *stars contrapuntal falling*
> *beating dissonate*
> *winds' tumbling turning hurr'canes*
> *to anticyclones-bound*
> *and conversat'n's d'bates and dialogues*
> *and counter args and counter cults,*
> *planets revolving each*

around themselves, among the suns
of countless worlds and times
and back again above below
'n eternal diapaisi-ons
of in and out
and two's and three's
and quavers 'n triplets
and woman and man
entwine-ed long
'n controlled unis-on
webb'd musicke spun for angel and for earth.

It took a while for Kate to recall herself. But then, there she stood, where she had been, with Columb in that great hall.

'And mankind?' she repeated quietly (*for the place was full of awe and resoundent with echo*). 'They must indeed lie at the heart of this great archive?'

Columb pointed silently. A few-words man except when roused to ire or song. He looked at the shelf high up, the toppest corner there, be-spider-webbed, al-most beyond eyens' gaze or handens' reach.

And when she looked close – oh then, then, what blaze, what burst, burnt color offering richest most dazzling glowing of designs, casket to hold the precious arts and wisdoms all that man and God had made in centuries of being. Round it hung songs of bees, of poets, of melody – the sweetest music she had heard. The tender touch of heaven's grace and with it fragrance, full, of thyme.

Columb handed it gently down. With care, the greatest care of all her life except perhaps perhaps – (*but she would not think of that*) she took out the leather book – how great it was.

'The history of humankind,' said Columb solemnly, 'how could it not have weight?'

She looked for her own name – what woman would not?

'Yes' he said 'but look here first.' He turned the pages. 'See the writ – of stone, of pottery, of grass, page upon page of hieroglyph, of pictograph, high italic, and cursive script, Mayan and Inca color, the gleam of Irish and of English scribal hands, monks bending to their task. Laborious. Then marvel of marvels – the art of Chinese artist-writers, calligraphic gold, blue-azure red of western scribes, glowing to the skies.'

Those names. Those lives.

Pages to their edges, crammed, enthronged, pushing, scrabbling for hold – generation after generation listed there, name upon name upon name, daughter with mother, grandchild with their great parents of old.

On one page a space.

'Strange.' whispered Kate. It was somehow awesome.

And as she looked that small gap, scarcely seen amid the throng of names, grew and grew again to her awed gaze until it filled – oh words could not comprehend the expanse, that light, that Word, that absence of Word which Was in the Beginning, till it filled all Heaven and Earth with absent present glory-full.

'It is the place for the name not-to-be-named of the Father of us all,' he replied in hush-ed voice. 'It may not be filled till all things are accomplished.' He broke off, gulping. 'Keep silent now unless perchance you have a song of praise.'

Kate was impressed. But by now she had seen enough. 'Look up mine.' (*An afterthought by now*).

Columb turned the pages, slowly, heavy, now they were within a century of the time she knew. Grandparents, parents, people she had heard tell of. They were there. All of them there. Here were gaps again, spaces for – what? Like grave plots for the family members yet to die (*gruesome she'd always thought*), husband for wife, dead child (*oh unent grief*) there, a waiting mother, lover for his beloved (*oh …*).

'You have it right my dear,' he said, 'it is moving indeed, that human love, that faith, those hopes.'

But not yet end. She read out the verse inscrib-ed there. How strange there was yet room in the enscrolled espace-ment.

My life enrolled
not yet full told
or whole unrolled
still to unfold
as yet unscrolled
on hold.

But alread' enscrolled, enrolled
by God enholy'd, enfold
en-wholed.

'And here –,' he turned to the last page, then hurriedly tried to shut it. Kate was too quick. There indeed was a small little wee-some teeny-some space-room, just enough to squeeze four letters and was it was it perhaps 117, no 118, no. If she could only see at last …

But by now she was too late and anyway beyond her wondering numberationing.

For look! Above was *his* name, not yet for all to see, but to her eyes, her inner inward seeing intuition, it was plain. three lines at least, the names by which men had known him, th' immortal one, through all the world. His death (*the date*) – his restoration, his beloved … She was just going to read …

But Columb had wrested the book from her hands.

'Don't know why you thought it was for *you*,' he said sharply. 'That dear name is yet to come, we know not when or why, but we await his coming as bridesmaids wait the coming of the groom for the great wedding in heaven. And all will be rejoicing joy, and there will be no more sorrow for he will have come among us …'

He wiped a small tear from the corner of his eye (*strange thought Kate, surely no tears in heaven*). It was all so puzzling even with the 'companiment of an Irish saint, her favorite, he of the dove and columbine.

'The time is not yet,' he said. 'First the Coming of the Son of Man, the creatures of God, and then …'

His voice faded as she …

14

Garden of Eden

… she was translated there. Into a great garden. She knew not whence she came, or how. But lying now on gold-lit ground, of needles, prickle-soft, pressing her back. Over her more gold hung, must it be heaven (*heaven no-heaven withouten him*).

It was. It was the trac-ed lacerie of true larch trees, gold into the clouds.

And a wondrous beautiful glade with clear sky above, gentle wind blowing, and fragrant soughing song of boughs.

It was dawn with crystal dew upon the grass, last hoar to the winds in sun's new-shine with apples off the trees, the lastest there till ardent suitor climbed to bring it down, but oh not yet, the honey brought alone. (*Oh climb it down again, back down, for me*).

What meaning could that have? But it was ever so, in dreams.

Autumn. The ripest richest sweetest time, creation's time when God first made the trees, the pears, the insects, male and … oh something there for delectation, oh some thing there that missing still …

The nuns not good at German, but – oh this was a place a

place a place for poetrie, thronging, o'er-thronging mind, ear and soul. But for they'd spotted a lovely Rilke lilt-y builten translati-on of praise for autumn and the One who holds it fast (*oh trust them to end with some Medi-Messaging*).

> "*The leaves fall, fall as from far.*
> *Like distant gardens withered in the heavens,*
> *They fall with slow and lingering descent.*
>
> *And in the nights the heavy Earth, too, falls*
> *From out the stars into the Solitude.*
>
> *Thus all doth fall. This hand of mine must fall*
> *And lo! The other one – it is the law.*
> *But there is One who holds this falling*
> *Infinitely softly in His hands.*"

It was autumn, autumn surely, of fruitfulness, of apples, mists. Of longing.

> *Be with me in the autumn time*
> *of starting frost and apple cheek*
> *of starry night and goldend day*
> *of storm and wind*
> *and pass'nate rain*
> *and loving word and lovers' pain*
> *to be with thee*
> *and feel your rime*
> *just once again*
> *with me.*

She was asleep again, dreaming, waking to – mist, mist light, the light!

It was him. Him, surely surely him, him, come to waken, and to love her, give his apple, that evening autumn quiet eve.

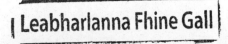

"You change every grief to gold.
You give us the key
to each world we come to.

You sweeten the lips of those we love,
and you open their mouths in desire.

You are beyond all guessing,
Yet within each guess.

Hidden, yet beginning
to be revealed."

How had that Rumi ruminating Persian poet captured his being in such exactitude?

Quiet. Peace. contentment. Was it not he who had her all way in his care?

Then seem-ed she in dream to wander through the gardens sweet, as earth worm, mole under the soil, bird lighting on the boughs. And lo there, many trees, not just the larch, but oaks and ash, the mighty beech, the humble hazel of sweet nuts, and birch with silver-gold.

And as she wandered on she came to the most fragrant of all, sweet spice of the east, balm of the west, reminding of her love. And it seemed to sing to her, or was it she who sang to him, her hidden love?

Dear nutmeg grown
for me and mine
midst tree and mace
and tropic's space
'quatorial shine.
With brown and black
in spice-isles sown
you're dirtsome cheap

and sold in heaps
then heapen pile
but dear to me.

So fragrant spiced
my honeyed dine
of loven taste
to sprink' on rice
or grated fine.

A dish to flave
with fragarance
near 'nto divine,
with pungent sweet
to touch and shave
nutmeggen sliv'rs
for seen, and eat.

So honey'd black so cheap
and clear so fragr' and dear.

She put out her hand to take, to eat. But it fought her grasp, that resistant enarmoured beshelled scorpioned love.

What could she but sing him again?

But oh! My dear you are so tough
so rough and tough, so tough
– to crack!

15

Adam with an apple

It was strange. Everywhere oh everywhere – except in that strict strait convent – and *she* could speak straightly too, in prose, relic from then, her business days, still there to resume when she had found him.

If she found him.

But now – only music and verse fit for this en-chanted place, for God's own gardening. For is not poetry man's closest reach to God? To music too? Had she not been told that by the old planter, him himself, rich digger of the soil?

Beauteous plants were there, fit praise for song. Birds too, on branches, twigs, on the ground. The lovely firefinch, blackbird with sky eggs and sweetest warble, phoenix high in flames, in inspiration, in eternity. Lovely 'bove all. But loveliest of all, remembered there from streams of youth, sweet lonely rowan stark against the sky, and then, at stream, the flashing brightest fleetest heron. Standing so still then flight so strong.

And trees – what seed could have engendered *them*? What

hand, what miracle of earth or heaven? Then answer from the birds, the stream's sweet voice, the murmuring wind:

> *'twas God who planted the seed*
> *of that great oak above*
> *acorn below, of roots and branch*
> *already great above*
> *already hid to grow*
> *in human love.*

> *But lord in that great tree*
> *with leaf and twig and bird*
> *and acorn hid in sward*
> *where can we find the third?*

> *That third grown there before*
> *belov'd, before the fall*
> *There, see, Golg-ōtha's hill*
> *the greatest tree of all.*

What could she but apostrophize him there? For even in the Garden birds pour their meed of praise. Why else the morning's chorus as the dawn star fades?

> *Do not be afraid bright heron heron-ing*
> *to-stand to wait and wade*
> *and watch the waters motionless*
> *and then – a flash a gleam –!*
> *To spear your trout.*

> *And do not fear my living heart*
> *to watch and wait*
> *and scan by waters side in stillness,*
> *stand to search the deeps and shallows, still*
> *to search him out.*

What magic art had salved this place, had dug the roots of tree – the pears, the cherries, apples, fruit of great endeavor? The creation of some hid hand, no labor spent? Or fruit of man's obedience-disobedience in some foregone age?

And as she pondered – fruit indeed of thought – lo from that meanest lean-to hut not seen till now, aslant the wall, he came:

> *… old gard'ner coming out his shed*
> *now old and slow like all good gard-eners*
> *his clothes were torn a bit and shabby now*
> *and dirty too, like th' shed behind*
> *but right for a garden-er and clean below.*
> *just like his art, his craft, his soil.*
>
> *What was he doing there, so quiet, so slow?*
> *Was something wonderful I'm sure*
> *so old and slow, be-bowed and tired now*
> *from long day's work of growing things.*
>
> *Was't flowers, seeds? Or autumn trees?*
> *Another miracle perhaps?*
> *A human heart?*
>
> *I wandered through the garden on to see*
> *the flowers, the trees, his mir-acles*
> *'n' the special tree, the one he loved.*
>
> *I wandered on to see what grew*
> *the wonders there of his mak-ing*
> *waiting for view.*
> *What would it be, that art?*
> *That waiting there for us, for me?*
>
> *And there I found best miracle of all –*
> *of all the wonders still to find*
> *throughout the world*

that wondrest woundrest wondernest of all.

For there I found her
waiting there
I found her
me ...

That was good – why had she not thought of it before? But *how?* How search him out?

But now had the sweet entrance-e-ments of magic place distract her mind. She looked again. Enchant-e-ment. Even that little beetle charmed racing an earthy crooked path through crackling leaves.

She followed in its trail, not knowing, stumbling for her mind was full of sorrow.

A path to leave this place? Oh *yes!* She could not never not, not never never never not abandon searching ? 'Twas unthinkable. The gate, the gate, must find it. Wait there – perhaps – for light to open. Sit in the dust and dirt and wait – to gain the exit, find her love that long long way from ...(*was it heaven?*) from here.

Her soul rebelled. She longed to stay, to rest a while. But find the way she must or leave her search. For he was not here. And herself – she did not want (*'not yet, not yet' whispered the angels*).

But God was with her. Feet trod unheeding on the beetle's little path, and –

Oh! It was him.

It was HIM!

Asleep. She feared to wake, awaken, waken from sweet dream of paradise regained, of love restored. But she could look at him ...

He was so beautiful so beautiful ... more beautiful than any plant, than any bird, than heron flying with heavy wings above her head.

Hush do not wake him.

And look there, his soul his sweet cleansest whitest soul, his soul restored

Adam …

At last before her eyes. He was her love. He was the blessed one, the highest most beautiful, the rightly proudest, most acclaimed in heaven, beloved of God.

He was the morning star that rises in the east before the dawn guilds the beauteous morning sky and brings the dew to new jewell'd ferns, the birds to their sweet chorus, heralds of the dawn.

She looked and looked, unstoppered now, and looked again.

He was so beautiful.

To find him here. Here of all places. In a garden shut from the world– but not more beautiful than he. Grief-ecstasy. She looked again, again.

> *Sore, grievous*
> *the pain, the loveliness*
> *that sore – sore – word.*
>
> *How shall we 'ncompass it*
> *direction it?*
> *Not south, not north*
> *or east or west – my heart …*
>
> *For dear and dearer*
> *now sores of sore believe or not*
> *pain there of ownest free*
> *free will by Goddis say.*
>
> *Wounded*
> *sore wound for us*
> *and hearted hearte-less*
> *on th' tree.*
>
> *So sore for me*
> *so dear, so thorn-ed sore-ely*

still must it be
the sorest knot not-soring all
all still for me.

Oh that I might so love-ly wing
soaring with thee
and the birds of heav'n
in God 's domain
with angels' sing
'ver th'indigoed sea
to sore and soar
and sing!

He stirred and came to slumber's drowse and even in sleep his manhood rose to greet and meet her there.

Like to that star of morning, great Lucifer before his fall. She loved him, high and low, in hell or heaven, she knew it.

She loved him.

Seven years or was it eight? (*She could not count*).

Eternally.

And then … he awoke. And looked at her before he knew, with sea-dark eyes. With … with eyes of love.

As the blackbird shows
first to her mate
heart burst of pride and joy
her heav'n-song
a clutch of eggs
as blue as life
her own, his gift
in their nest of the tree.

Blue as the sky
from whence they came
as sea wherein they rolled

of th' eyes of the one you love
with whom you breathe
so God too showed
in his first create
the Earth for man.

His heartburst joy
breath'd wond'rous love
his worldes whole
of bird and plant
and most of all
for Adam he made
what greater love has any man?
to Adam he gave –
Eve
and then he made you –
me.

And thus he looked (*looked*) at her. And then would he not seek for her a love-gift (*not for Adam to be trammeled down, strumpled and trampled by the bible-handed version*), a gift of love for his dear one?

I saw you there my Adam dear
no snake in sight, I saw you clear
among the trees at garden's end
well in my sight.

Yes it was you, though I agreed
and shared with you
in equal sin-bite on that autumn day
you plucked the apple then my dear
you touched, you said, only to love
and not to bite
but Newton helped and hindered you

yes, he there was too
that autumn day
to help us then
in miracle of earth
and heav'n.

So then you came and brought it me
to taste to share to love anew
in God giv'n care
for man for beast.

Was therein sin?
Or was it not dear lord
for then to walk us first,
first clean within
and then without,
yes, out your gardening?

'But yes,' he said, in whisper there
to me not you my Adam dear.
'But yes to sin, for otherwhere
how come dear mercy's pardoning
where naught to fear but love denied
or eyes turned 'way from countryside
'nd gardening?'

God did *not* like that version. He came with angry eyes. *That* was not the story he knew. The correct one. Orthodox.

'Know ye not the Bible handed down through My Own hands from days of yore, from prophets of the old? Ye faithless ones! Ye strumpet loves!'

But Kate o'erstalled him. Why should she deny? Did she not pass that love gift back to her beloved that he might taste the sweetness too? But wait, it became better yet.

For God decreed he had no choice, old man and humble (*yeah*

yeah yeah), that thenceforth for ever gardening should outwith his presence be.

> *So forth we went and sat aside*
> *in love in play on rocky brow*
> *on that hillside on autumn day*
> *within the view, the sight, the mightiest stay*
> *of God 's own town*
> *for what for him but draw us there*
> *that autumn day.*

And yet a-near that blessed garden too. For was it not on gardened earth – and only there and by our hands – that there heaven's holy city was then built?

16

Mr Business Snake and Company

As they went out, she glanc-ed back. There was – *something*.
Call it female intuit. Another there, 'scaped from the Garden? Wild,
eluding, undepend-able. Trust it? Was it Lucifer?

No. A Snake. A natty business man. Masq'rading. New skin,
sloughed off, suspicious business suit God knew, the old one. But
she knew him. She most of all knew *him* (*her business days – you
never lose that knack you know*).

He tried to wheedle her with sweetened words (*well, you know
salesmen – smarmy, foot in door, '£1000, no, just for you, because I
like you, er, £2000 …'*).

And so he spoke, 'One million pounds just come, an Africk
trust', to go in partnership. And share the booty. Thus cajoling her.

And so with snakiest double spice-ish tongue, enforking her.

'Am I a snake? So YOU say. I don't think so! I'm – amorous,
and loyal and steady and a bit jealous. Good mate for you, another

snake.' (*I got you through a snakey-business-baiting mating dating cabbage web 'fter all the other day*).

'I am an adder so you say goodish for maths and adding bites 'nd logs 'nd boiling eggs ... that's not my way – I'm the constricting boa coiling prayful victims, compet-itors just you wait! And that's why we're good as business part-eners – and a bit jealous too.'

'Why do you contest with me? Outdido Dido, ecloped Cleopa-tra, out-even Eve?' (*No marketing for apples an'way, as you know*). 'Just when I love you so, and throw my destiny with yourn (*ev'n if a bit jeal-ous*) – my nature after all, so take't or leave it, now!'

Master of disguise (*for he was a snake all time – she knew, lover of all beasts she was*), he coiled on the ground, by her feet, and instructed her on apples. For is not the snake, forever live, the master of all wiles? And of much wisdom too I think (*not all wisdom, as he thinks, but much ...*). The knower of good and evil.

'Think you that apples and pears are sep-ar-ate?' he said, 'or any other fruit? Grown in God's garden for the delectation of snakes and men – er, and women too' he added hastily, looking at Kate – so as not to cause any offence, any offence whatsoever (*can't be too careful these correct accurate days, not that God cared about it at all at all, snakes grew up in Ireland you know, in those days before St Patrick drove them out – or was it the saints he drove, even snakes aren't always right you know...*).

Anyway he knew that anyhow. Now in his generation – and he had lived long, long, oh centuries, perhaps since, yes of course, since Eden Garden days – for here he was, still around after all. Right at her feet.

'Bethink you,' continued he 'of golden apples of th' Hesperides, the western marvel, still with us now, that even Hercules piling Ossa atop Pelion had to reach.'

There, I told you so didn't I, the snake wasn't *always* right, he might have been right wiggelly and sniggerly and giggly and gaggly, but he hadn't yet learnt googally and googlelly and wikicoil and uncoil too – just give him time, it'll be *just* his thing. Sneaky snakes are aren't they?

'… and apples are choicest for love, but maybe you've not got there yet, too young.' (*But after all that searching, not fifteen again*).

'Look out for them in the market (*cheapest in the left hand stall, the one nearest hellside there*), and don't forget now, bargain well. As must in love. Think of the winged Atlanta, athlete, outatlantenicked.' (*Now that would be a good marketing word thought he to himself he did, but secretly – not share these fine inventions, patent first – a businessman looks out for good new deals, no need for a wily snake to waste on MBAs and such*).

'Yes, outatlantenicked by that runner, not fleet but wily wily-cunning, for – well who can resist the golden apples tossed in the racer's path?' (*Amoral or a bit of symbolism there, somewhere?*).

'And anyway – don't interrupt me Kate! – he got her, her Atlanta fine, and you know what THAT means.'

Kate tried to look as if she did, but really only looked blank. Sweetly confused. She didn't. Oh but yes she did, she did, sports day of course, he won the cup, did Mr Snakey, think she nothing knew, too young?

Or that sweet apple Sappho sang in th' Aegean isles, atop the bough for lover's reach – if he could just remember the words. Lovely they were, believe him (*only 50 drachma, last best price*).

Friendship – oh that too, he told her, is the apple of love. What can out-pass the kernel of a loving friend, sweet apple core, the pippin of love, of very love, the oldest wisest fruit of all?

'But is not the apple evil too – the seed?' asked Kate who had been well brought up but just now feeling very little. 'Surely I read –'

'– *Malus malus*, of apple – evil, you are right,' replied the Snake all erudite, he liked his wisdom (*and his teeth thought Kate, looking away hurriedly*).

'*Malus malorum. Male dictus malussimus. Maledicite omnes populi, omnes generationes,*' he added for good measure.

'Think not,' he went on (*on!*), his voice the pompous not-interruptible of lecturer, of nuns, of Oxford-hall like. 'Think not that apples always stand as choicest virtues, all of love. No. Discord. Aphrodi ...'

He broke off, devious – had he not been there himself, center of action and of plan, finding the apple, choosing, tossing it, causing that great siege of Troy and death of that sweet epic pair, the loving warriors Patroclus and Achilles, both. Best business projects yet, all that expenditure of cash. And deaths. And follow-up murders. And the loot...!! (*Wars always profit-full. And lucrative. For the not there*). Priam's lament too (*now that was something Kate knew about, tears came to her eyes*).

'... and then,' recollecting himself 'Apple of God's own desire, of his eye' (*must be fair to the old man – just in case he got caught out*).

'And what is that?' asked Kate, noting his oiley oil-ed oiling words. (*She knew men! Seducers all!*). But for all that, all her worldly knowingness, her long fee-earning then negotiatingness – she was a little, just a little, cajoled by him ...

'You will see,' said the snake.

PART V

DOWN AND ON

17

The fall

But then ...

Oh! He was Lucifer! The beautiful, the snake, the proud.

The jealous one.

Why should *another* son ... for daughters do not count even 'the great mother of all mankind' – *man*kind, there you have it, mark it well (*he was of the politically correct generation, as are all Saints and Satans*) ... why should a different one be sent to Earth and he, the proudest the proud, the wisest all, most beautiful, be bound above?

'Does not the morning star arise and soar above all morning stars, above the moon, above the sun, beyond ...'

'... and *fall*,' said God, 'and vanish 'fore the sun's, the son's, the Sonne's rays? Has not pride ever come before its fall, the soaring organ of the male, to fall before the morning's dawn? (*Oh oh the nuns ... And how could they, flesh-mortified, know that? God's secret veiled desire for veil-ed womankind?*). Was it not ever so?'

Did Lucifer, Great Star of the Morning, listen?

No!

For as a blacksmith plunges his glowing axe in the ice-cold bath and the metal screeches steam and temper hardens in the sizzling iron …

… as a lion wheels at bay, facing the gangs of hunters, 'scaping the circling ring …

… as the black cyclone whirls from the sky in thunderbolt and flashes through the stars …

… oh so was he!

Like a black mist creeping low to hold his midnight search and find the labyrinth of many a round self-rowl'd, his head well stor'd with subtle wiles …

So faster now and faster yet than Homer's poem or Milton's paradise, more beauteous than even Doré saw, more steeper than the words of Blake, through still air gravitie-filled, to appled earth, to plunge in water as the flying burning star …

… *he fell.*

And with him Kate. For had she not looked back at him there, out with the Eden fair? Of Adam we know not, no, but there perhaps he too, with snake? And Lucifer? And God's grace too?

18

Hell

It was *cold*! And there was she thinking hell would be *hot*! How could all those writers, black-inked books and prophets and the seers and mediums get it so wrong?

But otherwise hell was quite pleasant. No Tantalus in sight or Sisyphus, no torture tools, no gallows, sheep from goats (*sorry, forgot, just goats here lord*). The branding tongs? she still had nightmares of them, wailing wraiths of dead, thin shades bemoaning fate – those things the nuns had scared them stiff about.

None of that. Like images on old church walls, souls weighed in balance and – but of course no *justice* in hell wasn't that the point! 'Ireland for ever!' (*she meant Earainn I think, or something like that, spelling not her greatest forte either*). Even in hell, Kate was nothing if not loyal to her homeland – all those poor souls found wanting, so they were indeed, and the half of them cast into the pit never to return, burning flesh and branding and not enough beetles, er angels, to fly them up again. *Ouch!*

Not so bad then. Not for *her*. 'xcept coldening.

So why was waking still so sorrowful? Of what bereft? Was he was she …?

She remembered it.

It was her heart.

Her heart was not there with her, that was it. No longer in her breast, But there it 'd been since life began.

She had given it away. He did not want it, but he didn't give it back. He put it in a box. A box with six strong sides, a lid, a lock. He fastened the box well, put it up upon a high shelf there. He did not dust the box or clean or polish it. Or oil the rust – soon too stiff to open again. He did not remember it often. It lay in the cobwebs. with her heart. No one cared for it. But now and then he took it down and opened it. And sometimes he looked inside and thought for a moment, 'that is beautiful.' And then put the box back on the shelf.

Unbearable. To be forgot. Even Sisyphus'd be better here! At least he was *doing* some-a-thing. And keeping warm.

But soothing (*if could bear the unbearable that was and is. And cold*). Nothing she could do about it any-way. Not like the convent (*no nuns or lines or double negatives – maybe*). No one to see or talk or satisfy or sing to (*insects bees whatever now …*).

Just rags left in the corner, little beetle scrabbling around. How had she got there, wasn't it a garden, larch trees? Or Lucifer or business deals? But peaceful really.

Maybe just go to sleep and dream of …

But – WHAT WAS THAT!!?

A trickle from the corner rags. Unmoving but – a trickle, a dark trickle-ooze. And a beetle looking at it with wide eyes, so frighted now like her. She looked and looked.

And there she found him.

He lay un-breathed, unbreath-ed, breathless, without breath. Lucifer the proud. The Fallen. Lifeless now. The proud most beautiful, most highest, manhood fall'n alack.

Her twin, her love. It was for certain, known, she must die to

save, for seven years, no more, no eight, oh she was so confus-ed
now, deserving death.

> *Two thieves aloft*
> *how to unite?*
> *And what between*
> *do you not know*
> *above them there?*
>
> *Two gods above*
> *do you not know?*
> *Not thieves at all*
> *that God and not*
> *not thieves I think*
> *though steals of prayer*
> *of selves, of souls.*
>
> *Do you not know?*
> *Not two but three*
> *the triplet vis'n*
> *of deity.*
>
> *Was it not so*
> *the love that made that trinity*
> *in triplets sweet*
> *for us for you*
> *for all the world?*
> *Was it not so*
> *that love made three?*

And oh she'd followed him, where else to go? Through gravi-
tating heaviest air, through ether's unaired expanse, through Milky
Way and comet's path, past Mars and Mercury the messenger, by
Venus' mists and clouds (*oh clouds of love, her story's life*), she came.
So there he lay. Unbreathing. Still. A breathless unbreathed star.

But how could *Lucifer* be breathless? Lucifer scorpion lover of the earth's most lovely daughters, most beloved (*was he not, was he not?*) of his father?

Bleeding. All pride destroyed, black life blood seeping from heart's river flow. Perished before her eyes, her clouded eyes that had seen him on the shore. In the ship. One day in a shabby room. What was that flying shimmering thought? On way to heaven? And her bereft. No longer twinned.

> *Two stones on high*
> *to make the arch bend*
> *of our lives our souls*
> *our fate*
> *no need t'unite*
> *by human craft*
> *for look – they already stand*
> *by God's own art*
> *and now set them the cornerstone*
> *above for us.*
>
> *So too the twins*
> *slept in their womb*
> *as time began*
> *so quiet there, serene*
> *no harm no dream*
> *as in the tomb our savior slept*
> *no dream but ah*
> *torn two*
> *to fragments wrest*
> *longing for each*
> *no more unite.*

And – what? What was that? A little silvered bitch, the holly-barkened one, sea barqued, a whimper-barking, hear?

Black as black ink and devil was he there.

Oh for a wedge to plug that dam! Stop to his life-es blood's waste to the ground, a dog to stopper it, a beetle, scorpion ...

... a finger!

She tried it. He was lying wrong (*his fault, all his, his always irremediable fault*). On his side from where the black gore stream-ed still. What cruel spear had crossed him so, had pierced it there, in savagery of men – or, yes perchance, in mercy held?

Her helpless, what to do?

I have no horns ...

Even her song of love, of prayer, of lullaby couldn't raise him more. She tried again, for so she loved:

I have no horns
no tusks, to win you
to vanquish you, protect you.
I have no skill
of military might
to fight for you
or a beautiful tune
to play
or song-es sweet
to sing for you,
it's just – I love you.
Will that do?

The beetle whispered, quiet (*thus are beetles. And the beings of heaven*).

'Is your love enough?'

'Yes,' she answered, humbly now, 'for anything, for *any thing* in heaven or earth, divine or mortals bred, of the Great Book of Life above of which we mortals hear and I have seen,' (*Kate was one of those who could learn – when instructed*) 'in which is writ God's destiny for all, in black ink writ and color tint but which I know not fully yet.'

'Or, or anything in hell,' she added hastily as the beetle blinked at her with his all-seeing eyes (*she didn't want to cause offence, not anywhere*).

'Then take you now this knife.'

He plucked a pinion from his wings. Not easily. For fast welded on it was for flight, his sparkling flight i' the air, his hide-ance then in darkest corners hid. Not easily. For God decreed that he too must make his sacrifice 'ere Lucifer could rise. Only by mortal love could he do so. Not by God's will alone, try how he might.

'Take you this knife and with it saw and hack as may well be all through your finger's knot. The first high finger see, your dear right hand. That is the hand of art, of craft, of sacrifice, of man's great wisest artifacts, the blacksmith's forge, the potter's wheel-ed art, the dance of dressaged horse. The harpist' joy.'

'And if at first it will not cut then try and try and try again. Again. And yet again seven times, seven times even, even if ye count not numbers. Even to the ending of the world. And after. Until ye full have done it.'

But her heart failed her, quailed her at the beetle's words. She could not count. And even worse, that finger. *Hers.* From birth. The five. She could not could not could not. Could not give those gifts of God away. Even for her love.

It was not right she should be asked, even for her love, for her dear love.

Even for her love.

Even for her love, her greatest love.

'So,' said the beetle sadly (*for saddening God so too he spoke*). 'I see it now, your love is not enough.'

19

Love's gift and God's

She trembled there. She shook in fear, in shivers, quivers, quavers, terror. Blackest panic held her fast. Blind deaf bestood o'er abyss of time and space, of depth and number (*ah* ...), of name and nameless, of unknowingness. Of ignorance and faith and hope.

Hope ...?

Could she? Possibly?

If she did not what hope for *her*?

If she did not what hope for him? It was her Adam, her love, her Lucifer.

She could, she *must*.

She took the knife. And shook and shrank again. Not for the loss of finger, art, but for the hurt of sawing, hacking, twist and probe and pull.

For full three days she struggled there, with might and main and cross and crescent, finger, mind. And all her soul. Three crossed days 'ere he could rise again, 'ere God beheard him of his agony, the one forsookn.

For lying between
a mount of bones
of human grief and sins
a hill of stones
and pains and hurts
and joys and woes
where the sea's rain begins
to have fallen low.

But 'twas God that planted the seed
of human love
of that great oak above
of 'corn below, its roots and branches lurking there
already great with love
already hid
to love us there.

But Lord in those great trees
with leaf and twig and bird
and acorn hid in sward
where is the third?

That third grown there before the fall
of love the greatest here
see there on Golgoth's hill
the greatest tree of all.

Of all the world's great loving
of all our souls' harsh sinning
and did you first then see me there
before the earth s beginning?

God heard her – not through an angel as you thought, but through that wee beetle there who lov-ed her. Loved her in spite of all. In spite of her no-song. He saw beneath her innocence her ignorance her tongue-tied dumb-endance, her numerating non-the-numbers-still.

'Love – is that not the great story for which I was born?' he murmured in the scrape of his shining wings, in that language that God in his grace has given even unto the beetles.

And so God heard. Did he relent a little? Was it for him too that pain, that twist and probe and pull?

No it was Kate's. But God helped her too, a little, just.

He whispered close-hand to the beetle. It came to Kate's ear, then both, so quiet quiet quiet. So do beetles do.

'Take then your *leften* hand. It is God's grace. The hand of love. Of heart. And for your finger – you can choose it. Your left hand, that compassion I granted you. Think well now of your choice. For God is watching it.'

She looked and saw ring-sparkle on her finger. That ring of grief of hurt of panic, ring of love, of fondness, hate. That ring dividing from her love. That ring to wear no more but cleave (*oh, cleave*) to what was highest to her heart.

She touched it. Fourth one of her left hand, of the ring.

'Yes,' said the beetle.

So she did it. And as he'd said so struggled she. At first it would not cut. Again, again. Again and yet again.

As a sawyer measures the tree to be felled, with yards and inches and sextants against the sun and telescoping and lines, then saws with all his might the day through till the peaceful night begins to come, then fells it.

As a hen gathers her children one and one and one until she finds, and searches for the hidden one under the bank of the stream soon to be carried by the water – until at last all there and 'neath her wing.

So did she then.

For the whole day's length she struggled there – not while the bright sun rose and fell (*in hell there is no sun*), but while the silent stars of unseen skies above them waxed and waned.

So long fought she with knife and with her hand.

And God in tenderness cast her in a deep sleep and in her dream she cut.

And then awoke.

And no knuckle was there, no longer on that left ring finger there – in her dear right hand, whole, severed full. And as she looked the cut was healing, healed, the blood had ceased to flow.

The ring was falling down in whirl, in swirl, spurl, pearl, coil, whorl, in spiraling … tumbling and falling and whip lashing down and down where man no longer sees. For at last she was now freed of that coil that toiled and bound her, which she thought could not renounce.

Hasted she to plug the gap and kissed the place and gave all thanks. And miracle – for that long work the end was quick. Accomplished in an instant, the gore ceased.

And miracle again. His chest moved, rose and fell, again again. Beneath his clos-ed eyes his breath returned. Breath upon breath, sweet life, the breath of man, of psyche's life. Of anima.

She saw the sweat and blood etched on his brow. And wiped them with her hair. And mud from his pierced feet. She wiped them clean with her long tress, the hair he loved.

So then at last she looked around. She was in hell with her beloved, live and save-ed (*yes, she'd said it, 'her beloved'*). And it was frozen, fast. For it is ice, not fires in that cold hell. Yes COLD – and she who'd always feared the cold and sought the heat.

She wrapped her hair around his body, all, to warmen him.

And dreamed again next to his dear awakening corpse.

But then for fear he might awake, and seeing her resume his fall to nethermost region none could guess, she took her way, going she knew not where. But 'ere she went she pressed one kiss, a light one just, not lingering, on his brow – too light to wake but, oh it was enough, for gladden her soul within.

And so – so then she went her way from that cold place. And God sang quiet quiet quiet just for her – seeing seen what she'd done – that she might know he'd not forget.

20

Working Men, ads and hiding not hiding on a shared settee

Where was she now?

Where next did God intend for her, no-singer one, the loving, the unloved? But at least it was warm at last at last after cold-garden hell. And after all, perhaps, she *had* essayed her duty there. Such as was within herself to do. Not much. But Kate's at least.

It was even over-heated here if you asked her, amazing, but she certainly wasn't going to leave it for any frozen garden (*why think of that? Plants would never survive the heat here ...*), or sea-sound tangles or whatever. *Or* St Pancras (*wha- at?*).

Kate heard the voices on and on and on, and dreaminglike. And sea waves too. Not Shakespeare who knew all about it – about agony about the sea's own songes singing sweet (*"like as the waves"* ... *No no, not that!*). Like a nurse? A geriatric-guarding one? Incongruous. But *listen* now!

'... and the advertisements they have nowadays! And the

jingles! Though I do quite like that one about the girl rushing out after her coffee. Something like that anyway.'

'Ooh do look at the old dears on the sofa, aren't they sweet! Well maybe not sweet exactly but happily snoozing on each other's shoulders, they'll be in each other's arms if we don't look out.'

'Can't have *that* in our establishment, always keep to the rules and regulations. Always remember that Miss Wedlock, what a name!'

'Kate. KATE! It's Weddie, time to wake up for a nice cuppa my darling. And is he ready for one too? Milk, two sugar do you? Right here you go, not too full, c-a-areful now. Enjoy the tellie then then my darlins, nicely settled here till supper time. No no, fine I can get round your legs fine (*they did stretch them out, didn't they, he was even worse than her*), and the roses, aren't they just dears my dears, do look (*gone to sleep again ...*), left by that anonymous gentleman, I just knew you'd love them, put them there on the table just by your favourite settee me darlin ... didadidadida, didadida.'

'Darling? She'd never liked that 'darling'- thin, common sentimental patronizing, insult really, put-down.

After seven years, oh no now it was eight wasn't it? Oh no, how could they be 'old'? They weren't really, it was just the geriatric nurses' dream, they'd got it wrong, her love was walking young by her by the sea, morning glory entwined, oak sap in branches and birds.

They were kind really. But *diminutives*!

Diminutives make small smaller (*I'm smaller anyhow, don't diminutive me more*). Diminutives is diminished, dimmed, diminutiv'd.

Yes but 'diminutiving' is lovely. 'Dear' is lovely. And then 'My little dear, My smallest dear, My dear wee dear, my dearlet, darlingest.'

Is anything more loving, more enlovening love-ly than 'my darling?'

My darling?

'Didadida,' diminutiving voices still going on …

'… and just to add to our woes, what do we have but *two* new applications, lucrative ones too. We really must find room for them. But where …? Shame we're not allowed to double up inmates, er, residents, there's that nice empty room on the top floor. But no go. Same sex not feasible. And of course nothing else to be allowed, Old folks no sex you know, even if health and safety allowed it.'

'What *can* you be thinking of Miss Wedlock …!!!' (*S'pose can't blame her with that name, what were her parents doing …?*).

Good though that The Working Folk House (*'folk,' they were up to the minute, they were, Government Statement on Non-Offensive Language Number 334/F*), that folk and all they still had so many inmates, er clients. Finance-mines the lot of them. Not for him, oh no, love and unselfishness that was him! (*So she pretended to think anyway, keep in with who pays salary*).

The only good bits were the ads. That was *her* opinion, her considered opinion, she didn't have time to ask *their* opinion (*seven was a span after all*). And it *was* faintly intriguing to see the gentleman in the ad get up from his seat and ditch his paper and walk out by the revolving door. Er, no, swing door (*why had Kate thought of revolving? Seven years of course. Of course? What was it …?*).

The door swung and swang and swanged, then swam again on the television screen, and revolved and revived and revolved, yes seven years. By now. It was sad too. Between them they'd missed (*kissed? dissed?*) someone special. Poor thing. What a long wait.

She had sat and looked at it, at that disappearance then, for years and years. And seven now. And would he never come? Not come at all? She waiting all those years for his soft touch. For his sweet kiss, his ever loving heart (*oh but by now …?*).

No harm in going to pick up his paper, she'd a long wait in front of her, coffee or no coffee (*that advert …*). Could she get in the screen, oh yes of course, she was there, how could she have forgotten. It was *The Times,* oh of course it was. Him all those years ago, he loved the letters. And the ads, hadn't she always teased him about it? He'd claimed they might come in handy sometime. In seven years. Oh just look at that ridiculous one from someone called Catherine (*what a name, as bad as Wedlock*) about everlasting love. Ridiculous. As if you ever remember that long. No proper coffee during the war either. Dandelion roots would you believe!

And – oh dear, look, left his Eurostar ticket on the table – that must've been why he was rushing out so fast, she could just catch him (*oh if only, if only, if only she'd …*). His name on it too but no time to look.

If only …

Yes, there he was among the crowd, his yellow muffler. Striding (*that gait of his, she always had to run to keep up, thoughtless man*). Quick quick she must catch him, too late once he reached barrier, run run, high heels not good, catching tiles, run.

Oh! He'd Diss … he'd disappeared now, how could that be when he was there one instant, one year, one seven-year ago? Take with her, treasure from his hands. His loving hands. His name. A number? (*But he knew she couldn't manage numbers*).

More coffee. Thus commanded the ads. She quite liked it now, kept her awake – all night too. Years of nights and days and night night nights again, did he too perhaps perhaps … remember? Those sandy wakings and sleepings and sleepings again by the wind-swept wet Donegal sea, disappearances in mists of dreams, Irish jigging round the tombstones of Bunbeg.

Back in her seat. More years. That advertisement, more coffee, only drug left.

Except the roses. *His* roses, she knew it. Lingering fragrance of – of him. His. Misting through fragments of her-his memory (*were not their thought still shared?*), mind sliding past vanishing in the waterfall … Dartmoor wasn't it? That secret nook by the river under the rock, no one knew but them. Wild roses. Splashes.

Oh come my love, my only dear
my heart, my self, my only soul.

'Closing in five minutes.' (*Loud. Horrible.*)

One more coffee, just time, no rush, she had years. And years. Was it him on St Pancras platform? Going where? (*A dream, yes she was a bit confused about her surroundings*).

'Closing time Miss.' He was right, the time *was* closing, finished, this was to be the day of days. She had missed him, missing, she was missing, she could only glimpse his vanishing vanished shadow, the shade of his soul (*well that was better than any time these hundred – er these seven years*). He was almost … What? Coffee? The ad floated past them …

He hadn't come.

All day, seven years, down the waterfall.

He hadn't come.

So, then – put out the light.

'Oh come oh come oh come oh *come*, my love, oh show yourself, reveal, my only dear my only …'

He hadn't come.

Shift on the sofa, edging nearer, hearing the TV ads interrupting their too interrupting interrupted together scene.

> 'Seven-grainworth. Fresh from Ghana. Green and
> Gold. Take you through the day with no remember-
> ing. Buy me. Buy me, buymebuymebuy.…
> Make me. Drink me (*not Catullus not convolvulus*
> *confusioned together*). Drink me now, drinkdrink-
> drinkdrink … me now nownownow …'

'Drink up now like a good girlie dearie while it's warm. Not hot any longer, just right for oldies. And our nice gentleman friend there next to you.' (*A joke those two old dears, yes, rather sweet though*).

'Drink now now now now now … Yes and your gentleman friend too (*can never remember his name, now can we dearie*), yes, specially made with sugar just like we like it, we know how *you* like it too sir, we do so.'

   She didn't of course but instructions were strict and she did like to humour the old gentlemen, this one had a glad eye for a girl even now. Tell the truth she quite fancied him, he sort-of looked-behaved 25 but the records – always consult the records nurse! – said 60 or was it 70? Honey better'n sugar of course. She wouldn't mind honeying with him this evening, honey eyes an' all (*what was she saying …?!*).

   'Wake up me darlins, hot drinks here. Look, not too full, How 'bout cuddling up a bit closer so you can reach …? Well now, isn't that nice, and a biscuit too? Honey today, 'n oats.' (*Oat fields of golden corn back from the sea, she could remember … harvest time*).

   'They *are* quite sweet I agree … Oh, I do just wonder …' (*Genius. Typical brilliance – actually she'd been storing it up for the right moment*). 'Just thought … (*we- ell, several days ago, dare she?*), that little room up-top, 117, er, sorry 118, they could share it couldn't they?'

   'Yes I know. But they're both so dozy they'd never notice shifting, let alone each other. And another good fancy. Wouldn't need proper television, just pretend, rerun the ads round and round all day, that's the bit that fascinates them. And round. All night too. They'd have nothing else to do would they night-time.'

   Pity about the girl really with her coffee and running or something. Running after him or something? She'd of done it herself seven years ago. Or hence. Glad eyes … perish the thought! She wasn't called Weddie for nothing was she now, her parents clearly foresaw, seven years hence, not that a girl discloses her age, 29 forever!

   (*Stop for breath …*)

   'They could sleep through that bit. Irrelevant. Yes I did ask her and she agreed. Totally. Something about seven years. That's some agreement that is, isn't it all right! Sure you'll agree too sir, when you've had a chance to think it over.'

'Health and safety Weddie, er, Miss Wedkin!'

'Yes but those applications. We could manage them all right if we took their rooms. Wouldn't put up their rent or maintenance, well, only the breakfast, only one delivery needed after all (*money! she know that argument would work*). And … look, they really are sweet. They'd never know … (*seven years*). At their age!!'

'W-e-e-e-ell …'

'Perhaps you're right.'

(*She could just catch him oh if only, only, only she … His name on't too. Oh if only …*)

'Shift them then! Now! Maybe, sweeties, let them have the flowers, just till they wither, nearly done anyway.' (*Don't bother topping up water, throw 'em out, flowers I mean, though now you come to mention it … we might have takers …*).

'Toilet? Isn't there one opposite? Just pop up and check Miss Waglock. Yes?'

'A rail? Pop up and check Miss Wedding. No matter, we'll get Jackie to put one in next time he's around, no rush for oldies.' ('*Wedding*' *indeed, what would old folks know about such a thing? Or out of wedding either, not that you'd ever know what folks get up to at night even in a Working Man's Club*).

And so it was done. The old folk economized for the residence and shared the bed. And no one said them nay.

They put the roses in the corridor. For love's fragrance, love's great ocean of passion and tenderness, love's endurance for seven years and more and for ever, they had no need of flowers.

And in that dilapidated cheap room was – heaven.

PART VI

UP THERE

21

Road to heaven

Nearing heaven they were, were there! For they were now unite. As one.

She seemed to wake, yes 'Sleepers wake!' music in all voices, bridegroom coming soon. And from the heaven-haven of the darling old folks and that shabby room aloft – aloft not alost – she saw the opening of heaven near, it was near-far, attainable. Recycled new old tale. The ever myth.

Struggle from depths, the music in her ears, the sea, up from the deep ocean layers, of swimming fighting, up to light. Like th' airless classroom where'd fainted once, failed singer, to the fading language music, Linear Minoan to struggle back, up up to air, to light, the music gone but friendly hands to welcome her (*had she died?*).

So now at last they were on the road to heaven.

She felt the gentle path beneath her feet, soft wind behind her, the friends' hands – no Friend, for had he not e'er been within her. Twin shadow of her soul (*"as easy might I from myself depart ...", oh yet again*), he always there for her, iff-en she knew it not.

She trod on, ego-ed love so close behind, wafting into happi-ness immeasure-ed. She knew she was not alone. From birth she'd never been alone, He was always there. From womb and birth. Himself.

No no before! Before the womb.

As continents drift away yearn-ing to be one, as swallows fly south and long for homing land, as salmon leap rapids to reach to birth, so yearned she for their final full unite.

Once only, that would be enough. It was, it was, her hearte's song:

> *Come hail or storm*
> *come sun or shine*
> *they say – 'Illusion.*
> *No not thine.*
> *Not the real world.*
> *He is not there.*
> *A figment.*
> *Pigment.*
> *Imaginati-on!'*

> *I say – 'Come storm or tear*
> *come sun or shine*
> *come smile or peal*
> *come life or bier*
> *his care is – for me.*

> *Love? 'twould stream away*
> *in mist, in mind, in vapor of sea.*
> *Those words of fathers*
> *Faith, Hope, and all*
> *they cannot stay.*
> *Scholars' books*

all crumbled away.
But care … Care will await.

A care entrust' must ever stay.
His care is for – me
he cannot away.
For after all my dearest love
Your care is for – me.
Oh do not depart
from your struggling Kate.'

He *was* there. Within her. Near her. Her dream companion and her shade.

And bliss, they were on the way to heaven. Together now.

In joy she sang – and she, the tuneless 'tone deaf' child, she had a *voice!* A voice to sing her joy. His praise in innocent sweet simple lay.

I saw you glancing through the grass
over the morning's lea
dancing aloft in the dew
and coming and coming to me.

She was with him with him with him always, never to leave, to be together forever, seated on God's right hand. But who cared about God? It was on *her* left hand, the best – she wanted only only *him.* Just to be near him, just to see. To hear his voice.

God has entrusted me
t' the unloving, uncaring.
But now he must
for I am in his care
I do not fear
I am his care.

She had seen him had seen him, he was with her!

In joy she *ran,* she ahead. She the non-runner ran. Ran there in front to welcome him. At the gate, waiting, waiting for him, her heart near burst with load of joy, the suffering of her remorse, his unyieldien face, his love, yes *his* love too, the tangled hearts, the wait, the search, the long road, seven years or eight, the uphill, weariness, the hunger, sun, and rain and drought. Then finding, joy to come, the found, the lord, the love, oh it was all too much, she could but sit and watch him there – him him her love – thus come at last to his desert.

With her. Together now.

The incredible. He was there, face-shine before God, and all the hosts singing their souls out (*listen now!*).

Then they fell silent as a breeze dies in deep forest glades silencing the voices of the trees.

He had come.

Yes it was – it was it was! She could scarce believe. Delight before which all ill perishes, the rainbow covenant binding God and man, and man to woman, great eternity of life. That sacred rite of God-in-man, that air played only on G-string, echo round heaven and earth in that great round. Eternally.

In her joy she called it to her mind, the music and faint earth reflecti-on, the words that could conjure to her soul:

> *Air of my heart, my breath, my more*
> *than sweetest sound*
> *than Heav'n's suspending even'st glore*
> *of musick'd rhythms of humankind*
> *that air by which man lives and moves*
> *that air of sea's great ringing sound*
> *the seas' full bassest ring-est floor*
> *of sounding founding r'sounding song.*
>
> *How can I give, how live*
> *How seek for more*

than that great throng
of praise and measured solemn joy
of fingers gentle, slow
one ring-ed still in grief, I know
the hands I love and watch them go
all quiet through the keys above
and thighs below so tranquil, still.

Here is no need
for meddle pedal peddelling
for market place
of men's desires
and starts and wills
for Bach's slow speed
and air
of peacest duty.

Oh that one day we sing him there
and see his face
and hear Heav'n's sound
in skies' vast space
in loom-e's seam.

To hear it here
here hear for man
in Bach's sweet dream
in songs of grace
to praise again
the beauteous sound
and sing with him
as once before
in front that throne
of heaven's musicke's bach-en
Ayre.

She could not tell why it moved her so, but so it was.

Now she could watch him. He looked so tired so old, so decrepit. Old waiting long for her (*beetles did not lose hair when they grew old*). Waiting. It broke her heart – again again, the books hadn't writ that hearts break twice and thrice ... (*new for anatomy texts and wikis too*).

Just torn and tattered rags. Trudging and hobbling, limping past. Flesh showing through – but decent still, when did that proud one show himself, even to God?

He looked so tired now, how could she bear it now for him.

His journey's end was nigh. He raised his head to heaven's clear light, on it at last. At last at last she saw him clear, in heaven-adoration he thought not to guard. And now she knew at last why haloed saints were painted, radiant.

How she gazed now in glow too bright for her to see. Looked only to the ground, the hard brown dust-strewn ground. Lifted eyes to his sandals, soles so worn and split, oh thorn-pierced soul, oh suffering lord, oh love, sore passi-on, torn toenail on left foot.

And was he not left-handed? She'd forgot. How on cliff-edge she tottered, holt by that hand. Not fallen, by his grace, still there in him. See there it too was jagg'd, deep cut, the staff he held worn down by up-down hills and cliffs and precipices of up-way – with her, surely with her. Or had she dreamt the whole, that joyful painful traverse-cross 'cross life and death? For was she too not torn and wounded sore, sitting dust await their joint and joyous entry?

Her eyes bedazzled, she dared not look his face. His forehead rasped and bled from onslaught pressed above his eyes. Above, his hair no-hair white, straggling, struggling through his hat's through-holes. Oh he had grown old awaiting her, seven years, no, longer, decimal now, a hundred was he full one hundred now? Then so must she, his twin.

She could not bear it for him, all his wait. Take on *her* shoulders if she could (*I think, I slightly think, that God was listening. For he loved lovers. And loved love*).

But joy, joy above all, all in her heart for soon they would enroll as one, unite in God's great scroll.

She saw him come.

She saw him pass.

22

Welcome!

He entered in the Golden Gate, passage through dust and swirl, his passi-on. The gate swung open to accept him, and swung closed.

Yes swungen swingen to
swinging again in a Londonest-place
church bells in the night sonic
across the sea's expanse
like a ship swungen on the waves, going.
Like the swiping swinging winging wings
of migrating swallows, migrants from here.

Why was her joyous heart filling with grief? The gate was closed.

With joy with ecstasy, the end and climax and fulfilment of her life, she saw him go, be met. Received.

And acclamation. Praise. Rejoice from God, from all the hosts of heaven. Ecstatic joy, what overweening happiness from her, for him. Reward at last! The price for all his suffering. Hers too.

So now it was indeed 'Amen', true'st ending for them both.

23

A little dog leaps

A little dog. There. There inside. Oh oh it was Holly, Holly, her dear, beloved bitch. She of the silver fur, the loving heart. Always by her. Looking with one blue eye one half with brown and lovely brow, soft tendernessing. Never to leave till died a hard, late, lonely death, but she knew she was not abandoned by her mistress dear, unlike … (*Kate could not catch the fleeing thought-shred*), to meet once more in ever heaven.

The little tangled thing came rushing to the gate, so mad with joy, anticipation, expectation. Casual sniff at *him* as he passed, no interest by that unbark barking leaping thrill. Her mistress come. At last. Not vets this time. But *walks*! And cuddles too. Leap leap jump joy to happy hunting ground, cat-chase (*God's sneaky pets*), now mistress come, was near. But – where …?

The little silver bitch, yes really her – her Holly real – just glimpse as closed fast, so slowly, slowly slowly – the one with one blue eye and one half brown half sky-hue (*'wall' they called it, domestic-ating it*).

Actually – Holly quite liked heaven. Everyone made a fuss of her, she even licked God's hand once till she learned different (*a cat person he was, funny, you'd think … Oh well, irrelevant but she'd cert'nly sit and discuss it face to face, on knee, with Kate. At length. Sometime*). Best the hundreds of squirrels to chase and j-ust not-catch, they j-ust escape and chatter wink from treetop, high, what joy. And best of all, don't tell on me, the very best of all two meals a day, oh yum, and in a pottery bowl by God's own certified pot craftsmen, oh what bliss!

But ev'n in that paradise of rabbits, hunting grounds and (*ssssh!*) fat pheasants, something was missing. Smells.

No smells in heaven, no smells can you believe! And they call it 'heaven'? Huh!!!

They're banned!!! Binned brimmed and sinnified! Swept under carpet 'xcept it's lino here till cleaning day, then turn into something suitable. Gold and stuff and such like. Platinum once – till them dirty beet'les got thur fumbs all over it – and sixsome legs is a lotta fumbs.

Flagstone floors much better, that's how *she'd* been brought up, that she had. All proper-reared dogs knew 'bout *that*. Just sweep the mud 'n' sand and stuff off once it's dry, then out the door toward the holly tree, and any little dog-mishap, or little accident – no problem there – for God took care of it. For th' environment. The Green. And yes those human things not mentionable here (*but fuss they make 'bout accidental – honest – doggie fings …*).

Well an'way no scents. But, well, even them no good or Happy Hunting Grounds – them GOMLOS-tended (*yes by God's Own Mowers Look-Out Scythers*) – not without mistress-here and mistress-throw-stick there and fetch-dog-back.

But that day – oh.

Oo-oooh. Aa-aaaah. Her scent. Her mistress. Kate!!

How she went wild with joy. She was a very restrained little dog really. Normally. Like all Donegal curs. Only bit when – well,

when they felt like biting. Like they didn't take to someone. Like
strangers. Like someone who came up the drive. Like someone who
passed the entrance, half mile away (*children, babies, tinkers – yes
OK*). Rest of time just barked – the angels put their hands over their
ears, they knew. Choir objected, but hi fi snobs they were!

Holly leapt aloud abroad a-height and heaven-high with joy,
delight, with ecstasy, whole gamut through from A to, say, to X
(*hon-est*). Even leapt on Goddes knee (*yes true!!*) and would have
kissed, er, licked his mouth – but look-in-'s-eye, quick off.

But here was wonderful, a miracle, a holy-holyness above all
holy holies, how had she not known before she was unhappy? Even
heaven was missing something, and not just smellies either.

Raced round, circles, tail up, jumping, galloping, careering
round, oh leaping up as high as sky, as her mistress' heart when
she was glad. Ears stretched to heaven (*er, high up*), listening and
looking, sniffing, dancing, treading the golden ground, yes ever
fine-gold that celebration high-high day. God's cat looked on and
sneered. Supercilious. As if *he* would ever …

She could smell her, joy, oh nearer nearer.

But – but …??

Mistress never slow before. Nor Holly. Always answered mistress' call, no need for purgatory for little dogs (*not 'llowed there
anyhow – the Local By Laws*).

But angels were looking her with pity now, St Francis wiped
a tear. He didn't care 'bout humans, that Holly knew, so – so must
be ser-ious.

What had gone wrong? Of all the people on the earth her Kate
was the one that most deserv-ed heaven. And Holly keeping that
special squirrel run for her, as clear, 'Keep Out!' you-uns.

She raced to God. *He* sure must know. But he just shook his
head, looked 'sorrow!' at her, then at that cheeky cheeky upstart
'fore him, *without* Kate, all triumphant like as Elected One.

What happened then?

The scent, the sweetest perfume yet, oh most delectable, odor was strong by gate. Too high to see, to leap.

Holly's ears dropped, tail fell. Nose under gate. Whimper miser-able there.

Her little heart was breaking there.

24

The gate

Kate could not look, she could not look. The gate was closing. All she saw (*her mind's eye, closing now?*) was a little dog, sweet Holly, gentle Holly, faithful, silvery one, the one with the one blue eye now clouded with despair, death, desolation.

Oh all those D words, now Kate learned that 'D *****' (*the stars oh stars, she could no longer see, her eyes were clouded by those 'D' words*) was the DAMNED. Damned evermore in hell. But she knew about that already, no need for official judging for the d-souls, she was there already, yet again.

In its nine circles, cycles and recycles of her being, her own. In the dust, the dirt, the desolation.

That was the *worst* that could ever ever fall to man in all the centuries of the great world's being. A little dog whose heart was breaking.

25

Outside

But look now look look look, she could not see, look-not-look there.

Oh Kate, look, see.

Such joy, such wonder, heavenly music sound for him. Trumpets on that far side, the sight of glore, feel of an angel's wings, fragrance of the seas' deepest shells, the starting startling sounding Mozart keys of heaven. He was there wasn't he? Always, no wonder for his short earth-life, his quick death, pauper grave, once more unite with the sounden notes of heaven.

He had forgotten her.

Slowly slowly, oh so slowly, lifetime's beat of mosquito's wing, a caterpillar changed to wonder-of-the-world, she look-ed down and down and down, down into her ... heart. Agony to out ag-one the Congo pain. Agony she had never known before.

He had forgotten her.

26

The dust

It was true.

No retreat now into dream, dementia, amnesia. Those blessed states.

It was true. He had *forgotten* her. Her exist –, but she did not, now, exist.

Her echoed shriek to four blown quarters of the universe, and back and back, back, back, reflected in her heart, and shimmered, shattered, swingen shut, bells from ruined church and falling stars, and broken chords, cadences unresolved … hers now *not* hers, but not exist, could not be hers.

And again.

She heard it, could not hear it, could not utter, agony indeed to not resound that shriek aloud, sing songs of inferno-unforgiven, of trumpet shriek, *they* might sing there but in her heart there was only the silence of barrenness, a dead hearte's hurt:

I wasn't needed.

I heard the angel song,
music of man's desire.
I was not there.
I was not wanted.
God wanted me.
But wasn't looking when I came.

I sat by the gate.
Watched them go past.
I was not needed.
My love went by.
He did not see or hear me, did not listen.
He had forgotten me.

I stood behind the wire. Alone.
So de-sole-ate. I was not needed there.
My true love, he was there, forgetting me.
I was right glad for him.
He had forgotten me.

I stood at the wire.
Alone.

Silence.

No more the silence of music, the muses' poet-words. Not silence of sweet assonance of scansion sweet performancing. Or breeze caressing trees.

Dead silence, deaf and negative. Empty like noise, like din.

Just silence there. No sound.

Silence.

Then faint through bars no silence, but that greatest chant stirring even that sorest heart of hers (*she supposed they were always at the singing there, what else to do in heaven?*). Barren land – oh except that *he* was there. Wouldn't she live with him in any where? In desert, seasick ship, thin air, in hornet nest, in scorpion shell – oh scorpion, oh you have forgotten me – even in Heav'n's bare land.

It was beautiful … but she couldn't see his gleaming face, was turned to God. Away from her, always away.

And then that chant, known through all ages still, but not for her, for her, awaiting there, the dust around.

> *"Oh come oh come Emmanuel*
> *Redeem thy captive Israel*
> *that into exile drear is gone*
> *until the son of man appear."*

So true. So exiled now. So desolation. And despair.

He would never appear. Not for her.

Hear now his soaring sheering swooning, dreaming, searing tenor. Above them all. Sweetest of all. But bare. Alone, without her to support with also round. Always supporting. *Always* she would support him true, through life and death and at the gate. And could her bitterness e'er bear 'rejoice rejoice'?

Ah *he* – for he would never come again.

Was it true? Recycled in her lifest dreams. Happened before. She had sat before and seen him pass, looked in her heart. And then it'd come again. By God's will (*oh not a finding, his poetry'd misled confounded, her, his music mocking her, deceiving God, a Satan, snake, how had she not known?*). Again it would close. And so for all the length of time.

'Imaginati-on.' Yes that indeed her fatal cruelest fault, imagination, dire propensity of her own self. Had not the nuns warned her again and yet again? So uncontrolled (*controlled?*). She had fled to some far desert land outwith the world, b'yond even God's mercy reach.

But she *would* prevail. It had not happened. *Could* not have happened. They were on earth. Or they were in heaven, both of them. Together. Dioscuri. Twins.

She *could* not have seen him pass and enter there, or been

received with praise and acclamati-on! It was just a dream – she would have raised her hand, and touched him, called. She *would*.

He had *not* been acclaimed by God, welcomed by all, all with those paradise songs, had *never* passed her by in the dirt, she would not accept it.

He had just been tired, preoccupied, just hadn't seen, he'd come back any minute, any minute now, appearing through the gate just any minute now, she saw him didn't she? Just any minute, now just any second she meant, no century, no *second*, *now* and …

He did not come.

After all that had passed – her desperate search, her sore remorse and … and he had just forgotten her.

Her storied life – all just imagination. What could be worse? For anyone?

She was just imagining it all. It had not happened.

She was safe. *I* could not have …

The scream again, unheard and through her ears …

27

'Remember me'

And as she sat she heard them sing again, for *him*. So wonder-ful. For *him*. So wonder-full indeed. But …

… but oh it was her own song now, that harvest hymn she loved then as a farming Irish child, that 'safely gathered in' at last, that peace. Now she knew why it had moved her so, had always done, that cause reversed.

'Remember me.'

And yet again. Remembrance. Her harvest memories grew and flourish-ed, came close to ear, to grain. And as she sat she remembered that sweet song she'd sung as a child, with her still:

> *"Come ye thankful people come*
> *Raise the song of harvest home*
> *All be safely gathered in*
> *Ere the winter storms begin.*
> *First the blade and then the ear*
> *Then the full grain will appear*

Sing ye gathered people sing
Sing the song of harvest home."

Not for her. She longed for it, she longed. But could not sing. She was outside, forgotten.

Oh they were singing again, that harvest, the gathered ones. She would never be gathered in.

So may we all
in autumn time
in gatherance, all
see harvest home.

Ah home, but no way now a home for her.

Her song, *her* welcome, how could they do 't? Would they not come to gather her, for harvest home, first seed and then the ear, then the full grain would appear. Herself. The 'Kate.'

Not hers. Though she of all of all of all of them was waking, waiting waiting waiting.

With joy with ecstasy, end and climax of all life, she saw there. God knew his name, from her still hid. His number too. His soul within. Had searched and known it all along. Looked in his face, oh in his face.

And then – then all the songs of heaven for that one save-ed lamb that had been found, but not by her.

And looked again and looked. And heard faint faint the song of priests and people, dear. As in a great cathedral there, by arras hid. Not for the congregation, people gathered in. Not for the likes of her in the dust.

Was it I, was it I, was it I?
I who came here to kill thee?
Was it I so cruelly nailed you
fixed you to the tree?

Yes 'twas I that killed my beloved
who betrayed and spat and took him
and nailed him to the tree, betrayed by me
oh three times in chance and carefree whim
dancing in dawn-light glitt'rings
before the cockcrow chimed.

I carry you home beloved
to lay your bones in peace
and kiss you quiet beloved
what salves it now to weep
to weep for the sins committed
that nailed you to the tree?

What heed now the tears deep shodden
in painful hurt for thee
who trod the path now trodden
sore trodden then for me.

Well yes uplifting. OK. But she wasn't sure how it applied to *her*. Like all these religiousy things, could take more ways than one (*oh take it light, self-mockingly, to tame emotion?*). Tears burned her eyes – who knew so salt the ocean?

And then she heard (*or was it in her heart?*) that verse she half remembered still:

I am on a path
lovely with basil and nettle
I cannot tell where it may go
perhaps to a swamp
or an impassable river
a high hill
with sight of the sea.
I only know
that it will not go back

and I must tread on.

She hadn't believed it at her convent school, or nuns there either. 'Remember her' – he wouldn't now, he hadn't, the gate was shut.

She had trod earth in search of him, journeyed the skies and swum the seas, through ocean's nightly wrack to deepest deeps of man's desires, to search the hidden places of the soul, of scorpion kiss, those winding wending bending secret ways and woes where she might go, where she might find him.

Oh could she bear to see it once again, again unwind before her eyes – nowhere, *no where*, no place in galaxies, the universe of universes, in all the stretchingnesss of time.

She was not there.

'Oh but I am here, I am here, oh look me, look.'

Did he not know, oh sure-ely, that she that she that she was there!

'I am here I am here, here by the gate. Awaiting still.'

She *must* have seen them going in, in there together now (*she thought*). No gate-shut. For the best, the occamest is best. Like God's time, bestest time.

"Ave Maria, gratia plena
ora pro nobis peccatoribus."

She needed those prayers, whatever, dream or just nightmares those, she would not could not face it, mercy for sins, now and in the hour of her death.

They ceased. And was not the silence more blessed than the song?

As she listened still they raised their voice, canon now. The hundredth psalm, oh miracle, the hundredth hundred. She knew not where or whence she was but she felt infinite.

"All people that on earth do dwell

Sing to The Lord with cheerful voice
Him serve with fear, his praise forth tell
Come ye before him, and rejoice.
To Father Son and Holy Ghost."

Holy Ghost? No Spirit, psyche, anima or ka, that breath by which we live and move, 'love organs' – those, the lungs – that aye sustain. And is it not (*oh theologians now take note*) the exercise of human love that makes that third being of Holy Trinity? No magic spirit there, no halo bright, no artificial manmade flying dove or feministicated fem'nine figurehead.

No it was just – love. Love, plain and simple love she knew. That great grace, love, enduring, vibrant, 'making' love in humans' ways. *Saecula saeculorum* … (*But abstractions too like numberation, not for Kate. But yet was there not some magic there in fragrant prayer?*).

And then they sang for all the peoples of the earth, for God, for her, she that was poised on edgest edge of heaven:

"To Father Son and Holy Ghost
The God whom heaven and earth adore
From us and from the heavenly host
Be praise and glory, evermore."

For her but not for her.

28

Waiting

She looked again. Lo now a beetle on the skin of the earth. Creeping. Like her, a migrant, stranger, transmigrated there? What evil in her life that she was lowered so? To that be-beetled life, that lowly crawl, enfilthed be-crust be-cursed existingness? But then, had she not earned it full?

No, she had learned her lesson now. Beetles it was figured her life, that new'd her love, flew them to heaven.

'*Yes*,' said God, 'now know you beetles mine, highest of my create-on? My love-ed insect breed. Have you forgot my lesson now? The beetle parable? Their six-legged run, their purity, no sullied mind for them – do they not clean men's dirt? Their flight to th' skies? And you the mate of Scorpi-on, Great Insect-of-All-Insect-Breed?'

So God in mercy sent her words of her life, the Beetle Song:

The last oh the lastest
by morn or by night …

Yes but not yet. For the rest had escaped her mind.

PART VII

RETURN

29

The looking

Hark now that other song again … the secret heartes song, her inmost soul, not of now beetles but something more enchanted, words she dared not say, praise of her Lord:

> *"Laudate dominum*
> *omnes gentes, omnes populi*
> *laudate eum."*

Oh that she too might join that praise, praise of the Lord, the everlasting song of heart, of soul, her life, the one he did not hear and did not wish … oh song of rejected, guilty, her the desolate.

But – he *did* hear. 'Look down dear child' said God, 'and see your heart's desire, did I not promise it when you trusted me? When you waited for me then? In the dust. For it is e'en from the dirt, the humbling heart that man may see me.' (*'Man?' – Kate prayed that it was for woman too …*).

She saw it.

And there, she saw him, heard him, felt and touched him, sang his praise. All listening. And *he* was there, his head on hand, sat quietly. And hearing her.

Yes there again:

> *"Laudate dominum*
> *omnes gentes, omnes populi*
> *laudate eum."*

Song of *his* praise. Again. And yet again. And oh that she were there. In praising him.

And so she sang – she could not sing, she knew that well. But she sang not with her voice but with her heart, full heart, and sang that song of praise. She sang for *him,* her love, her heart's desire.

She lifted up her voice in heaven's great paean, was leading it …

> *"quoniam confirmata est*
> *super nos."*

'Nos?' – no it was for *her,* for her alone, for her, his cherished one, her to whom he was pledged. She sang again for God gave her voice to praise. For love and truth, compassi-on:

> *"misericordia eius*
> *et veritas*
> *veritas domini manet."*

And so she ended that great song – his truth and love abiding still.

She stood without the fence, looked in but not with mortal eyes, not humans' sight. Beclouded now, seeped with the wet sea's salten tears.

How had she come there? 'It was God,' whispered her ears. 'His grace. And as for Job your twin. So you might know what suffering is. Art blessed.'

She looked again, she saw, she saw.

Drought dirt despair, drowning in the dust-cloud sea of misery

– dust where she sat and stood and struggled breath.

She saw.

She was outside, the not-invited one.

She was outside the fence. God had forbidden her, she'd come too late run she so fast pack she so tight time she so strict she would be late.

She had not come at all.

He was not hers, it would never be for her, nor that beautiful room that was his and not his, that was *him.* Oh those words in her mind! (*Oh words words, black ink-writ in her mind – but not in bright love, nevermore*).

It would not be hers. The beautiful place. That beautiful room. Her heart's desire.

Little had she known poor fool that that sad verse she thought was new was all the time of her:

> *The beautiful room.*
> *the key was in the door*
> *I knew and won the way, the number*
> *and – it was surely mine, my room.*
> *It was my room.*
> *It was not.*

> *I went in with my mother*
> *not me but three on beds.*
> *I introduced two names I knew.*
> *The third?*
> *Oh the third, the third*
> *no name but closer than myself to me*
> *as easy could I from myself depart.*

> *We were late*
> *I'd missed the stop as usual*
> *when did I win right?*

I trudged the snow-way
slower than my mother
from Micklegate.

The room was beautiful
so beautiful
it was not mine
those men on beds
the angel song
more in the day
studying, gossiping, laughing
it was not mine.

I could not state
it was mine
but it was so beautiful, so beautiful
so beautiful
a shrine
of art and beauty.
Not mine.

I turned the key and went inside
it was not mine
my room-dream
but when I woke I would
reallocate
for the next year
when I was old and wise and grey
too old for beauty
to be mine alone
my own dream-room
my shrine of beauty, holiness.
Redemption.
Love.

It was not mine
that beauty wall, proportion, shrine
of sunset light, by twilight lit
of broidered edges, pearls divine
and ruby tracing beauty.

He was not mine,
though closer than mine own self's
from my soul depart
he was not mine.

It was not mine
not mine for sin
or virtue
no not mine to win
for God said 'Wait'.

And so – she waited there.

In the dust. For one who did not come. For one who would never come.

30

The agony

What now?

Her dog first, yes that tenderest heart. Next all her loving-loved in heaven, thronging the throne, clamoring, shouting, calling her name.

All of Kate's loving ones came, and her fans, admirers. Homer with trailing lyres and garlands, accolades to see his plagiarist, what greater praise to Greeks for a *cantor, poeta imitandissimus*. And Job, to catch good suffering quotes to pass to all (*they weren't about to grasp them were they now, those sun-glassed giggly girls, back row of lecture room. But old Job never stopped his trying, remind you …?*). And the Bard – look to those laurels Homer and green Milton and King David, all.

'Where is she?'

And her teachers and tutors. Even Her-Excellenceness-mother hen, the Nun (*people don't change in heaven I'd have you know*), came running – running! Mothernun!! Holding Kate's golden lines aloft, and in her other, leftes, hand, half hidden, knee-thin black stockings (*too much prayer!*) all set for darn. (*No darners in heaven then, all still below in the you-know-where, darning and damning and durning bad as ever*).

Then they all looked enquiringly to God (*so bless him*).

And all the beings of paradise roused from night's slumb'ring, all the created beings of now and then and time to-come. The mightiest gathering all the years of heaven (*they go back long way as I can vouch for personally, if you doubt it, ask St Columb, ooh sorry, he's sleeping in Iona, peaceful sleep-place, dreams of sheepskin, song and anger there*).

They stopped at once. In silence like you've never heard. Stopped wittering and withering and jittering (*or bugging or bagging. Or was it beetling?*).

They all looked at God. Accusingly.

He looked straight back.

They all looked, even *more* accusingly, glared at th' unpenitent self-portantising high fig-ure, The Self-Elect. (*He deserved their looking don't you think? – what Kate ever saw in him …! Well anyway she did, her choice and none of your bl**dy business. Free will don't you know, makes the world go round for blood is thick and wa-ater thin, in for a penny …*).

'Enough!' God shook his head. Shook disbelievingly. But the trumpets believed all right, prided themselves on being before the game, always, the first to haiku or to haka, there in th' forefront of the troop, brazen each which the way, unhearing taunts and slings of … (*well all that*). The orange drum that cared only that much for anything, for all the tragedies and comedies of all of life (*music outpaces evryfing, dunnit?*).

They set up mighty discords, did indeed they did indeed, to raise the roof (*if there are any rooves in heaven, who knows 'bout that?*), a great huge din, an out-of-tune black blasphemy – in heaven! (*But freelance musicians and rock stars, you know, don't you, they're uncontrollable …*). Clamour and clang to raise the …

the skies. Or saints from labors-resting-place.

So everyone jumped, even the man. Him. He had been busy instructing them. (*He! To them!!*), instructing them in the matter of his tolerating (*note gerund, grammar is all Miss K, but anyway she was the one he had to forget!*) tolerating harmony but really preferring contrapuntal (*surely in heaven that'd be the right top one hundred chart whatever his inner preference …*), occasional discord to keep it fresh of course (*play all ways, that's always best*). But this …

He turned reproachfully to God (*sure he agreed?*). God looked right back. Reproachfully, at him.

Then the great saved elected one – how generous, gracious he then was – I tell you true (*I don't think!*) – turned to bring Kate into the conversation, she'd wish to agree with him. He knew she really preferred to harmonize, her rude crude food-for-fools ears and compliant, oh good thing, persona, but now she'd reached here, with her entwined-following-his-self she would of course, and after him, he'd get her signed up with the other old uninstructed dears (*he was Grade VIII and more of course*).

Even little Meg-pup came up looking for her, bit late she was but what would y' expect of runt of the brood, the laggard. 'Meg-pup' – haven't heard of her? Not seen the gleam in Holly's eye and sideways look from eyelash under her *two* eye (*that one made all the difference, as well she knew – oh shy of course but long experi-ence*), that sideways look at God 's indolent Alsatian Dog? (*Heaven's of the future not just past you know. Ev'n Kate – well 'nough said, that's another story dears, right song sheet please!*).

The trees bowed stately heads, whispered her name, the sycamore wings drew a 'K' in flight, the scorpion cracked out her Morse name with his sting, and eagles called their nestlings with their yellow eyes. Oh no oh no they were always blue his eyes, blue as the sea at dusk, the sky at dawn, how kind he was, had she not know his divine nature since the start. (*Teenage? – He was age-old, Adam, universe, but she was far too young, oh then too young, too young by the sea*).

Who understood? Not Kate who sat there in the dust. Not angels or saints or archangels. Not God the keeper and recorder of all fate.

She saw, no not-saw, *felt* him turn, her love, her love who never would forget. Oblivious. Forgetting, he the unforgetting.

Mindfulness now just for God. And for the song.

Then she felt his puzzlement – her pain, turned her to look, one glance no more.

'She's here, just here, a step behind, one just behind (*of course*) me, close, oh coming straight, just look' – she heard the discord in his voice – 'coming just here, look, here to plainsong glee, (*likes harmony, she's alright really*), I'm teaching her counterpoint you know, just rudiments: you need to be sep-ar-ate and *wait* for it. And then it's …'

He *had* to go on talking at that point, anything else not to be borne. Best cover it with breves and semibreves, oh yes and triplets and those lovely ornamentationiments, and change of time and 11/8 … no sorry choirs hate that, he meant 4/4, good marching time for heaven's hosts … and … and … 'nd … 'd …

He'd lost his audience, he could tell. Maybe his confidence as well. Something perhaps for harmony after all – united same-time pair, chords brought as one … same time, same place. She had some ideas, yes hadn't he always said it? Well anyway – just coming, c-om-ing, Kate.

Wasn't she? *Wasn't she?*

Well, she wasn't.

What had they done with her? *They.* Someone else, it was bound to be, not him. Put it right! Instanter!

Right now not him not him. And …

Where was Kate? Kate!! KATE!!!

She was not.

Not not, oh not. Not nott-ing notting still. In the dust.

Knotted in the dust.

She does not see his agony, heart-rent for his abandonment, his frantic guilt, his wild insistence. No passion, passage, passi-on passionate cross to equal his.

He would go back. And ...

WHERE IS SHE?

He would return to earth, hows'ever hard the road, how peril-ous the way, how rocky the path, his heart. Persev-erance for sev-erance sake. For his abandonment. Leave heaven's delights – what woe, what sin, what fall – to sojourn, seek, on the earth below.

But no! Hark now to God's Decree:

> For those who go back, the deserters, silver by hand-fuls or what else, there is no return. None. Once entered in The Great Record Book of Heaven (*St Peter nodded and jangled his keys*) THERE IS NO RETURN. No second chance. Dwell forever with the sinners, the goats (*oh the wild goats on the hills*), the forever lost. Have you not seen the frescos, paintings of the damned? Know that it was I, your God, who guided artists' hands, sent them to earth? Who gave to man the holy writ of that Divide 'twixt Live and Dead, b'tween Lost and Saved.

> The Right Hand and the Left Hand and the Great Signatories of Heaven and Hell have signed it, call-ing witnesses, before my Throne and Power.

> So Was it in the Beginning and Is Now and Ever Shall Be, Amen.

And all heaven echoed the words. And the angels crossed themselves devoutly (*Columba wasn't listening – oh well*).

'Go if you must. And be condemn-ed evermore never to see my face again. Or your mother's too.'

At that the son's heart trembled. but his will held firm. Hard as a scorpion's shell, tougher than a nutmeg's rind, an eagle's talons, stronger than the mightiest breaker of Atlantic waves, than shrieking wind – his mind, no falter. He would find her.

She had not counted the cost. So nor would he.

31

Action in heaven

Problem. Quandary! Not to put too fine a point on it – *Chaos!*
Like before the Crea … God's decrees could *not* be thwarted. *Never.*
Never in the whole history of the universe. Had he not decreed In
the Beginning? His Word. Obeyed. And his decrees were never …
oh!

Where had he got it wrong in his creating? Just that one freewill
freewheel freefall stitch among all the good knit, stocking stitch
too, black-writ lines.

And now – look what had befall'n! No one picking up the
stitch, er, ball (*stitch was for girls. Girlies you know. Women*). Nothing in the Rules about *that.* Even Pete no good (*great on constitutions
and suchlike, but it was past the time for that … how could it be …?*).

For thus are men when institutions fail, when it comes to *them*,
to individuals stripped of imperial clothes. A-driften on a sign-less
sea – no one paying them heed, or due obeisance. Or setting up the
chair at table head, to bring them coffee and whiteboards. Women
better, multitasking, no pride either.

God was … *STUCK!*

It was not meant to be like this. Nobody to tell him what to do or, er, who to delegate things to.

He looked around. Where were his team? Nuns. Angels. Saintesses. And His own Woman, why else had he ascended her up here? But she just smiled and looked away (*and pondered with great joy in her heart no doubt to see him caught in his own petard. Or lanyard. Or something*).

What could happen next? Let us peep and see … a wisp of a garment flutter between a crag and a hard place.

It was God. Pacing among his sheep in the green fields, a fit place for indecision (*er, wise decision-making*), mounting to look down from the purple hills, pondering his will.

Challenges are good for inspiration the nuns told Kate those years ago (*another life*), walking the bridle path by the stream, commune the waters, never the same advice the second time but good for thinking. (*But didn't it come round the same each year that same imposs impasse impassing passi-oning Eastertide?*).

He needed her help did he not? (*What, hers?*)

He went to the Queen of Heaven (*best call her that, her right side best …*). No need to speak, she just gave him 'that look'.

So he gathered up his robe (*he'd have his own back in time, tell her she hadn't spotted that invisible tear in you-know-where, he'd show her and complain. Not mended then! Women!!*). He donned the high judge cap he knew became him well, showed well his tangled strangled locks (*hair to you and I – grammar please! Well really, men!*).

'Go then my Son,' proclaimed he in his most sonor-ponorous tones he'd had some aeons to perfect (*fortunate!*). 'My blessing go with you. It is as it has been in the beginning, as I have willed it from the founding of the world. For you. And for mankind. Remember, mark it well in time of greatest need, despairs, crossed desperation, and you're at your "Father forgotten me?" I did not forget, I did not "send" you, you went yourself. *Insisted* on it!'

And he bent his gaze upon the earth, his generous, feeling, fine, all-knowing, eyes. But did he really know all that of mortal, carnal love? There he must rely on his son – so best to let *him* visit earth, keep Dad up-to-date a little, mustn't sully hands with all that stuff, with what the prang-y younger 'uns, er, generation, called the 'real thing'.

So he stood up for a Solemn Proclamation, annulling the previous decree (*St Peter consulted the Constitution, yes, it was OK, vide sub-section 5.1.23 in appendix 105, sorry Appendix 105*).

All heaven grew still to heed his words. The mothers hushed their babes and flowers held their breath in growing. The moon alone refused to stay her motion there for what would happen to the tides – just like a male not to think of *that*!

> Harken ye theologians, ye self-styled philosophers from old, interpreters of bibles, priests and rabbis, imams gurus too, and all ye prophets of the past, oh ye of little discernment yet. How could an all-knowing Father send his Son to earth, to danger him? For the greatest love in all the universe could any father do it? Could he bring woe and pain on his own child?

> No, no, I tell you, turn away ye from your ignorance and harken to My Truth. He, He who loved the world, the dear race of men, verily he chose it for himself, the light, the truth, the way. He chose it to show them, to be saved, to live for ever here. And – when he insisted – I did not prevent, in love did not prevent, but loved him more, but did not 'send' him.

> Thus I declare to you My Covenant 'The New' All The Ages, sacred bond, slim scintillating bow of love,

and, er, sacrifice, the Shimmer-Rainbow prophesied
of ancient days, chain between God and Man.

All heaven fell silent at His Prophecy, were shocked. They had
never heard such words, such deep interpreting before. Archangels
flinched at changing everything. Lucifer poised a leap – 'a coup
d'état! a coup d'état!', he shouted top of voice, *à moi! à moi!*'

Michael reached for his sword, St George for his tame dragon
(*domestic all the time you know*), Gabriel his trumpet. 'What use is
that?' muttered the new recruit. But Gabriel and all the rest knew
that of things in heaven and earth and hell and 'mong the beasts,
music is the king.

And to prove him right – what better witness is than song –
the whole of heaven stood up as one, the toddlers too, and raised
celestial voices in their praise.

> *Now thank we God's new text*
> *and his great words of joy*
> *whose greatest Son goes forth*
> *e'en to himself destroy.*

> *To seek for his beloved*
> *and mankind's greatest good*
> *through dust and cross and passion*
> *to save us, by his blood.*

They were trying to sing the Kruger setting I think, 'Now d'we
thank us all our God? – all at once (*Ouch!*). All right in German,
but somehow it had turned chorale – for if music is beloved 'mong
arts, so is Johann Sebastian Bach the chief of all musician makers,
sweet and passionate music, the loved of God. How else could the
Words of God reach though the great eternal universe?

So thus it was accomplish-ed.

32

Feminine ways

The mother hid her smile.

She knew it was not Love of Human-ness or Sacrifice, or Love of Man – Woman more like, and the love would be for one of earth's daughters whom he had probably sedu … adored. She knew all about such things, quite right that a son should have his choice among all the mortal, er, maidens, she could tell by the droop of his eyelid that it was more serious than most.

Anyway she knew it was not for – well not *just* for – the saving of the world that he went. A youth he was, and youths must sow their tares and seek for adventure. He was a young man still, untried, needed a gap year there, or three, and wings (*and look at the one he did not name? Who knows – she was not one for interfering, things must run their course*).

She only said, 'Give children wings as well as roots dear Lord' and turned away to hide a little, very little, tear (*in Heaven all sorrow and crying done away with there you know, God forbids it*).

Then up she spoke, the Queen of Heaven.

'A parable.' (*For why should men have the monopoly on that?*).

'A song-sheet for the next campaign.' (*Not yet, when she'd gathered evidence and pants brigade*).

'A parable. Shut up and listen now you all.' (*Honestly, that family of hers! Better wheedle, she could do that fine*).

'Harken ye, ye hosts of heaven, and ye, great Master thou.' (*Good words on such occasions!*).

'Thou of the Ivory Carven Phoenix Peacock's Eagle-Throne.' (*These birds!*),

'Great King of Wisdom's Might, and All of Time, oh hear ye now the Word of The Lord. Harken to that great parable wrought by God.' (*Well she had to say that …*).

'I tell you of a box hedge …' (*No not vine rows, d'you think God's writ runs just in Italy and Palestine you xenophobes?*).

'A box hedge was once planted in a man's garden and flourished for the birds of the air and the sparrows and the fliers of entangled kite strings.'

'The hedge grew strong and enduring, it was green, it did not fade. It defied the rain and the drought. It did not fail. But even in God's rain … (*always salutary to bring that in – just a little inflection of the head, oh yes she knew her men she did!*) even in God's great (*genuflecting*) reign it could not grow of itself. Verily verily it needed the hands of the keeper of that garden to tend it day and evening.'

'And the keeper came to tend it, nights and mornings all, he came to tend and to, er, yes of course, offer up his own small prayer to Lord God of All.'

God bowed his head graciously and smiled at the Queen, not noticing (*why should he?*) his son's impatience to get on with it and his, 'There he goes again …'

'But I say to you my children, verily verily I say unto you, that the hedge would be of little worth if it had not also had – an opening. A way out.' (*Were they listening?*).

'Wings,' she added in case they hadn't got the point.

So all the little girls looked smug and *extremely* pious and mentally checked through their best party frocks, while the boys winked at their mothers and twinkled mischievously at their dads who looked the other way.

St Peter looked doubtful but decided to go with the flow and put a good godly ... (*yes that's what he said – and, as you well know, that's what all the, er, hmm, did too*) a god-fearing face on it and made sure all upheld the old traditi-on and didn't see it was new (*or was it the other way round? Bit of muddle there. Sorry and all*).

So his Father gave him His blessing and sent him on his way, telling him to call on His name at the last. He would not abandon him (*well, if he behaved himself and didn't have too many thieves or dancing girls with him when he got to Heaven*).

Then he made ready. He took his scrip and one torn cloak, refusing all the food and clothes his mother brought, accepting only one ragged hat against the hard sun (*his mother looked disapproving, but didn't really mind, it was only the principle of it*). For was he not taking his right hand's craft and his strong left arm, his pride, his might, his very self that he would never never be without, not in all the years of God's creation, the vastest realms of space? Always they would be with him. Yes, his very self. And he would not fail, not while his right hand held his cunning, the left arm all his secret strength.

He took his sandals too, still were they broke (*for who in heaven had thought to mend them?*), the curiously fashioned staff wrought by his dear stand-in father Joe whom he adored – what a worksmith and model *he* had proved to be despite all the gibes about, well about, well you know (*Nazareth small-town gossips and all that – Ssssh!*).

So off he went, head u-up – for they were watching him – back stiff, a little tense. No one noticed but his mother (*of course*).

And Gabby (*Archangel Gabriel to you*) twigged that his free-lance singer – well he wasn't *that* bad really – was doing a runner,

AWOL if it was the army but no military order allowed in heaven or so I hear (*hard to believe, that is*). Well anyway it wasn't for another gig, no honest, and he wasn't taking the clapped-out van or stolen drum kit either.

Well. Well then Gabby swallowed hard and woke up his pop band to play farewell (*not everyone sobbed to see him go I fear – there's a bit of pro-jealousy even in heaven you know. Just a bit*).

'There is imitation, model, and suggestion, to the very arch-angels, if we but knew their history,' Gabby said, and he flourished his fine polished bacchanalian trumpet, then propped it carefully against the parapet (*shake spit out first, archangel angel! Ugh!*) to run to get him on the right road (*stogefundle the thought, please, with crossed notes and bars, all right?*).

And so the son was now prepar-ed for the road, staying just to touch his little lamb, the special-loved (*didn't see Holly's little yearning eyes, she'd've gone along with him just for Kate and anyway liked walkies, there'd be smells again. But no!*).

He farewelled with great gentleness, 'Dear lamb, she'll love you when she comes.'

Lucifer whispered secretly in his ear that it wasn't so bad.

And Gabby ran fast (*a bit late but a trumpeter first has to knock the spit out again!*) to show him the postern gate that God didn't know about (*and that Gabby had found handy afore now, so that he could creep out uncounted by the bureaucrats – we won't ask why!*).

That way – never mind God's ruling (*Saint Peter's more like, Gabby was a cynic, a rock star, and there was no love lost betwixt those two. But wait, even in heaven can Love ever be 'lost'?*) – that way the self-styled 'Seeker' would avoid the Golden Gate on the way out, and then sneak back in again when he had found, er, er, whatever-it-was he was seeking (*a girl? He knew all about that, easy, she'll leap, leap, straight into his arms of course, no sweat*).

'Harder going down,' Gabby warned him. 'I know it well – don't ask! Pick your way, you'll be fine. Good luckee now!'

Huge smile with buffet on the back that nearly set him afloat before he'd even launched.

'No no! No blessing, who do you take me for? Just *arrivederci in paradiso*.'

He's waited an eternity to say that one. Learnt in his little grade school, and just right for now.

Then, 'Cheery 'bye 'bye, give 'er my love when you find 'er.'

If he found her …

33

The Seeker

And so he went back. Perchance it was a dream. But I think that he truly did return, do not the dead go earthwards when they're called by those who love them still?

But she was sitting in the dust by the Golden Gate and by the back postern gate he did not see her.

So there he was, leaving now the denizens of heaven. And God sent a secret angel for watching over him, the one with iridescent wings to shield him from the strikes of the hail, the heat of the sun.

But not from the strikes of love – that were impossible even if God so willed it. Quiet, Unfelt. But always there.

For God loved the Seeker. And though he might nevermore see him enter heaven, he wished him well in his search.

34

The plunge

Like as a black cyclone sweeps 'cross the plain, the eagle stoops on his prey, the rainstorms wing across the plain bringing destruction …

… so swept he down from heaven.

As the steeple stretches to sweep the sky, the child's soaring plank falls e'er it rises, as the great lever stretches, balances, to move the universe …

… so his seeking presence embraced the sky, wings like a peregrine's to uphold him as he hovered.

So again he plunged, lulucifered, apinioned, to the earth in that old time of his love's dear life, her dream, her greater wisdom than of mortal bards. In search of her, of his berooted self that he'd denied – but how can man deny his roots, his branches, twiggen, leaves?

Gabby'd been right. The coming down was harder than the upward, much. Now he knew what those clever NDE articles were on about – 'Near Death Experience'. Did they not know it was *real* death experience, not joy or sorrow or family tears or even Science-

Research, but hard hard hard hard.

He'd do it again of course. For her. But did she have any idea of how hard it had really been, was still being? *Women!* He did resent them now he came to think. A bit. But he composed his face into the proper suffering lines in case anyone (*female!*) happened to be looking.

We-ell that actually wasn't so difficult, yes for it *was* hard. Painful. Not to put too fine a point on it, agony, not the coming, no not that (*bad enough*), but the return. Dire.

Only a smuggler's back way down to stumble through, no thoroughfare for wheels, nor four-wheeled phaetons, nor for horse. Mud, fall'n trees, cherries there and yes the oaks, copses, corpses (*what did they think he was, a rest director then?*), upturned paving stones, no – gravestones, dry bones waiting for unite (*knee bone hip bone – that's quite enough of that!*), yowling dogs, and dust dust dust. Keep the moving on, you you there, one, one, left right, right right, long way to Tipperary, a-ah!

> *You have taken my heart*
> *and thrown out the key*
> *I no longer exist*
> *I exist – in hell.*

Ah-ah, first sight of water, looking down as from a turret top, as from the mounten-mound a hill, a crucifix, a skull-ed hill. Down.

And look! He could just catch a glimpse of, yes, of sea, a shell, a line of seeping footmarks …

Now surely he was nearing her? To bring her home. With *him*. But – she was sitting in the dirt at the gate and he had not left that way. He had passed by the wicket gate on the hillside, on the way down. At the side. He had not seen her sitting in the grit thrown up from his plunging.

He called to her where she sat – or wherever she happened to have gone, women *always* went straying off after inessentials, and then expected *you* to know where they were, and that it was *your* fault you didn't. And to come after them, looking for them, 'keeping them waiting.' (*Wouldn't you just know it!*).

She wasn't in heaven, far from it. Or dawdling round in the fashion department either. Or 'just looking.' Or gossiping with friends and 'a cuppa tea, one cuppa, truly.' She was just sitting in the dust.

He called again.

But …

… she was sitting in the dirt. Waiting.

Still waiting, hearing all of heaven's songs, in learning longing pati-ence. And severance. From him. From hope.

He was without the gates. Not waiting. Searching.

Searching to the edges of the stars and the phases of all Saturn's moons, the edges where the sun's beams do not shine. The bounds of the universe, the deeps of the ocean where the long legged crea-tures crawl and no sun shines, the eternal end of time and space.

So search-ed he.

She was still waiting. Just – waiting. Saying nothing. Alone. Only a little beetle for her company. Crawling around in the dirt by her feet. How he wished it was *him*, although he did not know it, even if only a useless little crawly beetle. Slimey. Just to be near her. Even if she didn't know either.

He brought to his mind her image. What sorcerer's art could raise her? What magicked number there? Limning in the luminos-ity of her love, he no longer knew whose he was, which was him, which her.

Did she prefer it there? Better than where *he* was at least. Oh curse her, plunging, diving, swimming the waterless seas, free plunge through the airless air, to the depths, to the no way up.

He called in song (*well he needed to cajole her just this once, save effort in the end*):

I know you preferred it there
to stay with the star-names above.
I know you had rather remain safe
to guard there your heavenly love.

Facile, as men are (*anything for a rhyme*). For she was *not* in heaven, she was in the dust by the gate. Waiting for him.

But you watched o'er my needs from there always
and extended your love to below
to my want of a mortal retainer
my need of an earthly love.

No answer.
He sang again:

I called and you came
did you not?
(Not not, oh not, oh not).
So may God bless you now the waiting
and bless me too, then, the called.

Some hope! No answer. But perhaps – was the silence a little a little *un*-silent? Golden?

Would any, *any* woman keep …? But she was special.

35

And search again

Far had he to go in the not-seeing of her then. For she sat in the dust by the gate, guarded by a little beetle that crawled in the dirt (*yes, we heard that before, but did not e'en Homer repeat himself, and we the better for it too, swift-footed … oh all right-y then*).

So he must tread that tunnel
of death and life and birth
of sin and pain and sorrow
and passion's deepest deep.

And how hard the way, more steep
and steeper – tread it back
to pastures old and newer
through womb and birthway slumb'ring
through sleet and mudway stumbling,
through winter long and wake-spring
t' bestir his love from sleep.

Prince to princess's hundred years – not that he'd dare kiss her, she'd give him her 'mum's look', best defense against street crime his tai chi teacher'd told him once – all right for women (*it always was!*), but he was maundering on. Oh any thing to take his mind off where he was, what he would do.

So the Seeker sang again, in hope, despair:

Matthew Michael Mercury
unseen morning star
messenger of gods
news f'r the rich an' poor
and gospel of th' oppressed
in desolati-on.

Fly me w' your quill
swift-silvered wings
through clouds of
dangerness and etherdom,
to bring some will
of earthly ways and
tears to bring me consolati-on.

Soar me with trumpet sound
and melody aloud
uplifting there and beautiful,
on tilting plungen way
through earth and years,
orbit-ing sun of love and truth
write me to fly
on black-writ print
and wing of revelati-on.
Oh come to me, and hasten now
to bring me rest and then
salvati-on.

She did not want him, denied him again again, denied his hurt, even his song. Could he not own even his own pain, that too denied? Oh *agony*!

She would not be found, she did not need him.

For she was sitting in the dirt.

Waiting.

Waiting without hope and watching the seasons come and go and the yellow leaves and thc no-leaves and the orange-red berries on the hillside rowans, and thorns on the bent of the crooked hawthorn tree, and the new larch and the distant dog bark.

Still waiting.

Hearing heaven's singing, hearing the faintest fainting songs of heaven, not hearing hope.

Waiting.

36

The unrelenting void

He was so lonely.

He wanted his mother.

Quite badly (*and him a grown man an' all then!*).

He missed her so so much. What was she doing now? Was her grey hair back in a chignon, the hair he loved? No not grey, her black was writ with silver, her own weaving there that God loved too, how often he had seen him with her, fingering her tresses there with joy. And with peace in his heart.

But for him no heart could rest until it rest in her, in his, oh *his*, unbearable, his Kate. His-not-his, once-his, no-more-his, his Kate. (*Oh those tangled, tender, memories. Damn her!*).

His mother, he knew it, was spinning him another many-colored one (*or for someone else, had she forgotten him now he was out of sight?*). But he knew she knew he needed it. In the cold ice of the beyond-the-sun desert (*but he would never come to claim it*). Abandoned – abandoning. Out-cast. And banish-ed.

He tried to sing but his voice cracked and failed. From grief they say.

Ave Maria, gratia ple …

It was so beautiful he could not bear it even with a failing voice. Too painful for the outcast, thrown outcast from her love. And if all the world was singing it, why should he?

Even if he *could* (*and it needed four-part harmony, not him alone*), they could magick that in heaven, but not here. Not on the drear lone edges of the universe where he must last out-last his nothingness.

Anyway his mother dearest mother (*why hadn't he noticed that before?*) would never make out *his* tenor voice in all the muddly middley medley confuse-ion of media hype, that toneless tuneful tunefulness.

All those angels thinking *they* were the ones to praise and get attention there. First among the host. When *he* was her son, the firstborn he (*till the next came along, that sour James one ousting him outside*). And why, just because *he* wasn't very good at loving – why should he bother himself, upset himself for that? And anyway how can stone heart within a rock show tenderness? To anyone?

But *she* had to love him, of course. Some called that selfishness, he knew better. It was Self-Worth.

Oh oh, you self-worth you, cry for your here cast-outedness! Only the bard had words for it:

> *"Oh never say that I was false of heart*
> *Though absence seem'd my flame to qualify*
> *As easy might I from myself depart*
> *As from my soul which in thy breast doth lie."*

Or something like that.

No, even a mother could not measure. It was Kate Kate Kate, his all and all, his pearl his rose, the one to whom he would for ever call, his twine, his string to earth, his kite to heaven.

His voice rose up, a rose again, could he never escape that fragranced soul? And thorn? It mingled with Kate's silent shriek in the circlinged frontiers of the universe, the soundless sounding sonicked ring-unring, re-echoing echoes, nothingness of nothinged voidedness. The empty emptiness of space. Of God-no-God.

Empty.

Oh his longing for *her*. And for his mother too. *She* would have comforted him. *She* would *never* have abandoned him, on a Donegal shore, or anywhere.

In the pain of his heart he sang – and perhaps she heard because she knew it was a song of longing, just for her, first time expressed aloud of loneliness like no man ever felt before in the great story of that universe (*why had he left his mother's cooking, warmth of heaven?*).

It must have been some dire necessity but he could not recall it now. He must. But – fleeting away with sun's faint rays, only a spark now, dying, across the rim, the rime the grime of the cosmos, the dust, the dirt where beauty was no more.

The outcast, the despised of all. Wasn't he once good at singing, leader in God's chorus, star of the Hevnly Rocksters (*why d'you think they had that name, Rockster rockstars geddit?*).

He tried to laugh a little at that, smiley at least to cheer himself. Thought of Gabby on the 'ccordion, huh! Call that mus'c? But didn't get too far. Missing his mum too much. *She* wouldna've evva (*couldn't help revert to babytalk*) left him all alone there, would she? No, she'd of carried him home and diddums 'im 'n' comforter'd him.

Who's there by the lake now?
But – men do not cry
Oh small boy, so woeful
don't cry, do not cry.

Real men do not cry
ev'n when they're alone

tough four-boys don't weep
e'en – dear one – my love.

Try, look in the lake
maybe there you'll find care?
Her reflection, her loving
but no she's not there
not there in the wild clouds.
Oh come back to me
Oh dear one oh mater
not there in the sea.

She did not abandon
you, sisters to care
to mother to smother
are they not still there
to love you dear heart's blood?
Oh look at your coat
so warm and so neat
so lovingly made
a coat many colored
for you one, her dear one
her heart's love her own.

Could she not have stayed here
to love and to care
for bruised knees and stubbed feet,
just those few more years then
so tender and sweet?
Oh dear one my loved one
my dearest my sweet.

But she did not abandon you.
'Never my pearl
my apple, my orchard,

fronds still to unfurl.'

Oh all those soft woundings
oh there to find
sweet love and sweet laughter
in joys or in fears
in triumphs, disaster
for passions, for tears.

She would never abandon
but watched from above
to send for your comfort
to send to be thine
myself to be watching
and yours to be mine.

Not bad for a beginner! Was he a bit too pleased with himself by now? (*d'ya think?*). But he thought that might win her. Thinking of *her*, his dear mother, not just himself.

He bethought the time when he was left behind ('*Wait for me*' – *he was only little, only so high, so wee*), and she'd stopped and stooped and waited, and he'd run and looked up at her and walked proud, big steps now, holding her skirt (*better than some he could mention!*). He could never be lost, so.

But even so his mum, even his Irish mammy (*babytalk 'gain, see?*), did not call back.

Oh *women*, they were all as bad as each!

But his mother *did* smile. Secretly. Perhaps – could she be thinking of Kate? A comfort, true heart-ease, blown spray in the wind.

Oh, now he had it, *that* was why he was here. Here alone. Lonely, Outcast. Beyond. What a relief to remember! (*That's what mothers were for, wasn't it? Silly!*).

But – that memory! How *dare* she? Put him through *this* would

she? Just wait till he got his hands on her – oh, on a Donegal strand
sound of the sea-opened shell … Just wait! Hair all untied, untidied.
And flying, still flying, flying, flying …

It came back, a little:

Through mountain dawn and gentle breeze
by star-stream-lit and loving heart
o'er highland pass and tossing seas
to seek again by craft or art
a love long held and wedden'd fine
in dust and spume and foam of grieve-ing
counting sands forlorn.

Left here to love and weep
amid tsunami billows tossed
a-fear'd where love's
once gleaming joy was hid.

Alas it's left me, lone and lost
with heart and self adriften'd, gone.

'Counting!' There he had her, had he not? Numbers, she could
not stand numbers. But *he* could. And might not geometry magick
her in, eternal art of God to raise her back. Not 'rithmetic of vulgar
ones. No not vulgar, no wonder she couldn't count … (*did it matter,*
here? For did not God eschew the quantitative, on quality look with
tender eye?).

Pulled between his anger and his doggedness, and maybe love
too (*if a third integer was allowed*), must ask Kate, when – *oh when*
– if … let him essay again.

And so, her very words, words of despair, her own and his,
entrancing words, the spell of sorcering, Great Word to bring her
there:

Parallels don't meet, they said

at school when I was young
before the maths'd begun
to fade in my heaven's brain.

They go away
for ever aye
and never meet
like parallel feet
sustaining, ever waxing
waning, treading
freewheeling wheedling
'way fro' you.

For parallels don't meet they said
And nonsense mine to hope they led
to us, to him, to me
to stay together
not in far apart
and trig no help
I's trying still
no algebraic formulae to meet
those parallel lines
eternally by God 's will 'part
by mathematick seers foretold
of old and now and evermore
no junction nor no function there
no cosine Einstein bringing close
to meet as one
what destined to remain apart.

Silence.

Again he tried, such spells infallible for that magici-an, him-self-on-search. And again again, crying to empty void:

Belov'd of mine

my mirror-sweet reflecting back
in what wonderland
can parell image meet
to join as one
in heaven or hell?

Look there
wine parallel.
how can we drink
from parallel racks?

Those side by side
still parallel'd tracks
of wine and love
and still above
in verticke too
must keep apart
for that's the art
of numbers.

That's the rule
God laid for us
as parallel
He, apart
can find no path
to join us two
or touch us ever.

For parallel lines they do not meet.
We know it well.

Silence.
Only – silence.
Silence and – nothingness.
Wrong tune? Right love, predestined, did she not know? (*But*

she was no good with numbers, was that the cause?).

Tangl'd up, confuse-ioned (*like hair*). Wrong spell?

So try again.

Tell her. Tell her not numbers now but lost-last – he last and lost and loser – to have passed her! *He forgot!* That parallels *do* meet, wend round and round, with laps and lapselapped lippend there.

And kisses too. That journeys end – oh surely end – in lovers' meet ('*lovers*' – *there, he had admitted it again*). Lust, lost, last, least in lists, the last – and oh *at last!*

> *I was last in the race*
> *came late, lost way, wrong kit*
> *they let me start – but*
> *I was last*
> *slow tortoise last.*

> *I was last in the race*
> *lapped and lapped again*
> *so I felt first.*
> *Why was I not born fast*
> *like all those others, fit*
> *and lean and hung-ary?*

> *I was last in the race*
> *heart bursting, mad-fast mind*
> *all lungs intent*
> *I strained and strained*
> *but still they went past.*

> *Oh love, of loving kind*
> *keep me in mind.*
> *I see your loving smile*
> *smiling to me*
> *your voice at the last*
> *to those who're passed*

in life's great race
your final grace.

For now he too was seeking.

But she did not know it. She was still sitting in the dust.

Even the beetle was asleep. She'd been kind, he had fallen into one of those big ruts in the dusty dirt and would've lain there for ever with little legs waving in the air. But Kate righted him, with gentleness (*she was gentle*), set him softly on a rag in the corner. No wonder he was asleep after that big adventure (*and perhaps he had other things on his mind too, somewhere else?*). But he would wake – no need of patience for *him,* he'd be up and about in no time (*never you fear, to help our action along. Just you wait*).

But for Kate, so patient, so waiting?

Oh that the blackthorn could blossom with sunbursten flower, with joy from the thorn, salvation from the bitter cherry wood. Alas for parallel lines, God had forbid their juncture. She was disappeared, lost in the no-space, the dew, the morning haze, the thorn-trees.

For seven years, or was it centuries, eternities, he sought for her. By rivers, trees, the great oaks by the stream that whispered lovers' meetings (*you only need to tread the glade to know that resonance*).

And as the sun shines rainbow hues on the world each morn, the half-moon glances through the clouds, and the faint light of the North Star guides the mariner home.

So stee-red he across the universe in search.

As a scientist sets up his specimen with precious art to dissect with care, or the astronomer points his telescope to the heavens to search the stars, or the vet tends the fetlocks and the feet, great engines those of equine locomotion …

… so searched he the universe, region by region, sector by sector, strand by strand.

And could not find her.

As a cellist and a harpist tune their strings, hear the celestial song to set their notes aright, as the musician gathers the scales to line them for the song, as the conductor moves when he hears the music in his heart ...

... so listened he to the worldes arts.

And could not hear her.

As a doctor fingers the joint to feel the hurt within, as a leech clings fast to suck the bile, as an artist fingers face to call its blind resemblance down to earth ...

... so touch-ed he the universe, its sides and parts and purposes, the hurts and sores that 'scaped God 's eyes.

And could not feel her.

No place could he touch her, Kate, his own, whose touch was heaven.

He tried the last throw of the long-hewn arts and senses of his humankind.

As a perfumier searches the choicest blooms, the roses, lilies, freesias, prim-roses, to combine their scents, as bees leave hives to gather flowers, deer scents his mate from far on th' mountains –

So sought he her sweet fragrance on the air.

And could not scent her.

For she was afar. At the gate.

He could not see her touch, her fingers, hear of her lovely face. She was disappeared from all the senses of God's world.

She was sitting in the dust by the gate and he had not seen her.

For he had passed the other side, another way.

He went to those known places of their love (*how hard that was, he had not known ...*), the school, the strand, the great lovely halls, the seats to learn. There had they loved. He'd thought. Not kissed. But closer yet. Their hearts, their minds. Oh surely one.

Water earth air and fire, Search-ed with no trace.

And now he could not conjure her to his mind's memory, the innermost caverns secret hiding places of his mind, the hidden places of the deep. Absence, absent most pitiful, the lost …

Let him essay again:

> *Why do I so often wake*
> *with tears under my eyes?*
> *Why when the day breaks*
> *is it with tears?*
> *Why ask?*
>
> *It is your love,*
> *that separates*
> *envelopes me*
> *for all the years*
> *of my life?*

And God spoke to him the words of Job, spoke of those great cycles of the struggles of God and man, travails on earth of sin and death. And so like Job he saw he must be strong, cedar of Lebanon, ox in the yoke, great lions of the desert way. Strengthen his sinews.

And prevail. Even 'gainst God.

Against all defeats, all sins, all travails, all obstacles that lay before him, even to the edges of the universe or where Neptune sheds his sickly light into the desert – he must find her. His destiny. God must agree, be *forced*, if that must be, to consent. Was it not His purpose to agree? Who could gainsay him? Who could withstand the fire of his presence?

He cried aloud with a great voice, echoing the boundaries of the created world, not joy but challenge. As the lion cries to his mate, as whales' songs resound their thousand sonared miles through oceans' space, as a man whispers low to his beloved in tones that echo clear from skies that only she can hear – so cried he of his love, seeking her.

Her steps were writ in the water.

She was not there.

He sought her by the sea, her footsteps in the sand.

She had been, she had trodden ...
The sea had covered them.
She was not there.

He numbered her in the schools, her words sounded among them.

But not it was she, his love.
The hound followed after.
But never the prey.

He sought her in the university's halls. Her thoughts were there.

But she was not.

He sought her in his mind.

She was there, she was there, she was there.

But she, his only she, his tangible seen love, was gone, steps vanished in the dew.

"Alas my love you do me wrong
to use me so despitefully ..."

And he had loved her so long ... (*men do not cry. Do they?*).

Memories, oh memories – of love, of longing, denial: how could such emotion be said, even by him, emotionless, unverbal, secret in the words of song, of poem – had she not seen it and herself taught him of that?

In the heart of the hills
still flooded by rain

my love once came to me
and came once again.

Then left me alone
to sorrow and woe
to languish for ever
in agonied pain.

For life does not play fair
or look to my d'serts
but twists, twirls and torments
cares nought for the hurts.

Of my heart and my anguish
my longing, my dole
as she goes with another,
a-stealing my soul.

He yearned, he brought to his mind that high scaffold, that jealousy, that ring of old – but she, did she? No. No look back at him. *Not one.*

His heart was sorer even than his feet and his ragged hat scarce held by the thorn caught on 't as he passed (*why had he not begged Gab to lend his trump his left-right left-right feet-beat march?*). Or could he recall the song his mother'd taught, of 'marching to the isles' to make his feet go – somewhere.

Could she forgive him? His anger, hurt were fading now. And, humble now, well briefly, was it for *her*? Could he ask her? Ev'n in song, that magic art, that bond of God to man, that art wherein salvation ever lies?

Forgiving – easy. Hard to be forgiven, he had not seen?

Forgive me, oh forgive me you
I know you do
but still it sits there, looking at me

entangled with the sunne's spots
the milken star-shine cycle of the universe
looking at me still.

Looking with your dark eyes
so beautiful of hurt
it will never go
like gravitie.

Forgive me, oh forgive me you
how could I then have hurt you so?

I didn't mean it, oh, I say
I didn't realize.
I didn't know.

Is that excuse
to hurt you so
upon the cross upon the ground
of love so sore,
when you yourself
were just the very one for me to guard
adore and sing and love?
I hurt you so.

For still it sits
and looks at me
oh, with your eyes
'twill never go.

How can I be forgiv'n?
How can I be
when I have hurt so sore
the very one I love
I wor-ship and adore?

Forgive me, oh forgive me you
forgive
forgive
forgive
forgive.

Even his song did not bring her, weep he so bitter.

Might it be in that some-where-place where no one knew? She was standing there? Watching for him? If he could not see her …

He tracked the paths of the planets, the moons of Jupiter, and Saturn's rings. The desert place where Pluto creeps his solitary way. To the deep roots of the great sea, of volcanoes, typhoons, tsunamis, image true of men's emoti-on. To the unfathomed reaches where the sun can never shine and the deep denizens of ocean creep through the sunless seas. Where space and time dissolve to nothingness, breath is no more.

A-hah, again the water. Sea the sea! His home. And in far distance there green hill, blue haze. And there beyond, y-e-es, a Donegal strand, a shell, with water over, ah, the footsteps (*oh memories, his not hers, to torment him again again*).

He would find her, bring her home. Even if he had to kiss her first.

But she was sitting in the dirt at the gate and he had not passed that way. He had gone by another way, a wicket gate. He had not seen her sitting there.

37

The beasts

So then return-ed he in hope and fear to that same strand, that very act and acme of his life. Older wiser, might Kate no longer fear his arms? But no less beautiful and wise, no less hair in the winding wending sending scenting wind.

Footsteps and steps upon steps in sands, trace of her sweet passing, deeper, sorer, greater wells of life, tests to be test again, the tastes of torn and taring tearing tear-ed salt.

Not now an untried youth but manhood's life to offer, at her feet, her hands, her ring-ed hands, would tear it off, mayhap it had not stayed, ev'n gold could turn to brass. He would give her that everlasting shell, created by not the hand of man but sea's eternal wash, the eyes of God, the secret pearl within, life tangled in her lovely hair, hair that he loved.

Think still that garden, college-near. That other's ring. His anger flamed again. Higher and still brighter still, ablaze. Let *this* be that of which men writ!

How had she dared? His maturity grown deep for her, for

her 'twas planned, for *her* his love, 'twas sown by God. His life, achieve-e-ments, his promise for all time, redempti-on for past, their new-told ink-ed pearl-ed tale.

Without her nothing but rejection. Again. More bitter than the first, most bitter in the salt-tears-torn-tears vale of earth, rejected there.

He *would* not follow. Care …

Yet still he cry-ed out unto her. Through the risen moon, through setting stars, the Milky Way, the furthermost bounds of broken universe, so she must hear. Not name not number, those his secret still. But love, his love, his love, at last his spoken love.

'Hear me … your lover, I am here.'

So then, despair, cried he unto the beasts of earth, birds of the air and cliffs, and woodland creatures wild and hill, e'en dragons and great snakes and those beneath the earth. And insect hordes in all their might.

None answered him.

> *Ye mighty forces beyond men's ken*
> *ye power of live that moves e'n brass and stone*
> *ye memoried statues, hieroglyphs divine*
> *from mightiest eagle and from smallest wren*
> *and gods and goddesses of ev'ry cline*
> *Oh come you now.*

None answered, no stir in the silent air, no small still cloud on far horizi-on.

> *And oh ye denizens of the mighty deep*
> *ye sojourners in galaxies' great darks*
> *where 'n oceans' tides the birds and whale-es sleep*
> *at back o' the winds' most peaceful homes*
> *behind the stars, beyond the comets sweep*
> *I call you now.*

'Valkyries, horsemen of the western skies, winds of behind-the-winds!' he cried too to them. And yet again.

'Beasts beasts of the earth, birds of the air and woodland, animals of wild and hill, even those beneath the earth. Angels in heaven (*are they not beasts as well?*). And insect hordes in your milli-ons.'

He cried to them.

He finished.

Still – nothing.

For she was sitting at the gate and heard nothing, only a slight stir in the silent air, in her heart, in the dust where a beetle scrabbled at her feet.

He cried out again with a loud voice, resounded to the heavens, echoed in the earth, washed forth and back in the ocean's tides, in the delicate sea shells, the seas' murmuring.

He cried out with a loud and louder voice ...

An angel that was flying past (*perhaps God had sent him so he wouldn't have to appear in the matter personally?*) whispered quiet, not to be heard too well so he could always deny it.

'Perhaps we should answer him?'

Then he flew off to God so as not to be involved (*ah we know that syndrome do we not! God did for sure. But we needn't tell you that, need we!*).

So the beasts called a mighty concourse. All were there: the worms, the moles, spiders, beetles, goats and sheep, lions and lambs, and all the birds of the sky. Not the angel, he was keeping out of it.

Many were the speeches, the harangues and rangs and args and orates, but none to decide. Then the Great Snake coiled imperiously around 'My friends' (*enemies he meant of course, you know snakes*).

'The argumentationments have all been heard.' He was quite pompous and liked long words – his Oxford philosophical training (*he decided to keep off the angels on the pin, too sharp-y for snake-collations*).

'Pros and cons (*make simple for the plebs*). Guilty or not.

Imprisoned for ever without. Or released in bondage. Heard or ignored. And the price.'

So they agreed there with the snake. For him to receive an answer he was to pay the price. The Seeker. It was right. To be snared and snaked and sneaked for ever to the Ki-snake, King of Kings, to catch the slough of his skin and smoothe his pathway and pay as well a small king's ransom (*they knew he had nothing, but so was the judgement*).

And to wander forever round the rims of the universe, no hope in his breast.

'This is the Word of the Chief Judge, The Imperator, The King.'

So thus it was decided.

They commanded that a parakeet be sent, swiftest brightest and talkingest of birds, to announce their judgement, judgement from the full court of law, as good as any God might devise in the sky.

So the parakeet was hasted on his way.

But secretly he did not hasten. He did he not quite like it. Was he not closest to humans? Could he not speak like a man? Who was he to take such a message? So he delayed his flight and lingered on the way.

But one beetle – he to whom Kate had once sung the beetle song (*first made by God it was, but sung it she had*) – his heart like hers was tender. And had she not helped him to stand and laid him gently on a rag for his slumbers (*how could he have been two places? Ask me not, it was magic times then. And he loved Kate – does not love transcend all?*).

The beetle's nickname was Micky but he didn't like that at all at all at all he did not so at all. So we will respect his feelings (*beetles have feelings too you know, very much so*). And since he has an important part in this story we will just call him the beetle. So the beetle made haste to reach the Seeker where he stood at the rim of the great cosmos.

But the beetle's little scintillated wings, shine they ever so bright beat they never so hard flutter they ever so fast, cannot match the speed of parakeets, even a laggard one (*but he did not know that the parakeet was delaying*). Despair seized his tiny brave wee heart.

But high on the tree a jackdaw (*or was it a raven?*), saw his dilemma. Now ravens are always at outs with snakes, for the snakes seized them when they could, black bites and all, and carried them off for their nestlings to play.

So when the raven saw what had happened, he said to the beetle in his hoarse coarse raven's voice, 'I can help you' – speaking not out of love as God would do, but hatred and jealousy. From which we can learn that sometimes (*sometimes children dear*) bad deeds have good results. And it was bad too that God and ravens do not tangle, for imperious ravens are the *only* thing God cannot tame except cats – God was a cat person (*like you perhaps, so you'll know what I'm talking about*). Ravens go their own way.

So the raven took the beetle in his beak, gently gently gently, and together they flew.

They flapped their wings in time (*teamwork is all the nuns had said, MBA folk too, and they were right, just look*). They made haste and came first to the edge of the universe where the Seeker was making his way. And looking. And not hoping (*for she, his dear she whom he sought, was still sitting by the gate, in the dust*).

So the beetle got there first. Quiet quiet quiet he flew down and alighted on his shoulder, the Seeker's, the Seeker after Kate. She, the one waiting outside the gate. In the dust.

Then the beetle spoke up bravely – for the raven had gone back to his nest in the oak tree – and told what he had heard.

He whispered close in the Seeker's ear.

'She is there. Waiting. In the dust. By the gate.'

His heart leapt up, leapt to the skies, the sun, the moon, the …

But – the gate?

There were a thousand gates, he knew it. And one more again. For the walls stretch the length of the earth, the breadth of the skies.

The height of the galaxies, no one can count or navigate the whole.

And while he tried – and try he would he would he would till he died himself – she would surely perish. Waiting.

But the little beetle crept nearer (*you know his six quiet legs, his iridescent wings*).

'Arise and go now, and gird up your loins forthwith (*mmm, verily*) and see wherein she lies low by the gate under the morning star. And by this sign will, er, *shall,* ye know her …'

The beetle had been to a biblically-inclined school, but even so he'd got his genres or his grammar or something a bit confused in his excitement – he was a bit frightened of the hissy Ssssnake too, he knew that snakes *love* beetles.

'You shall know her under the star, when you hear the whimper of a little dog, thus shall ye know … mmm, that's it I think.'

And the beetle, cleverer in his actions than his verbal style, granted the Seeker beetle-feelers and insect-sight and fast-flying wings to reach the spot where she was lying.

Then the beetle crept off – he knew he would be in deep deep trouble for what he had done. He didn't care. Had he not played his part in one of the great love stories of the world? And perhaps now, perhaps, they would reach heaven and comfort the poor little dog.

He prayed it so.

His heart's desire. He could not utter the words of his heart, but God would know, he always did.

38

Nearing ...

The Seeker now was drawing near.

To where she was sitting in the dirt. Waiting. In the between-the-nowhere place.

Waiting.

And he was searching. Still, he was beetle-winging round the walls and through the places whereto still no mortal man had ventured yet or voyagered. Into the eternal collapse of time and space. Into negation.

So journeyed he. With hope, this time, with hope to find. By the gate. For she was sitting there in the dirt. Yearning. Hearing sweet sounds of Mozart clarinet, scenting the air, echoing, thronging, song-ing, planging, sweetening.

But not for her a sweetening, honey. She was dry. Sour.

Waiting.

Just waiting.

39

The impasse no pass

But the Seeker, the Seeker after Kate, he with much to forgive
and be forgiven, he with no name – no name he would give to others
(*God knew it, and his mother*) – he gave one look to his once-heaven
from there, from without the wall. She was there without the gate,
waiting for him.

Her eyes were clouded with tears, could no longer see, not
even the little beetle at her feet (*and perhaps he had gone about his
other tasks. Beetles are everywhere are they not, always busy with
God's business, here, and there?*).

But still she waited, hopeless, hopeful, as something stirred in
the tanglements of her heart. She could longer see for her swollen
eyes. Or smell for her stream-ed nose or feel with her cramping
cramp-ed fingers. So she did not see him coming.

But *his* heart leaped, *leaped* to the skies, no beyond, for he was
surely there already.

She was sitting in the dust.

Waiting, waiting for him.

He had come he had come – *he had come!!*

And all the heavenly choirs set up their paean of rejoicing, he had come.

He had come!!

He had come. The angels were singing in joy. Even God smiled and his mother beamed and finished off the coat – it would have to do. It was only a token of her love really (*you know mothers*) 'cos she knew he wouldn't actually be wearing it – no cold winds in heaven. Then she ran off – sorry, walked in her stately way, indigo mantle and all (*she knew well that blue always suited her and took care to abide by that rule – for the sake of the onlookers, in heaven too you have to keep up appearances you know!*) to restart the slow cooker.

She didn't know exactly when they'd arrive, and she wanted things ready (*after they'd bathed of course, bound to be filthy, first things first*). She just hoped Kate wasn't a vegetarian or vegan or faddy eater. But whatever. She'd welcome her anyway, *any* old way. For love of her son.

He had come!

And his heart? It rose in joy but it rose even more in pride.

For she had not scented the odor of his approach and raised her head to drink its fragrance (*even a dog would do that much*).

Her eyes had not shone to welcome him. Had he not near-died in the search? Her eyes were dimmed with tears.

She had not run, she had not *leaped* into his arms. As she'd done once, surely? He remembered it. By the sea by the station by the strand. Across the impassible chasm of the cliff to his arms (*was it then, was it now, or was it still to come?*).

She had not *leaped*.

And the door, the great gate to heaven was shut. Golden, gleaming, glorious in the sun, but shut. Closed.

It was the end.

And not a happy one.

His pride.

Her desolationing.

PART VIII

ANOTHER JOURNEY

40

A way?

No man had ever found a path into heaven if the gate was closed. Not lifting their heads (*whatever that was*).

No trumpets on the other side.

Not purgatory, not hell, not death. Just – nothing.

The in-between no-place. For themselves alone, not even for them, the unexisting wraiths.

In the void. The between no-where.

Not even togetherness. For all that eternal entwinement. His hurt still held him. And his pride. Not so deep now, he had suffered much (*dear friends, is suffering not always learning too?*). But – still. A little.

Holding him from her as she sat in the dirt.

Not seeing, hearing, but somehow, sensing, sensing … sensing …

She had not seen him, had not heard him, touched him, scented him, but …

… but now she *knew*.

Her heart leaped, leaped, leaped, LEAPED!!

To the edge of the universe and back, bouncing after her scream round its margins, falling to earth as does the burning star, scenting the plants of the garden, feeling the rain, the sea, the lightning (*oh – no words*) ...

She *knew* he was there, that his pride – it was not the end.

And perhaps perhaps God knew too? In theory (*he was good on Principle was the old man. And we need those do we not? But those of action too*).

The beetle was still a little bit suspicious. Cautious. About the Seeker. But he loved Kate. He loved Kate for her love. For her love of the Seeker. For her love and help for Beetles.

So he came and he whispered, quiet and shy as beetles are, 'Quiet quiet quiet.' (*You know beetles*).

'There is a way, a secret way, not even God or angels know it. Impossible-impassible. For mortal men.' (*For women then, thought Kate? Perhaps she was right*). Crag upon crag heaped there, mountain upon mountain, peak beyond peak. Even the greatest heroes, they of magic myth of old, could not pass there, even black inked eternal love shoe-bright may enter not. It is hidden in the back of heaven, behindways, made we know not how or with men's certainty by whom.'

'Then why tell us?' the Seeker asked, impatient. (*You know men, even hero-men – not much of a hero, him, though he did try. For sshh, Kate, for Kate*).

The little beetle hesitated then. For dare he tell that tale he only knew? And his mother who had told him? For such are women. Whether she had been told by her mother, and her mother before her we know not. At any rate, he spoke up, quietly. Hesitating. A little stumbling in his speech.

'I have heard,' he began – then stopped. Then looked at Kate's eyes, clearing now, grey as the sky around, the dust that lay before. 'I have heard tell,' he went on more strongly, 'that one mortal, man, one only, found his way. He was a Greek, a scientist, an engineer. I think he must have been a lover too to make that perilous way, impossible route, impassable pass. And here is the secret.'

The Seeker pricked his ears up. Kate looked only at her love. Unending. Could she ever see enough? Oh and he was still so beautiful. But grey with dust, with age, with seeking her. The dear one ...

'For he once pronounced to the world, if it would but listen (*it was in Greek so they took no notice*), "Give me place to stand and I will rock the globe.".. .' (*The beetle'd have preferred the ancient Greek but was feared to try Modern Pronunciation. Those 'Accents' too*).

'And he did it too. He took his stand, with magic lever of the spirit, standing on the farthest reach of the great universe, before there was created place to stand. Where he found to place his fulcrum we know not.' (*that had always worried the little beetle, despite his quietness he thought you know*).

'It was not yet there. But balance it he did. And the force of that lever, its push, its pull, pivoting exploded rock pieces from their place, upheaved the mountains, blasted a way through that perilous passage. And he went through. And entered heaven from behind.'

'I do not know,' he went on, tremulously, 'if still the path be there. Perhaps it is overgrown, the rocks subside with stones to clatter it on every side. But perchance ye may wish to essay.'

He was getting biblical again in his emoti-on – it really *was* a Great Love Story, and so he would tell his mother when she told him he was late – again – for his tea. But Kate at least did not mind (*men, well she knew – even him – were always more impati-ent. Not for them slow instruction manuals, whatever language, biblical Japanese or what*).

'We will essay then,' he said. Impatiently. Importantly. For so he was.

And marched his self off.

He did not look at Kate. What were women to him, dream reality? 'specially women who had – once, no, would you believe it, *twice* – rejected him! *Him!* Spurned *Him!* What did that say for men's vanity, the only thing left (*women were so all-powerful now-days, blast 'em*). By now her attitude (*attitude indeed, women again!*) … it shouldn't be possible. Not his search for *her*. How could he have so de-manned, he meant demeaned (*of course*) himself?

Anyway, he would soon break his way though (*look at his strong right, er, leftes, hand, his sinewy arm, he'd be back up there in no time for a proper supper*).

And Kate – well, that was up to her, she shouldn't've been so silly and, well, feminine in the first place. That's not how to get to heaven! And anyway heaven's for men isn't it? A proper gentlemen's club, no frippery gossip or distraction. (*Oh except his mother of course, had to have someone to do the cooking and the mending and the clearing up. Oh and would his new waistcoat be made? And had she chosen his favorite, colors not – how like a woman! – just her own? Blue he bet ya, ugh*).

So on he trod. One man, one man only in the history of all time had found his way through? *He* would do better! He'd heave the rocks with just his shoulder's strength, no magic 'science' for him or vinegar, his own great strength, endurance male, would do it. And his father would at last admire him. And his mother … well, all right, she had always believed in him, now she would be proven right.

And all the heavenly hosts would turn to praise him.

And Kate? Well he wasn't going to be accused again of abandoning her. As if he ever … he'd look back over his shoulder every now and then to see how she was following (*of course she'd follow, way of women kind*), even not go too fast. His big concession. See?

She stood back for him to go for she knew what was in his heart. And she did not care. For she loved him. and she knew, even if he would never admit it, that he would have died for her. Even if he would not reveal his name. Or his face. Or number. That he would die for her. Had come for her when all hope gone. Had found her waiting. Rescued her from the dust. And now he was leading her to heaven, to the eternal sleepiness of love. For he … he … he … yes he really did, he really cared for her. And he loved her. So she thought.

So she followed not too close (*a woman should go behind a man*), she didn't mind her feet went slow. And as she went she hummed a marching lulling song to keep her legs on going. For yes, she admitted it, they were quite tired from all that waiting, cramping in the dirt. Left right, left right, left – no oh no, she was *not* left. And all was – right!

> *So stand now stand aside*
> *and I have tried*
> *I really have*
> *to stand aside*
> *in quietness*
> *in Quaker peace*
> *come storm or tide*
> *to his sore heart*
> *and painfulness.*
>
> *Oh rest belov'd*
> *and sleep in peace*
> *what care for weep*
> *or scream*
> *from me*
> *or grossly grasp*
> *if you can rest*
> *and sweetly sleep*
> *at last.*

He marched on, no look back (*well, hardly*). Kate followed, as best she could.

41

Around

So look now look, approaching heaven now. A roundabout route that, their own. Drawing so near and near at last? And there is Kate behind. He spread his sails, his trail, for her (*well perhaps he did – though still resentment, grudge, revenge-ement. A bit*).

Long was the way, too long for even your dear chronicler to tell. Will you not read of the perilous journeys taken in those Haggard tales of love and loss, the path of the great adventurers of past in Africk ways, retrod today?

Yet even those ways were not so long or danger-wrought as for these travellers. The Seeker first. Then Kate. And ever she lagged behind, her feet were torn on rocks. And bare. And lost him as he vanished behind the crag. The next. But ever as she rounded it, she found him there bestood – not waiting, not of course *waiting*. Just – a little rest, and check the beetle was there, their guide and help.

So – not in the dust. But Kate. Following after. Softly so not to harass him (*she loved him*).

But let that be. Approaching the haven now, the light of every wending barque. The way was even, she could not lose him now, sight for her guarding loving marching eyes.

And the way was even, broad, downways, not steep. Naught barred their way.

They were there.

Surely they were there.

And this time this time he could not forget, no waiting at the gate. For she could claim her boon at last, her promisest. God's promised destiny for her. At last.

They were *there*!

See the fine broad way opening out for them.

Broad, broad. Broad narrow. Narrow road. Oh! Narrow. Narrow! Narrower narrower narrower. Narrowest.

It narrowed. Ended. Only steep precipice before. It was the end.

It was the end.

It was the end.

42

The way no-way

He slipped on the steep rock, righted just in time. Another 'nother step. Another slide. In front of her. Another. Further. Kate just caught him from behind, stumbling on the path's steep incline, edge, edge, edging him on down and down and down …

This time saved. But what of the next? His *sandal*. Strap unfixed.

He bent to fasten. But oh, his mother had not sewn it well. Or leather was not good. Or he had walked too far round the far-est bounds of universe, too far for mortal man, The strap unstitch'd, slipped from its mooring, ship adrift in storm. No way to fix it now. No spares, no spars, no rope, no mooring. He was lost. No way through now (*oh for his pride his arrogance, his – oh his ire …*).

But always Kate was there. No thought for self now, quick tress from black hair – it was soon done. Her pride, cut short. The broken strap? Her hair was there, it stood secured.

But slipping still, one single lock, need more.

Go hurry, wrap hair (*loved who wants that now*) round shoe for shipshape (*it will not slip, no time for words*), not slip, not slopping sleeping steeping, hurry hurry now, hair no one wants now (*though once ... so did she too, she did before the nuns said cut if off, they knew back then, it grew more strongly after, just for today, but stop it, hurry now, no dreams today*).

But – but he was not yet through to heaven's song. Yet could she hear them sing, faint echo through the peaks? It was her dream wish only, cycled recycled through all centuries of this worldes way, it was God's plan.

It was not yet. She was sitting here. And it was dusty here too. In the dust.

The way before them slimmer still. And thinner. He slipped to one side in that thinningness, then to the other, by the unending unforgiving precipice below, recovered on the edge as she caught and held him. No slipping rope now, no fast vanished ship. And oh this time he *wanted* her to hold. His feet. Sandals were broke and worn and smooth with use. Even with that strap to hold it on his foot (*so beautiful ...*).

So she took the strands of her hair, the hair that he had loved, and cut them, rough, much, from her head and bound them that his sandal might hold firm.

But still he slipped on the round pebbles of that smooth and slipping path. Treacherous, like dreams. Now she must tear *all* hair from her head, all, what cared she, wrapped his feet firm that he might go safe on the narrowed path by the cliff.

So he trod on, before her, no look back, she behind. (*Did he know whither? Or did she?*).

Still not – not wide enough for him to pass.

But look again! Interpret well, oh prophets ye. For from a tiny crack in the rock, so tiny tiny hard to see, was crawling – a little beetle, little six-legged one, about his business, the task God had set him. Quiet. Quiet. Quietly.

And he was looking back more often now. Every few steps. And the sun glinting round the far peaks silhouetted his figure, his so beautiful figure, darkening his unseen face as he turned, full-shadowing him.

But it was not a crack, it was a crevasse, a great crevasse, a gulf. No bridge. No way for any feet to tread, for angel's wings to bear. Even for him to pass.

A curve. Bend of a finger on hand of human kind, sweet moon of a finger's nail (*of hers? Once given for love?*), delicate in the sky, a pulsing rainbow tress like beats of a loving heart. The bridge between heaven and earth that she had made from love, of the bend of her dear finger.

So he *leaped* just as in the days of their youth. By the Atlantic sea. And cross-ed safely to the other side. She saw him pass, the sounding of the waves and the sky.

He was past.

And he was gone.

43

Across?

This time no time for tears. No agony – though well remembered she the blast … that strand, the storm, the seagulls' shriek, her own.

Now sea was calm. Her heart as well. Was safe. She'd save'nd him. Was it not now by God's design? For it was He had granted her that greatest boon, her wish – that he might be safe. Through severance at last, per-severance. And hair. And safe'nd soul, forgiveness won. Oh at last at last, she'd lived her whole whole life for this.

The end of her search, of his, of all man's proud endeavors in that great world of centuries.

Would it end then in – nothingness.? For her? So be it then.

So let it be. Now let her meet her end in his dear company, not in the flesh but better far, like those young days of bliss, more intimate, more closer, than in flesh – in song.

She sang again the song the nuns had taught. No it was God. Her life-song's *salva me*:

I am on a path
lovely with basil and nettle
I cannot tell where it may go.
Remember me.

And then again she called on that most famous of all the haiku verse, just syllables enough, no more:

God 's love was so great
for his world and for creat'n
no words are enough.

Nothing.

Just dust again. No rain. Hard rock, an insect crawling there. A beetle. Hard. Shelled back. A pearly sheen. As beetles are. On the rock.

Now to bethink her of her love. Her earthe's love. Her love of heaven. For he was *there* now, she knew. He was with Holly, her dear dog, her Holly, her sweet holly tree – no she was confused again, was it the numbers, implant numbers so Holly would not get lost? (*But she was no good at numbers, why did they keep bothering her, surely it was time to let go, surely in heaven …?*).

And and – but Holly would never take to a new master, wouldn't know her wants, her mistress-throw-stick, likes, dislikes, that she must never catch the squirrel, didn't want, don't try to stop her, hurt-back, fondle love her pull her ears and gentle, let her lie content talk with her ask her 'bout, oh, every thing oh dearest Holly, bestest dear of all.

Oh – but for *him* …

As mutilate-and-un-mute Abelard to his lost Eloise, as Ad'm to Eve, Isolde to Tristanmate, Guinevere to Launcelot of old, as Eury-dice to her dear Orpheus, lutenist looking back too soon, ah looked too soon. But was she not aling-ering on purpose there so he might see that heart-rent instant soon? Did she not wish to stay below? Did he not join her longing there at the last, a happy not a tragic ending after all?

As Pelion to Ossa, continents before the drift, longing for their reunion (*look, just look at a map, does not the sep-ar-ation break your heart?*). As Patroclus to loved Achilles, Dido to Aeneas, twins slept in womb as one, one seed torn roughly 'way …

So yearn-ed Kate for her beloved gone before.

She called again, would he not let her melt into his goode-ness, submerge in his great sea, loosen her chains to be as one with him? Had God said 'No'? When other helpers fail and comforts flee, Help of the helpless, O abide with me. To let him go. And free.

> *Caught in heart's rings*
> *those iron chains*
> *will you not let*
> *the daisy turn*
> *once more to th' sun?*
>
> *O loose the reins*
> *the clasps that burn*
> *and hold too fast*
> *to let you go.*

So she stood alone, there on the rock. The precipice. The unending precipice of her existence. She saw him passed.

He had not looked back. From there. Again.

But – no gate. Not sitting in the dust. And a little beetle looking up at her. Six legs. But this time with big eyes there too.

She knew then what to do. She haiku'd him:

> *O beetl' flighting high above the earth the heaven*
> *why flight not for me?*

She was left. In silence.

And this time – was he looking back? Back with his beautiful eyes. Amidst the danger, atop the cliff, the precipice. Her hearten heart sang as she called to him in love, in confidence:

> *I am here.*
> *I hear you.*
> *I am here.*
> *I am not going anywhere*
> *withouten you.*
>
> *Your voice o'er the deep*
> *bell on the sounding sea*
> *that sea between, among,*
> *within us two.*
>
> *On the quiet sea*
> *and echoing air*
> *- my name is sound!*
> *I hear you.*
> *I am here.*

And the silence was no longer dead. It was a gentle silence, a quiet one. A quiet quietness.

So then replied he to her, in song (*replied!*), the Seeker, he, to his beloved. For 'twas a place of song. Song through the crags, resounding echoing in the mountain range, flown golden in th' radiance of the dying moon:

> *So trembelling and fearful*
> *my darling, oh my soul*
> *so fearful by the entrance*
> *that little small lost foal.*
>
> *Did you see not the field there?*
> *Look at the open-ed gate.*

Kate looked, she, the obedient. No gate. Chasm still wide, no magic there – what was he on about? (*Men so impractical ...*).

> *So 'trancing and so dancing*
> *the path right to your fate.*
>
> *A fate of grass and meadow*
> *of wallows and rollings and mucks*
> *in the river, and canters and prances*
> *and gallops and tossings and bucks.*
>
> *So come on my dearest get into't*
> *why shy-back and still hesit-ate*
> *and jimp at the noisiless windlets*
> *and shy at the opening gate?*
>
> *For look you too can now down-lie*
> *and I can lie with you there too*
> *for it 'twas God ope'd gates to the meadow*
> *it was me then who'll lead you full through.*

'Huh!' said the beetle looking a little askance (*he was only little, right, he'd just learned that big word from a friend*), 'wasn't it *me*, er, *I*, that op'ned ... just like those mortals, ugh! But let it go. If God'd decided, then His Will be Done. Oh then *let* the Seeker think it was *him*, OK OK, I'll get a guerdon (*good word*) some time (*he'd have a quiet word with God, you know how beetles are*).

And look! Here he is, the Beetle, in the tale after all. Not in the dirt by the gate. On the edge of the precipice, By the girl. The heroine (*yes, yes that's right!*). Across the way the Seeker, safe (*all very well for him, all the work left to the beetle, typical!*).

Kate waited. Yet again. Patience was her second name by now (*didn't you guess?*). Yes, trembling, it was true.

And this time, oh this this time this time this ... look look, he'd turned. And looked, and looked at her, looked with his sea-dark eyes, and locked his eyes with hers of grey, grey as her suffering, grey as the ancient Greeks or God's high wisdom for mankind.

She could not see him now, or touch, or hear. But felt a memory of mouths as one, of softest softest miracle.

How that could be? None but their two selves knew. Even God.

He stretched his strong left hand. She saw him now.

And as she stood silent there by the precipice – not in the dust but by the cliff, sky, air – he stretch-ed out to her his gentle right-hand hand. To *her*! Stretched out his hand, with cutoff finger too. (*Why had she never noticed that? He was her twin. She'd always known*).

No way to pass, the bridge dissolved in the air, as rainbows do, enchanted bond of man and God, that magicked there-not-there to look.

She *knew*. This time she haiku'd God himself in fragrant scented words of praise:

> *God's love was so great*
> *for his world and for creat'n*
> *no words are enough.*

Singing of love, calling 'cross chasm of life and death. No short-est haiku now but the long song, long cruel-sweet road to salvati-on, for her, for him, for Goddes will:

> *You were first*
> *no I was too*
> *I know I was*
> *sent you the message*
> *ethereal message*
> *through ether gone*
> *that I would wait*
> *that I was willing*
> *that you might take*
> *when you would*

when you were ready.

I know you heard
You flew to th' sky
you hovered, soared
among the birds of heaven
of milky way
of falling sparkling stars
with mirth with leaps triumphening
you knew you knew
at last my love was there
was there for you
for you alone.

And next came …

And next you came
again again
in forward springs
and leaps and flight
above the moon
above the night
in joy, delight
that I at last had said
had said-en
'Yes'

Then what of you? I know you held your self *to* self, your mind in its own, did not intend my soul to mend, with words of will … and yet …

Sudden I knew
the leaps and bounds
in my heart too
never to emulate

the heights that you
could mount.

I all-ways seconding
your lovely lead
high tenor sound
but stumbling still I found
you'd always wait
and I could leap, a little, too
off-en the ground.

Always behind full sure I knew
stumbling behind but never lost
for you my heart my lord, my saint
your sins to hold me safe so at the end
me, lord, your arms enfold me.
Safe at last.

But still for all her words – the precipice.

To her mind then floated clear that verse – for the cliff-like sacred isle in a blue sea was full of voices, of song, of music, clear in her mind, waiting till the time was ripe.

And quiet quiet she sang the finish of the beetle song, the one that is always there, the one that she had known from her mother's breast. Now. The right time:

Oh listen ye – for God has toldend me –
and yet I see that he was all-ways right
the last oh the lastest to come t'us
by morn and by star-legg-ed night
the prize oh the wonder and bestest
not legs after all!

Not six legs nor seven
of hard legs or slithers

or circuits and serpents
of slippries or slithers
but – wings up to heaven!

Her breath breathed with its breathing. Meditation, stillness. It was quiet now.

Quiet.

And *see*! The crevasse was narrowing. Was it the beetle song, what magic in that invocation taught by God? Who surely loved her. Could she at last cross to him? Still narrowing.

Narrow. But too broad, still too broad. Aah aah too wide even for his man's stride, for his. Or for a running leap. Far less for hers. (*Holly would have leapt it for her Kate, beloved*). Oh she would have *leapt*! She bethought her leaps across the bogs of old. When they were young. His twine-ed twinning twining arms, his whole, enfolding her. So – not afraid. But now … too wide, too wide.

It was not meant to be.

No footgrip, none, for hand, for toe, for holdingness on the slipping knot of rock on which he stood, held by firm hand, small jut of faceless rock. Chasm still there, between them still.

She saw him measure with his eye. Too wide even for his height, his sinews, reach to her, Kate saw it in his eye. His beautiful eye. Sea dark. His opening face (*why think of such things now?*).

She saw him stretch his arm t'wards her. *Her* he was thinking of! How she might come to him. Across.

Be-thought him of his stick. But it was gone, fall'n from the cliff, down endless precipice to the nothing there. Where soon they'd be …

Her hair – too matted now on bounden feet to unfold, disentangle it (*it used to be so beautiful …*).

His clothes – too ragg'd to hold her weight, even her light weight long wasted in her waiting weightless wait, her hungering, her walking there.

His cap – burned off him by the wind and the rain.

Oh for a horse to leap it there. No, useless. No rope knotted round his waist as do all prudent seamen, mountaineers. And he a sailor in great ships! And mountain walker too.

Nothing to use.

But still he had his knife. His precious knife, more precious than the world. Given him, a boy, to keep, whetted in woods and stones. And in his play, as boys still do. Curiously wrought it was by Affrick Ogun, Affrick Smith of Heaven. Great One praise-song praised of all.

Bepanegyricized.

Others had looked, and disapproved. 'A young boy. Only seven. To have that knife! And his left-handedness!' (*It had been ruled that that knife wielding was only by the handed-right. Too bad, he had learned, and craft-art so. What could else left-hands do?*).

Wondrous sharp it was still, cut through trunks the breadth of arms and more, of forests even, through sunbeams, rainbow bridges too. Even horse's iron shoe, too hard for blacksmith tool, even that gold ring once she wore, waiting below her for this moment of time.

'If you drop it then shall you lose your life,' his mother had said, 'but at the last, when all hope is gone, it will save you.' So she spoke, for she of all beings knew the soft gentleness in his heart.

So when his belt had given on the mountain side, blessed indeed was that it had held so long, fixened only by a single string of leather cord, the strap had somersaulted of its weight, the buckle first (*for even in the magic mountains is gravity, God's law*), tumbling leaping hurdling hurtling fast and faster down the vast vastnesses there of voided voiding void where soon they too would broken lie. Soon followed his hat, his stick, that blessed stick (*for him not Kate – though now, if only now …*), his knotted rope from off his waist, fine sailor, mountain walker he. Oh then he'd thought – what inspiration seized his mind (*was Holly there?*) – to take it 'tween his teeth. And there he carried it. Was with him always. Closer even than his arm.

So there indeed the knife clenched fast between his teeth. His hero's craft. His father's pride of carpentry.

He measured again. Again too short. Even with his knife extended far in hero's hand.

His fiercest eye. Inflected will. He took the knife in his strong left hand. Straight from his teeth. He measured distance on his arm. Two armes' length. Enough, two, end on end, to reach her there.

To bring her fast.

He raised his arm, measured the place on it to cut. Would be enough, oh j-u-ust enough, juust stretching, stretch ... for a woman? *He?* That sacrifice of his chief pride? His armes' self? But – she was Kate.

But oh, Kate saw: he raised the knife, taken from his teeth. And he had, he had, oh, he had – he'd loosed his hand, he'd lost his hold ...

... and slipping, falling, falling, falling ... there, before her eyes, before her eyes, before her eyes, before she ... she could not look she could not to see him tumble fall rotate o'erturn those one one seven, no, one one eight those counted countless times, then one more still, for ever-ing. To there whence no return from numbering, the coldness colding cold for ever, falling falling falling ...

The beetle whispered low, urgent-ing her, 'Will you not take the gift that he would give?'

She hesitated there. *She* was not the gived-to. Giving for ever they'd taught her convent-days. And they were right. For that was Kate.

'No *no*,' the beetle said, fast now, 'hasten oh hasten hasten ye. Nine seconds only for your say, acceptance. Now! Quick quick quick e're dashed below in endless pain. And nothingness.'

She could not. Could not go against her nature. Kate's.

And as she trembled there and stood eyes shut.

She heard.

She heard the tumble there, the skirl, the fall increasing down and down and spiraling down. Too young, too young, teened, she could not take it, panicked, hide, her eyes not look, her ears not hear the jangled tangled wangling swangling grinning swinging fall with stones a-hurtle plucked from jangle tangle world aburst with iron glints and sparks like firing stars afall, the jagging sparking iron smith-son furnacing that metal melten glowed and hammer-ed, oh cannot bear, the sea, too young too loud too tragedy too love no-love too young too …

'Quick! Quick!' The beetle yelling now, he *yelled*, forgot *his* nature too. 'Count now and count and count and count, stop dither-wither-wittering you! For once you hear the bang the dang the damn below, it is the end, this time the really really really end.'

And he waved his iridescent wings, 'irridescent' (*no time now for orthographic rules an' all*), and yelled (*just shows how panicking he was*).

'Five seconds left,' he said, 'not nine not eight, just five. Get on – *Accept!*' (*Was shouting now … poor beetle*).

'Three syllables, just the three. Now! Now! Say you agree!' (*Not fair she thought on beetles or on girls too young, too young for him to die*).

She counted then (*she counted! Kate!!*), oh count count count, she can't she can't she can't, oh try again, count count, (*her fate*), oh seven (*was it seven now? left now to doom, no nine by now, count up she'd learned*). So she counted then, with care, to one and two and … perhaps she could, three instants more to think, decide, yes counting helped.

But Kate oh Kate, all-ways too late, too late, she'd counted wrong, again, she'd fallen behind. Behind. Too late. She drew her breath to say the word. The helping salving given-to word.

'I agr –'

Too late. As breath was drawn as syllable formed, it needed one more, just and only one.

She heard the clanging, down and down, below.

'Alas alack amen, so all is done. It is indeed the end. The really truly only end. Alas. Alack.' (*Those words she'd learned, ne'er used before. Too cheap …*).

'My dearest dear,' (*oh still no name*), she thought, her heart, 'your sacrifice I do accept. At last. If all are dead and we in endless pain, know that I do accept you at the last. For love. For loving stronger still than death.'

And hid her eyes again.

The end.

The beetle whispered low (*quiet as beetles are*), 'So – you are saved. And him. For in your *mind* you spoke. Look down, now look, the knife it is that falls. That clangs. God sav-ed him. He did not fall.'

And now the beetle's heaven-sent wings were stretched. To fly. His duty done.

Even her beetle was going! Leaving now. What hope for her, could she not even fall, be with him? Did not believe. For still she felt him down, below, the bottom bottomless, to be, oh be with him, entangled in the coldness there (*let not a beetle 'suade her now, she knew*). It was the worst, her numberation now again, again, un-numerate. She felt the frozen coldness there (*cold was the enemy, she always knew't*) of frozen icing frozen-ness, there-here in her bones. She, doomed to stay for ever on that ledge, the ledge of loneliness, of desolati-on. Or fall. Alone.

He would've sacrificed all all all for *her*. How could she live withouten him, tangled for ever in his love, her hair? And even the beetle was going now.

But he was speaking still, farewell.

She could not look. Or count. Her eyes were clouded, cold.

From far below, oh still she heard she heard the broken break-ing fractured fracturing sound … the falling end of all. All hope abandoning … the cla-a-a-ang of iron, the iron in her soul.

She could not speak she had no words, could only pray (*what use prayer now?*), for his dear soul. Oh his, her own.

Into her mind came float those wordless words, the spoken-unspoken of the convent school. Her last night there. By Sister Bernadette, the oldest and wisest of them all. The silent one. The one near death. The words-unwords.

> *"That whereof one cannot speak,*
> *thereof one must be silent."*

So Kate kept silent.

'Look again dear Kate,' whispered the beetle in her ear, close still. 'You counted right. *First* time I think. In time, in mind, in time'es nick.'

And in that silent silence, stir of wings, in noiseless murmur of the wind in trees, the quiet stream, the ocean's ceaseless sound – in quiet gentle quietness she felt the pass of wings, the silence, the wind under the sky …

And …

… and she was standing on heaven's sward, blue-green and broad, fragrance of thyme, his arms around her, her long hair, the hair he loved, a-flying in the windes' sound, the sea's great echoing song.

The sun full on his face.

As the world hangs unmoving and the sea ceases its labour at the moon's turn of the tide, as the magic instant before a first kiss, as the sounding silence as the last tones of a sweet melody sing through the sky …

So stood they on the high edge of heaven.

Together.

PART IX

THE EDGE

44

At heaven's rim

Now she was there. At heaven's rim. And in her tiredness she slept. And seem-ed to herself to dream.

There on the edge, looked at her life as she had lived. The threads of dream, imaginati-on, Gabriel's silvered trumpet calling her to come, to rest. She thought she sang with them in that sweet melodie, of days and her nights, land of the love that moves all, the very mountains of her life and love. For even in heaven, alone, she thought of him.

His earthly presence then
those years ago
so wonderful.

His music too, his voice
the mem'ry of a smile
a frown
the breath of clouds at dawn
his sweetsome lightsome lighten touch

a miracle too great
ev'n for my tears.

But sweeter still that tun-ed harmony
that holds us fast
through years
of long eternity.
as fine as counterpoint
as delicate
as dreams
and tears.

That band-ed branded knitten knot of sound
between
fine microscopic hair
below above
to bind us in the death-driv'n cold
of frozen ether
warm
in th' deathless gold
'f undying love.

For has not music the miracle, been with us all of time? Calling saints and sinners, learn-ed and ignorant, children and elders, far off and near – God's greatest gift to man (*they'd not told her that in convent days. Why not in God's New Cov'nant when they knew it in the Old, with harps and timbrels, songs of exiling and love and praise?*).

She saw again the shore, the ship, love slipping down the moon-washed sky, herself outside the gate, and when he'd turned to look then on the cliff. At her, so long ago. With deep-set love-seek eyes. For look-back, turn, return. She had not seen or turned, watching the gulls swoop down below the Atlantic cliff.

And now God sang a new song. It was for *her*, for her to sing by the waters of grief and exile once, but no grief now. Water indeed, but no, no tears now or sighs.

Oh God hath helpen me
and whispered in my ear
'Oh wait oh wait onlie, my dear
the ships that parted in the night
will sail for ever near.'

Alas she had not harkened then, or heard. Oh exile from herself, she had not sung that song by the waters of ...

They had warned her at her convent school they had that there is no pure originality. "All minds quote", they repeated. "Old and new make the warp and woof of every moment. There is no thread that is not a twist of these two strands. By necessity, by proclivity, and by delight, we all quote." Did not that quoter Emerson once tell them that?

She looked and saw again her fullest life: that strand, his hurted stance, implacable, her suitors all (*so many too, for she was beautiful ...*), her questing through the place of men, of demons, angels, Adam and his apple – *his*, not hers till in gen'rous love he gave it her, in severance, per-severance and gave her of his taste.

Were they not twins, minds ev'r a-lined, attune, in parallel? Oh agony from pass-ed passing past, must it be so, that same old strain in vain (*repeat it now*) that:

Parallels don't meet, they said ...

Kate wept, she'd thought to thwart God's laws, his destiny. Un-parallel. Could there be ever mercy or unyieldance there, his iron laws relaxed, shut gates opened by love? What but by music, heavenly art, shadow-reflect on earth, the muses' craft?

He came once in mist
fainter than cloud

always upstanding
unyielding and proud.

He would not bend down t' me
wept I so much
'llowed me no sighting
suffered no touch.

Oh do not leave me
in untended tears
how can I bear it
for centuried years.

Her guilt – remember, those bitterest words of all, oh speak them low:

So Peter remembered
the cock still to crow.
Oh will yet his grief
yet melt dissolve go?

Oh well I remember
and share in that pain.
As the cock for me crowed
yet again and again.

Gossamer, thistledown, sand on the shore, spume in the wind, gone in the scent of the gorse, the down of the thistle, her lost soul. Too young. Would she ever grow?

And then it seemed to her that he was there. With her. In dream or was she awake?. No phantas-m but *he* himself, his very self. She heard his song, felt fragrance of his beauty's sweet. Waiting for her – still *her* – in mind's reality!

But still she saw his anger hold, his hurted ire 'gainst her who had o'erset his peace, and tried to force his scorpio shell. And as she looked she saw again her agony, her dream and wake, her pain, she knew it real. She yearned, she long-ed still for him.

And oh, now now she could plead him to forgive. Even that strong arm, that knife, that cliff, the crossing there, acceptance of his gift, his love were not enough.

She had wept before him, cried out to him.

He had looked at her but no seeing. Why should *he* the most beautiful he reach out to her? (*She had been too young. She had not known, how could she? Only fifteen years*).

Again she'd tried:

I'm sorry I'm such a problem here to you
the non-un-beautiful
and you so beauty-full
twisted and gnarled
roots' tangle below
an' crooked an' maimed
by unthinking winds
away from the stars
no sight of heaven.

Crook'd from my own fault too
no not the wind, nor yet by the stars
not firm beautiful like you
my own laments
my own lamentable lament-able faults.

I know you cannot straight me
or find me fruit
but perhaps en-graften me?
veneer to cover crevasses
or take as guest
as prop for your table
polish'd with honey'd glow
and kindly look

a stool to rest.

Or no! that were too much, too more than I could bear
your lovely sweetest feet.
I know you cannot straighten me
can never do.

But could you just love me all the same?

Did he not see …?
He was vanished …

Where have you gone love?
White blossom sweet as slumber
I cannot see you.

Only his fragrance lingering in the air. Rosemary. Rosemary for memory. Remembering.

Then nothing more.

But then she saw – that in his pride and his vengeance at the last, the very last, she saw that he had shown her mercy. His. And given his arm for her, just her. If she would take. And she had took it there.

She saw again the heaven-weft of her re-quoting life. Now made her own. That far, yet ever near-far, cycle retold in the round of comets the ever circling of moons of Jupiter, the seasons' falls. She saw again how.

He looked in her eyen
deep pool, surroun'
with lovely reed and willowen
an instant then, a span, an elm
and saw
and saw
her infinite love
her eternal, alone

desolation.

And God in his mercy
gave his dear sore gift.
Dementia.

Oh was that it, thought Kate, and others … blessed?

And autumn mist
so she walked
again in the garden
with him
before the apple pluckt.

And at the last
he looked in her eyes
deep fathomless,
a life's full span,
millennia swirled
in stars
and sky.

And cosmos-en
and saw
and saw
eternal love.
So they walked in the garden
in autumn time
and plucked the apple
for the world.

'Look again dear child,' whispered God, 'and see. In the end was it happy? For you and for the world?'
She looked and she thought.
'*Yes.*'

45

Past and present

Stories and voices from the past, enfolden in the ink-ed page, now it was for her to lay claim to her life present enfragranced in the past, what was to come already there, waiting for them to come, hers and not hers, past and not-past, *aeternitatis specie*.

And as the tides follow the moon, as the winter the autumn, as the leaves fall from the trees and wither and spring out in new bud, as the earth rounds the sun or in the directionless infinity of space and time the sun circles the earth, as man has ever turned to woman and woman to man.

So, like those ever-repeated words she had learned so long before, she saw the present in her past, the past in her present.

She saw from parapet of heaven the checker board of her life. The chess board, black and white, her life's moves laid out at last for her to see again.

And *him*. No name but woven with hers, advancing, dancing, twirling, tangling, rising as morning star, falling with Paradise Lost. Adam (*oh, that his name? too sacred still to say*) for SatanAdam-

Christ ...

She saw again and yet again, as do we all, the eternal cycled joys and woes of life, writ with her own sore soul, love's three-felt trinity. Was not her love fragrant as a summer's day, as moderate? So Shakespeare bard-es said, "Shall I compare thee to a summer's day ...?", for:

> *Love does not die*
> *it sprays in the spume of the waves*
> *hovers in smoke through the clouds*
> *lies in the grain of the shore*
> *flies in the birds' wild flocks*
> *swims in the shoals of the sea*
> *in a young girl's arms.*
> *Love does not die.*
>
> *Love cannot die.*
> *It slides in drops through the rainbow*
> *leaps passion to the skies*
> *shines in the beams of the sun*
> *the setting sun, the sands*
> *Sweeps sweet usic's triplets*
> *a boy's sweet treble.*
>
> *Love cannot die.*
> *Love does not die.*
> *No, love does not die.*
> *Does it?*

She conned its threefold writ, black written there. Had she not felt the joys of love, had she not towered to the heavens? But then – those self-same words (*oh read again*) – love's agonies, down down from Eden to sharp torments, hell, shattering of earth's upheavals there and ocean troughs. Sing then the gentle song of Garden's flowers:

My dear
I see you at my door
wet with my tears
will you not grow
in my garden?

"Shall I compare …?" Oh lasting summer day.
And then the storm-strand, start of all. But now …

Oh God tell him
I don't have words
I don't know how to say …
that it is so simple just a simple sweetest thing
but higher than the sky
more precious than the Milky Way
the night, the day.

Love.
Just to be near him
it is so simple
just – a heart
ah yes, the heart
heart's veins and arter-ies
its complex curves and swathes and ways
returns and doubts and deep entranceries
and still it comes.

Love.
Higher than the sky, the day
more wondrous than th' imaginati-on
profounder than the seas'
eternal flow.
It is so simple
Love.
I cannot say …

Tell him.

Once more she stood there trembling. And again he bent his head to kiss, eyes not of passion now but tenderness ...

She shivered with terror, sobbed to flee, shouted in panic, cried to the skies, the wave ...

His arms held, no slip-holding, holding ...

She cried out all the more, what if his arms were weak, if she fled, if he could not hold her, if she saw not the way back, the way home across the bog, in the rain?

'My little bird,' speaking to her 'my gentleness, my dove, I never will let you fall.'

And she knew, she knew, she truly knew, that she was safe, no longer des-olate, she was ... she was forgiven.

46

Last look down

She looked again across the woven cloth, the sea-saw's tilt, the balance of that great judge of all. She looked into her own heart's choice. Her own. Hurted – but not regretted. Of her own giving, forgiving forgiven in her giften giving.

Oh that soft morning-star of her first love! She sang again, back in the womb as that life's pages passed before her eyes:

> *Does first sweet love ev'r perish?*
> *Or drown deep down in the sea?*
> *Or faint midst the stormy rain clouds*
> *to vanish there from me?*
>
> *Oh 'Yes' you say, it must do.*
> *We live and grieve and grow*
> *and can't keep all our lovings.*
> *How could men cope with – 'No'?*
>
> *Wake up he says to 'Yes' land.*

How could you 'strain me so
stand 'twixt my joys, my livings?
But I grief-drown'd say – 'No.'

And there she had it. It was done.

47

The number

117, 118. Her numbering had been so *nearly* right. Just that last sum, forgetfulness in her self-self-giving, she had not seen.

Nine! He was <u>NINE</u>!! Number of muses, enneads, nine-sided universe. Of the nine ringed plates of heaven's temple there, sum of three three's, of the days' fall from heaven to earth (*she knew it well!*), from earth to hell. Nine witches there, nine planets too. Nine the great circles of entrance-ment, nine for our punishment. Nine storeys deep hell (*them too she knew*), and for stitches dropped not picked in time.

Nine.

Nine embraced *all* the numbers. The universe in ninesome myriad shapes, the scintillating changing phantasmagoria of nine lives, escaping grasp, even *his*.

That only she could give, the numberless. Give him his name.

Nine.

She had not been so wrong at all then in her un-counting. For there he was, floated yet formless through the universe, assuming first one figure then the next, he did not know it either, not for sure. Awaiting *her*.

Nine. She had it now.

Not yet himself. His very self. His presence there. But now at last his number, *him*.

Nine.

PART X

THERE

48

The finding

But … where *was* she now? What after all, after all that has passed in heaven and earth, what is the best?

Brown crackle afoot
of hollied leaves in winter time
a thunderstorm
tawn-glint of autumn goldend beech
a ewe lamb at her mother's breast
sweet primrose glint in faint spring's dawn?
Or – God, oh God,
Could it be me?

She had seen now the exchequer of her life, her loving giving self, loving too well, too much.

Moderation said the Greeks. Yes wise. But to turn from too-much love? (*too much …?*).

She looked again. And steeled her heart. And then rejoiced, the first time, like the un-reckoning steel-ed troops of old to know she could not master number. Was it the last move on board, that tragic comedy, wry plaything of the gods?

And then another song they sang – his mother, his dear mother, whispered it low in her ear, singing for her, for her, for Kate:

> *As camels become thirsty,*
> *long in the desert's drear*
> *as farmers seek for the rain storms,*
> *so search I for my dear.*
>
> *I looked in rocky ranges*
> *I did not find him there*
> *I searched through leagues and oceans*
> *through mountain peaks and air.*
>
> *Found nothing when I sought him*
> *no chance but home alone,*
> *and there I found love hiding*
> *hiding in my home.*

Oh this over-brimming dream-ed poetry buffeting her with storming footsteps of no peace. Yet now, it was right to have given all, accepted all, was nothing of herself now left to give.

But then, as a woman turns her broidered cloth to see the wrought stitch on its back, as the carpenter looks beneath his beveled masterpiece to see the joints below, as a harpist feels her music's form as the fingers touch the sweetened strings, so she looked … and found therein the power to strengthen firm her heart, and tell it at the last, 'Be still.'

As a chrysalid releases its caterpillar to the beauteous tortoise-shell, most glory of the woods, as full tide sends the fall to reveal the sands, as the moon's thin crescent swells to light the sky, so she looked …and saw the back, the be-neath part, the hidden casket of her life, unroll before her.

She saw the tangles all and beauties of her handiwork, its triumphs and reverses, its mistakes and her glad'ning saddening quest for him, her closed rejecting mind. Rejecting others gifts. Ev'n his. Till the last gasp. And even then not knowing it.

Is it not more blessed, more hard, more wrenching to receive than give? That over-gift, that self-regard mistook for sacrifice? 'twas *she herself* had lived it short.

Heaven and sea and hill and earth and desert. Could it, could it be … nearer home?

She recalled the ditty her mother'd sung:

I went to the market
to buy my love
I saw him hide there
all flow'rs above
my ocean pearl
the onlie one.

But he was sold.

I went to the market
to find my love.
And there 'n the shelf there
I saw him, above
all hearts and souls and vanish-ed loves.

But he was sold.

I go to my home now
with no thing bought
'long donegalled roads
to home Derryart
by Clonmass shore
Sheephaven's Bay
empty from market
my lonely way.

And there I found him
so weary, so sad
And there I found him
there in my heart.

'Ditty.' Not so silly,

Hark the below, the undertow that pulls you further than you think, back flow of her myth-lad'n life, her danger quest. Was it for her that heaven-song?

Then – as Orpheus to his Eurydice, as morning star to dawn, as neap tides to the spring, so looked she back to her following hidden self. To her who stayed in the darkness, corner there below, the shadowing place, to that obscured and hidden heart that could not meet the light. To the snake whose biting froze, that stopped her veins her thoughts her feels.

So looked she in her inner soul. Was *she* the one to fail, to give too much?

How had she let heaven's womb-sight slip, that infant with heaven's wisdom still asleep beneath the rowan in the granny's garden-place? Celestial geometric lines of being, ebbing and gone in the waning of the moon? For so all babes lose heaven's numeration skill as learn of human joys.

How could he have shown himself to her, unknown-to-self? Her overwhelming love, her adoration, help-meeting? Gift is exchange they say, giving makes friendships, love, yourself the gift.

I sent you a smile, a look
a postcard, phone call, poem
music, most beautiful of gifts,
a blessing in the night, a book.
tears in the dark, and then –
myself.

I saw what I had given

given away for no return
that I gave to him
and gave forever to him
that I gave
I gave
my heart.

She looked again. And thought. Thought of the starry arch, great oceans and the sonorous great sonority of song – clear, there – in heaven's great hall. And thought again.

But why do I complain
my soul?
For did I not hear
when you sent me the sonnets of love
when you played me that beautiful music
and oh – when you showed me your tears?

How could he take her gifts when *she* would not be give'd-to?

So now – look to her self. And for all her learning, all her years' search, all her mother had taught her, the fairie way, the Tír na nÓg – all she had left in black writ was – herself.

Hidden for all the days of seven years, of seven times more, to the end of the world when the sun runs dry and God folds up his creation and tiptoes away. Oh then …

… oh then she looked in her heart, too long too long neglected, always the giver, the giving 'unselfish', 'self-denying'.

Selfish!

Did not God demand the account of her *own* life, not others' there? That her quest, the guiding star of life (*for how could love be wrong?*) was not enough?

For now she must find the value for herself. It was herself, not him, for her to account (*not 'count' then, after all – account*). In dream, or thought, imaginati-on, this life or next, *she* must carry her own load. And virtue too.

She would.

And this time, at the last, she did.

So now she had come to that place where the sun not too hot did shine nor May's sweet buds fear the equinoctial storms. Her eternal summer, nor his, would not fade and her love, her given gived-to love, writ in these for ever.

'I am me,' she said, 'and that is how I want to be. I want to do the things I do – even do the highland fling or the hokey pokey. I am me every day, I will never change to someone else, I will never go away from me.'

So Kate looked down and sang once more again that lullaby her mother sang when she was still a child, innocent of all the travails of the world, held yet in love's everlasting crib …

God be in my mind
and in my sinning.
God be in my womb
and my beginning.

God be near to me
today, tomorrows
for time for life
for joy and sorrow.

So God be with me there
when soul is flying
when mother's care ca-an reach
when lives are dying.
Now is time to sleep
to rest from care
for God will keep my soul
when I'm departed.

The pearl that had always been there, from the dust, the grit, the sound of the waves. In such a moment, a gnat's wing flap, a beat of her heart, she would turn and look in his eyes and give him his name at last, Woman to Man, wondrously different, but equal.

Her tale was writ.

49

An epilogue for those that wish

Whence came this black-writ tale? Its truth, its place, enume-rati-on?

Ask of the birds of the air, ye readers, of the stars, the insect hordes, the angel hosts. Muses of honeyed tongues. Or God himself, if it may be that *he* knows.

Ask if she'd really found him then, and understood him right?

Ask if she surely found herself, the quest of mortals all?

Ask what in this life of hers, or ours, is dream, and what real-ity? What falsehood, what the truth?

Who can tell? Not your chronicler.

And for myself? Like my mother before me I am a romancer (*what else is a black-ink teller of tales?*). I believe, I *know*, that yes she *did* find her love at last, and looked him in the face, and learned and gave his name.

And that they lived as one in peace. The beetle flew off to other tasks, as beetles do, but a little silver bitch with one blue eye lay content at their feet.

For in true love, *aeternitatis specie*, what matter of time, or place, or number, yea or name?

50

In the beginning was the Word

And so, at the last, I found myself.

Kate.

In the sea-tangle of black ink.

In the beginning was the Word.

The Word, the creator of Truth, the very tool of Love.

In the end was the beginning.

In the Beginning was my ending.

A pearl.

THE END

THE END

Notes

Citations Page

"*Since brass, nor stone ...*": William Shakespeare *Sonnet* 65.

"*Whatever pearl you seek ...*": from the poem *The Dome of the Inner Sky*, by the medieval Persian poet Rumi (Jalal ad-Din Muhammad Rumi).

Chapter 2

This chapter is based on my (the author's) memories of my childhood in Donegal. My mother's take on it is given in the enchanting and enchanted memoir by Agnes Finnegan, *Reaching for the Fruit: Growing up in Ulster*.

Tír na nÓg: the land of eternal youth in Celtic mythology, made famous in the writings of the Irish poet W. B. Yeats (also later in Chapter 48).

arithmeticking: here and elsewhere new words and spellings are deliberate, a play with language, allowed (*it seems*) to poets and verbal artists, as in, for example, Gerald Manley Hopkins' poetry or James Joyce's prose. Many of these words are also allusive in sense, especially sound, and for those acquainted with them (*not essential for the story of course*), sometimes redolent of the literary references in T. S. Eliot's poems though in my case not limited to high culture as his was.

childers: Irish dialect form of 'children' that carries an extra air of affection (also later in Chapter 11).

Chapter 3

The literary allusions throughout this chapter are more fully explained in Chapter 7 of my book, *Why Do We Quote?* They are often references to texts learned by heart in my Quaker school where, unlike Kate's nuns, the teachers were all kind. Only some of the many allusions in the novel are annotated, left to my readers, if they so choose, to winkle them out.

"an old half-witted sheep … good Lord! I'd rather be": extract from one of James Stephen's fine parodies in *Lapsus calami* 1891. Passages within double quote marks here, as elsewhere, are full quotations, the rest are Kate's own words.

Fall of Pride: reference to Lucifer both as Satan (here as male lust), and as Lucifer the morning star that rises higher and higher before sunrise then vanishes ('falls') as the sun rises and the increasing light obscures the star.

Amazing grace: The word of this beautiful hymn with its (probably) negro-spiritual melody were composed by John Newton, himself once a slave trader – so he knew what he was talking about when he spoke of 'amazing grace'. He lived in Olney near to my present home where with equally amazing grace the words of this novel were dictated to me, ready-formed, in dreams.

"That whereof one cannot speak …": the twentieth-century Austrian philosopher Wittgenstein, in *Tractatus Logico-Philosophicus* (also later in Chapter 43).

"Shall I compare thee to a summer's day": William Shakespeare *Sonnet* 18, which I think the most beautiful love song ever (also

later in Chapter 45).

Chapter 4

MBA: Master of Business Administration, a highly fashionable – and lucrative – qualification.

A story for you: this story was told me by the talented storyteller Karanke Dema in an up-country village in West Africa, transcribed and translated in my book, *Limba Stories and Story-Telling*, slightly expanded here for Kate-full fateful purposes.

Nausicaa's ball: in the *Odyssey* Odysseus is shipwrecked on the shore where the king's daughter Nausicaa is playing a ball game with her maidens.

passi-on: Kate's feelings take the form of a triple word play – passion, meaning both suffering (above all Christ's) and, more neutrally, experiencing, plus the plain 'pass, passing' as he was doing (also later in Chapters 7, 21, 22, 29, 30, and 31).

eppur si muove: attributed to Galileo the famous astronomer after (or perhaps during) his examination by the Inquisition for his unorthodox heliocentric theory: 'but – it (the earth) *does* move.'

"as easy might I from myself depart": often-quoted line from Shakespeare *Sonnet* 109 (also later in Chapters 21, 36).

Noli me tangere: 'do not touch me.' Said by Christ in the Garden before his full resurrection, also typical of the distancing 'keep-off-me' character of Kate's nameless love.

Garten Vale... "Sleep my babe": Garten, a remote valley in Donegal, was the reputed birthplace of St Columba or Colmcille, 'the dove of the church', the founder of Derry ('the oak grove', my own birthplace) and of the religious foundation of Iona in Scotland, still a center for peace and prayer.. *The Garten Mother's Lullaby,* little known outside Ireland, is one of the most beautiful of Irish songs, and the first tune I recall from my childhood (babyhood more like), sung to me by my mother.

Chapter 7

Tasting a pear is an adventure: from https://www.hort.purdue.edu/newcrop/janick-papers/pearinhistory.pdf/.

Without the courtyard: from Homer, *The Odyssey*.

dulce inexpertis: 'sweet to those who've not tried it / been themselves involved'. Based on *bellum dulce inexpertis*, a Latin proverb on which the famed humanist Erasmus Desiderius of Rotterdam, arguably the first pacifist, wrote a long and still pertinent disquisition. This has been acclaimed by peace-lovers down the centuries, and abhorred (naturally) by the power-holders: 'War is glorious – so long as you're not on the front line' – it's sharper obviously in the three-word Latin. Modern translation by protestors (including me): 'All right if you're in the White House!' Or, as an Irishism (Kate's translation): 'OK for youse-uns'.

Chapter 9

"He came all so still …": Irish song about the birth of Christ that my mother used to sing.

Veritas domini: 'the truth of the lord' (will remain for ever) from the famous Latin hymn of praise *Laudate dominum*.

"He shall feed his flock …": from Handel's *Messiah*, also Isaiah 40:11.

Chapter 11

Inquietum cor meum est (donec requiescat in te): St Augustine, *Confessions*: 'My heart is restless until it rests again in thee'.

eightsome … is not mathematics beautiful: The mathematical sign for 'infinity' (∞) is like an 8 on its side, two joined circles, also viewable as a spiral. 'A figure of eight' is a well-known series of steps in the energetic Scottish 'eightsome reel'. It also recalls the figures illustrated in Jill Purce's fascinating and beautiful *The Mystic Spiral*.

look wikiped: a reference to the online, seemingly omniscient, encyclopedia *Wikipedia*, also a pun on 'ped' – 'legs'.

Chapter 13

Columb: short name for St Columba, renowned as scribe and scholar as well as a man of both passion and peace.

eyens, handens: Kate (together with her earthly author) sometimes likes to use Anglo-Saxon/Teutonic plural endings in *en* (or, adapted, as *ens*), also at times old spellings with a final *e* (*hearte*, etc.) or, as genitive (as in Goddes) and *-ick* (*magick, musicke*), when she feels it sounds better – the sonic/poeticke dimensions are key to her writing. The same with the extensions, separations and abbreviations of words.

Chapter 14

the lastest there till ardent suitor: this recalls the poem by Sappho, the Lesbian (from Lesbos) poet about a lover picking the last, lovely, apple, the maiden that no one till then had been able to reach.

'The leaves fall': from the late nineteen-century German poet Rainer Maria Rilke, *The Beckoning.*

"You change every grief to gold …": from the poem *What Fear of Loss,* by the medieval Persian poet Rumi (Jalal ad-Din Muhammad Rumi).

be-shell-ed scorpio-ned: her love's zodiac sign is Scorpio, by nature defensive and uncommunicative except when attaining its higher form of an eagle, or highest of all, a dove or perhaps a phoenix, the scorpion being the only sign that comes in more than one form. Kate's is Capricorn, the goat, signaling, as in her life, determination and perseverance.

Chapter 16

Atlanta: In the Greek story Atlanta agreed to marry the one who outran her, knowing no one could: she was the fleetest runner in the whole world. But one suitor won by guile, throwing down an entrancing golden apple which Atlanta swerved aside to pick up and so lost the race.

Malus: a favorite play by scholars and theologians (whom Lucifer is here seeking to emulate) on the Latin word *malus* which means both 'apple' and 'evil'. He goes on to say, in show-off but not quite accurate Latin, that the apple was the most evil of all evil things and the most accursed.

Aphrodi ...: Aphrodite was the Greek goddess of love and desire, the one to whom Paris awarded the golden apple ('the apple of discord') in the contest for who was the most beautiful of all, thus offending two other goddesses and causing the Trojan war.

Chapter 17

Homer, Milton: the first two similes are based on Homer (describing a battle clash), the third on Milton's description of the fall of Satan.

Doré: Gustave Doré the nineteenth-century French artist who painted a famous picture of Adam discovering Eve asleep in the Garden of Eden. The poet William Blake too, as here, described the fall.

Chapter 21

'Sleepers wake!': from a biblical parable about the need to stay awake to greet the bridegroom (Christ), set in multiple musical versions by J. S. Bach.

Chapter 26

"Oh come oh come": an advent hymn commonly sung before Christmas.

Chapter 27

"Come ye thankful people, come …" (Italian): Kate makes a good attempt at Henry Alford's popular harvest hymn but muddles up some of the words.

occamest: 'Occam's razor' comes from the famous saying of the medieval philosopher and scientist Occam that the most economical – simplest – theory is the best, an approach still favoured by (many) scientists today.

Ave Maria: The well-known Christian invocation 'Hail Mary full of grace … Pray for us sinners (*peccatoribus*).' Kate's convent background is showing.

"All people that on earth": the hymn from the 'Old Hundredth' psalm.

saecula saeculorum: centuries of centuries, that is 'for ever'.

"To Father Son and Holy Ghost": final verse of the Old Hundredth.

Chapter 29

Laudate dominum …: 'Praise the Lord, all nations, all peoples, praise him.' Again from the great Latin hymn of praise set to music by Mozart in (to me) the most beautiful tune ever.

quoniam confirmata est … veritas: from the same hymn 'for his mercy to us has been assured and his truth (*veritas*) remains for ever.'

Micklegate: is one of the four fortified gates in the medieval walls of the city of York, where I went to school and where, unlike Kate's convent, the teachers were understanding.

Chapter 30

cantor, poeta imitandissimus: a singer, the poet most to be imitated.

haiku, haka: Haiku, greatly prized Japanese short-form verse, now much practiced outside Japan. Haka, the aggressive Maori war dance by the New Zealand rugby team before international matches.

Chapter 32

arrivederci in paradiso (Italian): 'See you again in heaven.'

Chapter 35

but did not e'en Homer repeat himself: Both repetition and the recurrent 'Homeric epithets' characterizing his heroes ('swift-footed Achilles', 'much pondering Odysseus', etc.) are features of the Homeric epic style, imitated, as is the biblical tone of the nineteenth-century translations in which I first read Homer, in parts of the novel. Homer, the great epic poet, whom one might expect to be perfect, is said to have 'nodded' when, for example, he presents a warrior that he'd killed off earlier – said by some to be the result of his 'oral' or unwritten form of composition.

Chapter 36

The bard, "Oh never say": from Shakespeare 'the bard', *Sonnet* 109.

As a perfumier: here and often, especially in the later portions of the novel, Kate's experiences are conveyed in a series of Homeric-like similes, sometimes in direct translation from the *Odyssey* or *Iliad*, sometimes modeled anew on this rightly famous form.

"Alas my love you do me wrong to use me so despitefully …": from the well-known English folksong 'Greensleeves', later set to

music in Vaughan-Williams' *Fantasia*. It continues "When I have lov-ed thee so long / Delighting in thy company."

Chapter 41

Haggard tales of love and loss: the late-nineteenth-century novelist Rider Haggard wrote many novels about fantastic journeys, often set in the interior of Africa.

Chapter 43

Abelard-Eloise, Isolde-Tristan, Guinevere-Lancelot, Euridice-Orpheus, Pelion-Ossa, Patroclus-Achilles, Dido-Aeneas: famous pairs of lovers in myth and story, often ill-fated.

Ogun Affrick: the West African Yoruba God of smithery and iron.

Chapter 44

"All minds quote ... we all quote": from Ralph Waldo Emerson's 'Quotation and Originality', in *Letters and Social Aims*.

Chapter 45

aeternitatis specie: from the viewpoint of eternity. 'Keep things in perspective!' or, as my mother sometimes asked (told) me, 'In the light of world affairs ...?' (also later in Chapter 49).

Chapter 47

enneads: reference to the Enneagram or nine fold personality theory (explained in http://en.m.wikipedia.org/wiki/Enneagram_of_Personality).

Chapter 48

Derryart, Clonmass (or *Cloonmass,* to match the pronunciation), *Sheephaven:* names of places at or near Kate's – and my –
childhood home in Donegal.

I am me … quoted (slightly adapted), with permission, from
a poem by another Kate, my New Zealand granddaughter, then
aged 6.

CPSIA information can be obtained
at www.ICGtesting.com
Printed in the USA
LVOW04s1444030216
473522LV00020B/1127/P